CUTTER 1

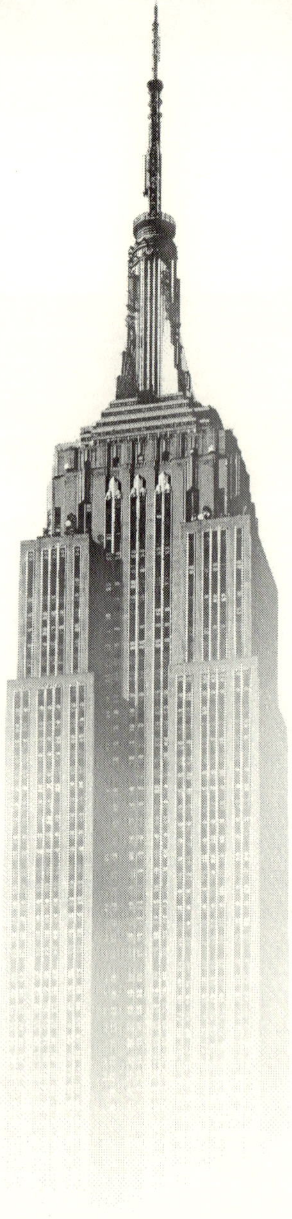

Cutter

DAVID E. GORDON

David E. Gordon
AATA 2023

Cutter

Copyright © 2014 David E. Gordon

All rights reserved.

"This book is a work of fiction. The characters, incidents, and dialogue are drawn from the author's imagination and are not to be construed as real. Any resemblance to actual events or persons, living or dead, is entirely coincidental."

No part of this book may be used or reproduced in any manner whatsoever without written permission except in the case of brief quotations embedded in critical articles and reviews. For Information contact David E. Gordon at: davidegordonauthor@gmail.com

Dedication

I dedicate this book to Christine, my wife and best friend in the whole word. She makes every day worth smiling about, through thick and thin she has stood by my side. I will always be grateful for the support and encouragement she has shown me. Especially while I have spent hours and hours writing, editing, and preparing this novel.

8 CUTTER

CAST OF CHARACTERS

Robert Cutter
Main Character

Simone
Original Girlfriend

Sam
Philly Cop

George
Philly Cop

Mr. Lee
Store Owner

George
Doorman

Sam Simmons
FBI Agent (Former Philly Cop)

Jack Franklin
Detective (NYPD)

Lilly
Nurse

Shannon Adams
Doctor

Joseph Brand
Right Hand Man

Jennifer Sullivan
Administrative Assistant

Lowell McDermott
Chief Strategy Officer

Frank Martino
Chief Legal Counselor

John Tower
Nevada Senator

Mark Thompson
Political Liaison

Roger Thompson
Senior Analyst

Captain Davis
National Guard

Pearl Franklin
Mother of Homeless Child

Mikhail Franklin
Homeless Child

Father O'Brien
Priest from Philly

Gino Caporelli
GC Realestate Owner

Anthony Salvatori
Philly Construction/Demolition

Anthony Salvatori, JR
Las Vegas Union President

Tom Dell
Philadelphia City Councilman

Martin Anderson, Sr.
CEO of Anderson Brothers

Chapter 1

The little boy sat on the stoop of the video store, long since boarded up. Yellowed posters of the newest movies available on video cassette were just barely visible through the grimy dirt covering the windows. He – if the child was even a he – was dirty from head to toe, making it truly hard to tell if he was actually a boy. His hair was long and greasy, his clothes so grimy it seemed as if the dirt was actually holding the material together. One sleeve from his t-shirt was torn away revealing his bony shoulder and he wore holey sneakers that were too big for his tiny feet, and only one foot had a ragged sock. Despite the heat from the early sun, he still looked like he was cold.

The man opened the corner market promptly at five every morning, so when the fresh bread was delivered he was there for it. The newspapers were delivered during the night and piled up next to the steps. From the small pile of papers it was obvious that fresh bread was much more important in this neighborhood than reading the news. By the time the bread truck arrived the boy had gone.

The man stood at the top of the stairs and looked around for the boy, a worried look crossing his face. This was not a neighborhood where anyone should be wandering around alone - especially a young boy. As the man looked up and down the street he remembered the days when all of the businesses were not just *open, but thriving. They had been busy with customers coming and going all day long. Across the street was the men's clothing store that had always had the latest fashions, the ladies clothing store right beside it with merchandise just as fashionable. There was the old appliance store always getting in a shipment of the latest gadgets like the Sony Walkman or the some other type of portable radio. And of course the video store where the boy had just been sitting which had the latest movies available to rent.*

Now, all that was left besides the memories, were boarded up windows, broken neon signs, graffiti, and trash piling up in all the corners, blown there by the winds of time. Even the winos and beggars knew that no one in this neighborhood could or would give them a dime. So, like the customers long gone they too had moved on to the major malls nearby and the more prosperous areas. Only the corner market still stood and the few customers that remained were barely enough to keep the store open. The store was not well stocked, but it didn't need to be since he knew what his customers needed. And these days, needs were much more important than wants.

The next day when the man came to open the store the boy was back, huddling in a corner on the stoop next to his. He appeared to be wearing the same dirty clothes as the day before. The man got a roll, with a couple of slices of lunch meat and cheese, wrapped it in a napkin and laid it on his stoop. As he put the sandwich down he glanced at the boy then turned back into his store. Knowing the bread truck would be there in just a few moments, the man hoped the boy would take his offering. When the truck came, the man went to get his day's bread and smiled when he saw that both the boy and the sandwich were gone.

Several days passed and each day the man left a sandwich along with an apple or banana in the morning and again in the evening. Now, after a few days he would also leave a small container of milk. Each day, almost as if Santa had stopped to leave his presents, the milk container would be empty and nothing but the apple core or banana skin remained. Usually the boy wrapped his trash into a little ball inside the napkin, as if despite the neighborhood and his appearance, he wanted a little neatness somewhere.

The warm sun was rising later in the day and the mornings were becoming colder, and still the man left the food for the boy. One cold morning when the boy finally got up the courage to thank the man and perhaps spend a little time in the warm store, there was no cheese sandwich. Instead the steps to the store had a funny yellow tape wound all around them. Had the boy been able to read he would have known the tape said 'Police Caution'. Even without reading the tape, the boy knew what police cars looked like and there were several parked on the street outside of the store. The boy watched quietly from the shadows of the empty video store.

Two policemen were talking at the top of the stairs leading in to the market, and since even dirty little boys could be curious he inched a little closer until he could hear them.

"Damn shame Sam. Damn shame. Who would want to kill an old guy just trying to sell basic food to people who needed it?"

"Yeah George you're right. And the thief probably didn't get much more than twenty bucks and a carton of milk."

"Hardly enough for any kind of high."

"From the look of the shelves, he probably came for some food. And knowing Mr. Lee he would have just given it to him. Mr. Lee was just that kind of a guy."

As the little boy turned to go his little belly grumbled reminding him that he would have to find something to eat and soon. Suddenly, he felt a huge hand wrap around his little arm. "Hey guys, look what I found hiding in the corner…"

CUTTER 13

***

Robert woke suddenly, sitting quickly upright in bed his forehead damp with sweat and his heart racing. Ever since the car accident the week before he had been having strange dreams and even more headaches. It seemed like his dreams were becoming more troubling and he woke more often from them. Thinking back to the accident he was again reminded of the fear and shock he felt when he saw the car coming towards him from the alley. It had almost seemed as if the car was aiming for him. Then to add to the uneasy feelings he had, the driver had run off. Of course, since the car had been stolen the police blamed it on joy-riding-teens and nothing more.

Moving quietly he swung his legs out of bed and listened to the sleeping sounds of the woman beside him. As he rose and got a silk robe from the edge of the bed he tried to remember her name. It would come to him he knew, it always did. He silently moved through the dark bedroom, then he glanced at the bed and smiled at the sight of her sleeping under the soft cotton sheets. For a moment he considered slipping back under the sheets with her, but recalling the dream knew he would not get back to sleep.

He was troubled by how vivid and real the dream had felt. Closing the door quietly behind him he moved through the dawn lit living room to the balcony. As he stepped outside, the fresh breeze blew across him. In the still of the early morning the city looked amazing. He could almost imagine the steel and glass office buildings waking up themselves. From this view he could not actually see the business side of the city. One did not pay millions for a view of oversized office buildings. Rather, one paid millions for a perfect view of the park and gardens below – which is what he had done. It was one of his first big purchases and it was for this view alone that he had bought it. Looking over his shoulder towards the bedroom, he realized that despite the woman's presence he felt almost totally alone.

As he stood looking out over the lush green lawns and tall trees, the colors from the various gardens all seemed to blend into one. He found himself thinking about the dream and the little boy. It was strange, not just because he almost never woke from his dreams, but never was he jolted awake and sweating. The vivid dreariness of the stores and neighborhood seemed to envelope his very being. He could almost smell the trash and taste the desperation, the grittiness and the dirt that was everywhere. Even more strange was that he could still almost feel the cop's beefy hand on his arm. He now found himself touching the very same spot as if willing the cop to let the boy go.

The boy looked so familiar to him, not just a passing familiarity but more than that. His gaunt cheeks, pale skin, thin lips, and long greasy hair. Everything about him had looked tired, except the bright blue eyes, which had seemed so alive. Those eyes seemed to sparkle with more than just a boyish curiosity for life; but with their own energy. Everything about the boy seemed to scream that he was alone in this world and Robert wondered how a boy like that could survive. But the eyes told a very different story. They told of a mind, hungry for knowledge, as hungry as the boy's little body must have been. And they told of a boy determined to do more with his life than just survive.

No matter how alive or real it had seemed, it was just a dream. Robert knew he was being ridiculous about it all. Shaking his head he reminded himself that he had no time for dreams. He had a huge business to run with people relying on him for solid business decisions. He walked the length of the balcony and through a different door into the kitchen. As he closed the door he smiled at the scent from the freshly ground beans of coffee made just for him by the Johnson Brothers. While it was known that they were perhaps the finest coffee manufacturers in the world, he still preferred his own blend of beans, and they were all too happy to make it for him.

He looked around the perfect kitchen at the stainless steel appliances, restaurant quality six burner stove, and double oven. He looked at the granite counter tops, and the special order cabinets. The glass fronted cabinets nicely displayed the fine collection of dinner ware and crystal glasses. There were enough dishes and glasses for a nice sized dinner party, all of which were always catered. He did sometimes entertain a few intimate friends, but even those dinners had been prepared for him so he would just have to serve. He smiled to himself thinking that the kitchen was perfect, it was just never really used for the family it could easily feed.

Obviously his habits were well known by his staff, as the coffee pot had come on automatically and there were already two mugs laid out. Glancing at the clock he grabbed a fresh croissant and chewed it while he poured his own coffee. He poured the second mug and not knowing her preference put sweeteners and cream on a plate beside it. He also placed another croissant on a plate and stacked, then carried them into the bedroom. He placed the mug and croissant on the night table on her side of the bed, brushed a hand softly against her cheek and whispered that it was time to get up. As he stepped into the bathroom he turned on a light.

The bathroom light cast dim shadows in the corners of the bedroom, but you could still see that this inner sanctum of privacy was done to his perfection. The cotton sheets were obviously a higher thread count than could normally be found. No, you would have to specially order these sheets. The oversized king mattress was huge and would have filled any other bedroom, but in this one there was plenty of room for the overstuffed recliner and ottoman in the corner near the patio doors. You could imagine sitting with a glass of wine looking out over the park as the moon rose effortlessly in the sky. The furniture was a dark walnut and there was not a speck of dust anywhere. On two of the walls hung posters from Leroy Neiman of his favorite sports - baseball and football, the largest on the wall behind the bed. The wall across from the bed had a large flat panel TV, the newest and best of course.

The room was perfect in almost every way, but as Robert glanced around the room he could again feel the emptiness all around him. Even the quiet soft breathing coming from under the sheets did not do anything to fill the void. In that moment Robert once again felt a stark loneliness as he had not felt in a long time. Despite the oversized room the walls seemed closer this morning than they had almost any other day. Robert's eyes were drawn again to the bed and the girl sleeping soundly, her name jumped into his head but even that did not help how he felt. He considered climbing back into bed with her, but knew that would not ease the emptiness. He shook his head and turned back to the bathroom, closing the door behind him.

Awake now and ready to get his day going, he moved efficiently and in what seemed to be one fluid motion put down the coffee, hung up his robe and brushed his teeth. He got into the extra-large steam shower and as he scrubbed himself began to think again about the boy in his dream. He stopped in the middle of rinsing his hair wondering if the boy had even known what soap was. "What the hell... ", he mumbled. It was a dream – what difference would that make? As the rain shower continued to rinse his hair, and the scent from his favorite soap reached his nose he knew in his heart that the closest the boy came to a shower would have been standing in the rain.

He shook his head to clear it and as he stepped out of the shower grabbed a thick towel. As he dried himself off he thrust the thoughts of the boy aside and pushed a button on the wall. A corner of the mirror came to life with the early morning CNN broadcast. As he finished getting ready he listened as the newscaster covered the top stories. The latest economic news – good for a change, the war in Afghanistan coming to an end, local and national political news, and then quickly covered the sports – Cole Hamels from the Philadelphia Phillies had thrown another no-hitter last night. Even the entertainment news seemed to bring him back to the real world and out of his dream.

Suddenly Robert stopped in the middle of rubbing his aftershave across his freshly shaved chin and stared at the television. The story was an alert as it had just come to their attention, but was not considered a "top story" because of its locale. It was just a run down, almost deserted section of Philadelphia. According to the reporter, there were several blocks of abandoned houses, warehouses, and businesses, which were burning uncontrollably. While the story itself was eye catching because of the number of city blocks that were burning, what had caught his eye was the sign over one stores front door that had not yet been totally engulfed in flames. Above the Korean symbols were the simple words "Lee's Corner Market".

Shaking his head and staring at the screen, Robert told himself it is not possible that this was the same store from his dream. There must be hundreds of "Lee's Corner Markets" in the country. There was no way this could be the one from his dream. And there was no reason to think that his dream had taken place in Philadelphia. Besides, it was just a dream and nothing more. Just one of those odd coincidences in life that make us shake our heads. He turned off the television and stepped back into the bedroom.

He paused looking at the girl still dozing under the covers and softly touched her ankle. "Come on dear, we need to get going."

Her beautiful brown eyes with flecks of gold flutter open and she looks at him mumbling, "Do we have to?" With a wistful look she leans forward smiling, purposely letting the sheet slip to her waist.

Robert paused for just a moment smiling, then nodded as he turned to his closet, and remembering that it is Saturday selects a more casual oxford shirt, a pair of tan linen slacks, and comfortable loafers. He quickly gets dressed, making sure that Simone is also now up and getting dressed. Afraid that he might change his mind, he looks away as she slips into her dress. Stepping to the dresser he selects his favorite Omega watch from the collection, slips his wallet into a pocket and selects a Mont Blanc pen which he puts into the pocket of a navy blue sport coat.

Simone slips her arms around his waist and asks that since it is Saturday morning – and awfully early to be awake – perhaps they could relax for a little longer before leaving? He gently slips from her grasp and turning he smiles, "sorry darling, but I've got a bit of work I need to get done this morning." As she pouts playfully and bats her eyes at him he knows that he would normally agree, but today he feels a strong pull to get to his office. He leans down and softly kisses her forehead, pulling away before he changes his mind.

"Will I see you again Robert?"

"Yes Simone, you most certainly will." Even as he says it he realizes how many other times he has said these same words and wonders if he will ever meet someone that will make him mean it. Almost as an afterthought he kisses her lightly on the lips and gives her his best smile.

Before she can smile back he is on the move heading towards the door; his long legs striding quickly and easily across the living room. He holds the door for her and as they step into the hallway the elevator doors open as if by magic. Not magic, he knows, he had alerted the lobby while he was getting dressed by pressing a button on his wall phone in the apartment. The elevator descends quickly to the lobby where he moves effortlessly towards the main doors. Simone has to hurry to catch up to him, and turning he says "I will arrange to have a car take you home after we get to my office."

The doorman approaches quickly, saying, "Mr. Cutter, this was left for you this morning." As Robert takes the package he hesitates for a moment and smiling says, "thank you, George."

Just as Robert and Simone turn back to the front doors the entire wall of glass explodes inward. Robert throws himself at Simone taking her to the ground under him as a million shards of glass rain down on them. His weight and the blast throw them easily to the ground like slips of paper. They slide for several more feet landing at what used to be the reception desk in the lobby. The doorman can be seen lying slumped against another corner of the same desk. The plotted plants and miscellaneous modern art furniture are strewn about the lobby like broken toys. As Robert looked around he found it funny that the furniture was only really there to look nice and fill the space, but would now make the designer cry. The last thing Robert thought of before his eyes closed was to wonder if the ringing in his ears would ever stop.

Chapter 2

The doctor held Robert's chart in one hand and was studying the monitor at the same time.

"How long has he been out?"

The nurse adjusted the oxygen and glanced at the clock on the wall and said, "almost two hours, Doctor."

The room was crowded with police, which gave the doctor a hint that the patient was someone important. Reading his name from the chart – Cutter, Robert – she was sure she had read something about him recently. But with her constant twelve-hour shifts and very few days off in between, she couldn't quite place it. That was the price she knew she had to pay for being in charge of the department, that, and not having a social life.

As she continued to read his chart she moved to his side to check the pulse in his wrist and looked around the room. There were two plain-clothes cops, two more people that she knew were FBI because they had made sure to show their identification to everyone. And there were two more uniformed cops in the hallway. Then there were the other two guys who just kept looking at everyone as if something was going to happen at any moment. Those two suits were from "another agency" and that was apparently supposed to be enough for everyone. Of course, the fact that the patient was already in a private room spoke volumes as to who he might be. All that, however, did not matter to the doctor: in her book every patient deserved the same treatment.

The doctor looked around the room, "gentlemen, we certainly have enough security here. Between the hospital security, and the two uniforms in the hallway the patient is safe. Please let us take care of him and get him healthy again. Now before any of you start to argue, out!" The doctor spoke softly but with extreme confidence that spoke to more than just her professional achievements. This was her ER and they knew it.

Despite her being obviously young they didn't question her, but filed out into the hallway. After a few moments of uncomfortable silence in the hallway, the two plain-clothes cops, FBI agents, and one of the other "no name" suits left to find some coffee. The other suit stayed behind with the two uniformed cops to make sure nothing happened. Despite the doctor's notion that the hospital was completely safe these guys had the look of being perpetually paranoid. There were a lot of questions to be answered, and even though they didn't think Robert had the answers, the questions still had to be asked. They had already had a similar conversation with Simone, and she provided even fewer answers than they thought Robert might.

After getting fresh coffee in the cafeteria, the five law enforcement professionals took seats around a table in the corner, away from prying eyes and ears. However, from the tight faces and sharp looks, the FBI agents were clearly unhappy with the un-named suits from the "other agency" even being there. After a few moments of sipping their coffees they began a tentative discussion of the events of the day. While it seemed that it was a personal attack against Cutter, they all agreed that a car bomb was a little extreme for an attempted murder. While Cutter certainly seemed like the obvious target, there were three people who were killed walking along the sidewalk and a dozen others that had been injured. In addition to the loss of life, there were also the hundreds of thousands of dollars of damages to the building, as well as the damage to the cars on the street and even the surrounding buildings.

In an effort to lighten the mood, and perhaps break the ice one of the cops suggested it could be a crazed fan of the Die Hard series. Maybe the fan was unhappy that there was not going to be a Die Hard five? No one laughed – least of all the no-named suits. Obviously not worried about making friends, one of the agents said, "Maybe you should go get fresh coffee and leave the detective work to us". Grumbling something unintelligible, the cop rose quickly, knocking his chair over backwards, and then leaving it where it lay, he stormed off. It was clear that if they wanted coffee it would likely be thrown at them.

The silence that followed was deafening and the elder of the FBI agents decided he had had enough of this cloak and dagger crap. "Look, you don't have to like the local guys, or even think they have any brains. But, they can give us invaluable local intelligence." The stone-faced look that greeted him proved that the suit had no idea what might be needed to solve this case. A good detective understood that you never knew who might help to solve a case. Then again he also questioned whether they were here to solve the case – or just stay in the loop, whatever loop that might be. Standing, the elder of the two FBI agents turned to his partner, "Stay with him, anyone too stupid to recognize the importance of local intel needs watching." His partner smirked, nodded and took another sip of his coffee. Then he strolled over to the local cop who was obviously still pissed off, got himself a fresh cup of coffee and patted him on the shoulder.

Extending his hand, he said, "Sam Simmons. I just got transferred here from the Philadelphia office. You been on the job long?"

"Jack Franklin," he answered, shaking his hand. Both men instantly sizing each other up as they gripped each other's hand firmly. "Nice to meet you too. I've been on the job for about fifteen years, a detective for the last five. I see your friend doesn't have much of a sense of humor, too bad, because that suit really fits him." Both men chuckled and took seats at a table to drink their coffees.

Simmons' glanced back at the other table and said, "don't really think he has any friends at all, which could explain his sense of humor – or lack thereof. I was on the job about five years before joining the feds. Sometimes I even miss it."

The cop looked at Sam through squinting eyes, the question forming in his mind. Sam answered before he had a chance to ask. "Yeah, that was me... one minute a simple cop being ignored by guys just like him," as he spoke he pointed over his shoulder. "And the next moment you get a serious bad guy off the streets and everyone suddenly knows you. Just doing the job same as anyone else, right?"

"Well, if you call getting a rapist/serial killer who had been avoiding the cops for over two years off the streets just doing the job, then yeah – that was just doing the job. From what we heard in our little town, it was really quite a piece of detective work."

"Something about the whole case just kept nagging at the back of my mind, so I went back to the streets and found the right string to pull on. Guess that's why I don't discount the local guys so quickly. We all have a part to play – even him." Again he pointed at the suits sitting at the other table.

The two veterans started comparing notes, the cop filling in the local picture for the agent. Sam glanced at his partner and winked at no-name who was glaring at him from across the room. Despite the circumstances both FBI veterans broke into grins and chuckled at his expense. The NY city cop and the FBI agent continued to discuss the case, with the detective sharing the list of other occupants living in Cutter's building, even those not at home at the time of the explosion would have to be interviewed. The cop noted that it was a fairly exclusive building, which meant fewer occupants than a regular apartment building in New York City. With the top ten floors being broken down into two penthouses each and the remaining floors containing oversized apartments there was only about 120 families living in the building.

Looking over the list Sam knew that interviewing the other families would be a real chore. There were two state senators, four actors, two he knew were on a soap his wife watched, three mega-corporate CEO's, a newscaster for one of the major networks, a baseball player for the Yankees, and of course, Robert Cutter. The detective pointed to Cutter's name on the list and said, "enlighten me here, Sam, I am sure you feds know our boy better."

"Robert Cutter was truly a nobody." Sam said, consulting his own notebook. "The first we heard of him he was working for a small Wall Street firm doing analysis for the partners. He apparently saw something in the Internet before anyone else did, or even before anyone else thought it was possible. The managing partner died and within six months Robert had left to start his own firm. Several of the firm's clients moved with him, which of course upset his old bosses immensely. We first heard about him because a couple of the partners tried to bring a law suit to stop him. Then he really ticked them off by being right about investing in the internet and several other 'dot come' start-ups. He made his clients and himself hundreds of millions of dollars in the process. After that, his client list grew and they continued to invest with him and have since financed several of his ventures – very successful ventures.

Although Cutter has reportedly made his clients hundreds of millions of dollars, it's known that he's also made billions for himself at the same time. From what we know he is involved in about a dozen different businesses spread across several industries, including internet companies, computer software, insurance, transportation, warehousing, and real estate. Although he generally lets the companies operate on their own, he also holds a board member role at some level. That is assuming he doesn't just simply buy and then re-sell the business – sometimes in parts. Our white collar guys sometimes joke around that he could be Richard Gere in Pretty Woman – but with real millions. We even heard that he and Warren Buffet have met several times in private, but no one knows why.

The justice department has investigated his company several times due to antitrust or shareholder lawsuits. They have never turned up anything more than him being an apparent financial genius who seems to have an uncanny ability to pick the right investment at the right time. Also, according to the Justice Department he is currently involved in the takeover of a private aircraft company, which not only leases private jets but is also bidding on outfitting some of the presidential fleet as well as other planes used by the justice department and government agencies. In addition to that, he is also reported to be working on a deal to buy *The Bellagio* in Las Vegas."

Jack whistled softly and then chuckled, "so, basically what you are saying is that you don't really know anything about him?"

No-name had walked over and was listening to the bio from Sam. He now spoke quietly and said, "anyone with that kind of dough spread around in as many companies as that makes us wonder what he is really hiding."

Both veterans looked at him and in unison said, "us?" No name hesitated, looked carefully around the room and then quietly said, "a division of Homeland Security."

***

The nurse leaned out of the room and waved for the doctor, "he's coming around doctor."

The two cops and the agent jumped to enter the room, but were stopped by a look from the doctor. As she walked over, she took the chart from the nurse, "thanks, Lilly, how is he doing?"

"He is stable, heart-rate is steady, but his temp is a bit elevated. His pupils are unfocused and non-responsive right now."

The doctor stepped over to the bed and taking Robert's wrist in one hand, checked his pulse against the heart rate monitor. Nodding to herself she used her stethoscope to listen to his breathing, she felt the patient begin to stir and shift in the bed. Moving closer, she placed her hand on his shoulder. "Just relax, Mr. Cutter, you are in St. John's Hospital. Do you remember what happened to you?" The patient blinked several times and stared at her, his mind not comprehending what she is saying to him. The doctor pointed to the nurse and smiled reassuringly, and then patted his arm. As she turned and started to walk away the patient grabbed her hand and trembling, mumbled something.

The doctor turned back to him and smiling repeats that he will be ok and to try and relax. He looked at the nurse pleadingly as she slips a sliver of ice between his lips. He looked back and forth between them, trying to find his voice. As he became more agitated the doctor nodded at the nurse who increased the dose of morphine he was getting to help him relax. As both the nurse and doctor looked on, Cutter visibly began to calm down. The nurse slipped another piece of ice between his lips. After several more minutes he tried to speak again, this time a tiny croak escaped from between his lips. A little more ice and then he is able to speak softly, "what happened? The last thing I remember is riding the elevator to the lobby. The doorman stopped to hand me an envelope and then lights out. Why can't I remember anything after that or how I got here?"

The doctor and nurse exchanged glances, then the doctor quietly said, "It is common to not be able to remember things in this kind of a situation. There was an explosion in your building. So far, it appears that you suffered a minor concussion but we are going to run a few more tests just to be safe. You are going to have a headache for a few days, but we will cover all that later." She glanced over her shoulder at the cop outside the door and said, "try to relax and get some sleep. I will keep the feds and local cops out for a while longer."

The doctor gave him a reassuring smile then patted his shoulder again. As she turned to walk away, he again took her hand in his. This time it is more in gratitude than fear, and she gave him a confident smile and said, "don't worry, Mr. Cutter, you're in good hands here, we have the best nurses. Now try to get some sleep."

Cutter watched the doctor and the nurse leave the room. As the nurse dimmed the lights, he saw the doctor stopping the police in the hallway. Standing beside the policemen he saw a 'suit', obviously a federal agent. He laid back against the pillows and struggled to stay awake long enough to try and remember what had happened. Robert's mind was confused as images floated before his eyes. First, a dirty little boy who suddenly became an older man, but just as dirty. Then, a beautiful woman dressed for an evening out who was suddenly standing in torn and tattered clothes smiling at him through tears mixed with dirt and glass. Last, there was a smiling angel with raven hair and emerald green eyes. She didn't change, just kept smiling and nodding.

As he was drifting further into the dreamless haze of pain medicine, the boy kept calling for him to follow him. But it was dark and Robert did not want to follow, it was too dark. He was losing sight of the boy, and the more he struggled to keep up, the further away he got. Robert kept following after the boy when he suddenly turned a corner and Robert found himself in the lobby of his building. But, it didn't look like his lobby, this one had broken glass and furniture strewn all over. Oddly out of place was the twisted remains of a car that was laid on its side against one wall.

Chapter 3

It was raining again. It was just a drizzle but the boy was still cold and damp. He shivered so violently that his entire body shook and he looked like he might collapse at any moment. Of course it didn't help that he was wearing nothing more than a t-shirt and jeans. The boy was walking along the trash-strewn streets, his eyes darting all around, watching for what lurked in the long dark shadows. Between the heavy dark clouds and early dusk it made the shadows even darker and longer. As he passed in front of a dilapidated house he glanced over the simple wire fence, looking at the mostly boarded up windows. Then, seemingly out of nowhere, a huge dog charged the fence barking and howling. The little boy was so startled that he almost jumped out of his sneakers. As he continued walking past the fence the dog followed him, barking madly, saliva spraying as his paws bounced off the fence, shaking it. Finding his inner strength, he smiled a crooked grin at the dog and kept walking. He walked a little faster as he passed the next lot that was empty, but slowed momentarily as he passed the now boarded up corner market. His grumbling stomach, an additional reminder of the nice man that had been there and how hungry he was again.

By the time he had reached the end of the block the rain was coming down in sheets so thick, he could barely see where he was walking. The sky was as dark as the inky black sea, and with the rain falling so heavily the boy was almost invisible. Suddenly everything was lit as bright as the day had been just a couple of hours ago by a sudden bolt of lightning. The brightness was followed immediately by a huge rolling clap of thunder startling the boy and making him duck as if the sky were falling around him. He looked skyward for a moment before quickly continuing on. The lightening continued to come, faster and brighter with each strike, the storm felt so close it was as if it was trying to chase him along his way. The thunder beating against the buildings made it sound even louder as it echoed all around him. The booming was so loud it seemed as if the sidewalk was vibrating under his small feet. By the time he reached his building he was so wet that he looked as if he had fallen into a deep lake. The roof of the building leaked everywhere making small waterfalls and the boy had to walk carefully between them as if he was trying to stay dry. Despite all the leaks in the roof and lake-size puddles, there was a small lean-to in one corner that managed to keep the boy's meager belongings dry.

The boy stripped off his wet clothes and hung them on a line so that if the rain stopped they could drip dry. This also seemed like a good way to get them clean even if he didn't have any soap. He slipped on a pair of dirty, oversized shorts, and laying back on his bed against the wall, opened the bag he had been carrying. He emptied the bag beside him on the bed – if you could call this lumpy old mattress a bed - and used the lightening outside to see what he had scrounged to eat. There were a couple of pieces of two day old bread, a mostly brown banana, and a few Oreo cookies. It wasn't much, but with his grumbling stomach as proof, it would have to be enough. As he took a small bite of the bread a slow lonely tear slid silently down his dirty smudged cheek and blended with the rain that was still dripping from his hair.

If not for the deafening thunder all around him, the boy might

CUTTER 31

have heard the footsteps coming up beside him. Instead, the first sign that he was not alone was the voice that came from the end of his bed, "try this... its fresh." The man then placed a ham and cheese sandwich beside the boy along with a small bottle of chocolate milk. The boy glanced down at the sandwich and caught just enough of a glimpse of the arm to see three stripes on the navy blue sleeve. The boy also noticed a very distinctive ring with a large black stone in the middle with a special symbol carved into it – it looked like two circles with a line between them. The only thing the boy could think about was the offered sandwich, and dropping his two day old bread he began to gobble down the sandwich from the man. Between bites he was barely able to mumble out a, "thank you," and had he looked up he would have seen the man smile.

The boy finished the sandwich and milk quickly, only then seeming to take his first breath. He then remembered the man and looking up realized that there was a policeman standing at the end of his lean-to, just under the roof. The cop was smiling and holding out his hand to him, "why don't we see about finding you a proper bed and roof to keep you dry?"

The boy hesitated for a moment before selecting the only dry clothes left that he owned and putting them on. He hesitated again, and then standing; he took the man's hand and started to walk with him. He looked over his shoulder wondering if they would put him in one of those homes he heard about it and if he would ever come back here. He looked around as if trying to fill his mind with memories of what was his home, in case he didn't come back. Suddenly, the boy's eyes went wide as he remembered something he had left behind. He ran back over to his bed and grabbed a small wooden box from under the mattress. As he stood there looking at the box there was another loud clap of thunder that shook the building. Startled he ran back to the man and held tightly on to his outstretched hand, while his other hand grasped his cigar box tightly against his side.

***

Robert sat up with a start, looking around, unsure of where he was for a moment. The only light in the room came from the glow of the monitor beside his bed. After a few moments he found the call button for the nurse and nervously pressed it. Robert had never felt so unsure of his surroundings and so confused. It was several minutes before the nurse came in and when she did, she briefly checked the monitor making sure everything was ok. She then slipped a thermometer between his lips, while checking the pulse in his wrist. Removing the thermometer, she checked it and made several notes on his chart comparing it to what was previously noted by the other nurses. Seeing the sweat on his forehead, she picked up a small rag and dabbed the sweat away.

Licking his dry lips, he whispered, "can I have something to drink?" The nurse glanced at her watch and then smiling said, "I am sure we can find you something, give me a few minutes." As she stepped out of the room he glanced towards the windows and for the first time realized it was night. He looked around the room in the dim light and saw there were no flowers, no cards on the table, no chocolates, no balloons, and not even one stuffed animal. For the second time in recent memory he felt truly alone. In that instant he realized it was not the first time he had felt this way. A silent tear slid down his cheek, and he could not decide if the tears were for himself or for the boy in his dreams.

About fifteen minutes had passed before the nurse returned with jello and juice. After finishing the juice in a long swallow, Robert chuckled and in his most charming voice said, "if you get my cell phone I am sure I can do much better, for both of us."

The nurse laughed and said, "I am sure you can, but it is 3am and you need to get your rest." Seeing the look on his face, the nurse smiled and said, "come on, doctor's orders Mr. Cutter." As she left the room she turned off the light leaving him in the dark – the only light slipping from the hallway under the door.

Robert lay back against the pillows, his normally quick mind struggling to process and understand what had happened, and, almost more importantly, why? Was someone actually trying to kill him? If so, who? What could he have done to piss someone off that much? With these questions swirling around in his mind he closed his eyes and slowly fell back to sleep.

The next morning he was woken by the nurse, once again checking his vital signs and making notes in his chart. He started to ask about breakfast, but remembering the jello and juice from the night before he decided to ask for his cell phone. The nurse just smiled at him politely and said she would look for it in a moment. But before either of them could react the door opened and his personal assistant, Joseph, came in. He was quickly followed by two young ladies carrying several packages. From the smell, you could tell they contained bacon, eggs, hash browns, toast and even a carafe of his favorite coffee. The smell alone was intoxicating.

Sitting up, Robert smiled, "this doesn't look like my usual breakfast, Joseph!" The man grinned. "No, Sir, but you need your strength".

The nurse had moved out of the way when they arrived with the breakfast, and looked surprised as most people did when they heard Joseph speak. The smooth educated voice did not match the wrestler physique, which was clearly visible under the perfectly tailored *Saville Row* suit. At six foot four inches and almost two hundred fifty pounds he was massive, and even the perfect cut of his suit could not hide the strength that seemed to run through every muscle of his entire being.

The doctor came in and looking around smiled, "you certainly do attract a crowd Mr. Cutter. Ok, let's clear the room… again!" Instead of leaving, Joseph moved out of the way, motioning to the two young ladies to leave. Seeing the look from the doctor, Robert glanced at Joseph. "He's ok, Doctor – hell, Joseph probably knows me better than I do." She nodded, and then began looking through his chart making her own notes as she read those of the nurses from during the night.

"You were pretty lucky, Mr. Cutter, other than some cuts and bruises, you have just a minor concussion. You will have a headache for a few days, and may also experience some blurred vision and dizziness. If any of these symptoms continue past tomorrow I want to know right away. Also, if you notice that you are having trouble remembering things let me know." She glanced at Robert, then at Joseph, who nodded. Stepping over to Joseph she handed him her business card, "it has both my personal and work cell phone. I want you to call me at any time if there are any further complications. I have already put through the paperwork to have Mr. Cutter released, so it shouldn't be too much longer before you can go. While we will be done with you in about an hour, I am sure the various authorities would like to have a chat with you also." Then added with a smirk, "but they don't need to know that you have left the hospital, just yet."

"Now, do you have any questions? I will have the nurse go through some specifics with you, but is there anything I can answer for you?"

Robert hesitated, the confusion clear on his face. "Can you tell me what day it is? Also, there was a woman with me – is she ok?"

This caught Joseph by surprise and he glanced at the doctor. She smiled and replied, "that is quite normal, Mr. Cutter. Today is Tuesday. And before you ask, you came in on Sunday, two days ago. As far as I know, the woman was fine with just cuts and bruises but I can have someone check." The doctor gave Joseph a reassuring look, and then left the room.

An hour later Robert was feeling better after eating and getting cleaned up. He was dressed and ready to go. Joseph had also brought a change of clothes for him, including a navy blue pair of slacks, white polo shirt, and loafers. As Robert checked himself in the bathroom mirror he smiled knowing that only Joseph could have selected exactly the right clothes to help him feel comfortable today. He was also glad he had foregone the tie. His first thought had been to get back to work; then Robert realized that he might not have any other place to go at the moment. Just as surely as he knew Joseph would want him to rest at home, Robert knew that he had to go in to the office. He smiled as he wondered what his peers and other Wall Street executives might think if he made this a regular dress code for his staff.

Before they stepped through the door, Joseph stopped him with a hand on his arm. "From now on I go through every door first. Your security has always been important to us, now it's heightened and there are no arguments. Are we clear?"

Robert looked at him, then without hesitating smiled, "thank you, Joseph, for everything." As he opened the door, two men could be seen in the hallway, although given their size they would have been impossible to miss anywhere. They were either six foot seven or eight and both looked as though they weighed at least two hundred and fifty pounds of pure muscle, if not more. There was no doubt they were security, and the earpieces they both wore just made it more obvious. They both wore perfectly tailored suits that still could not hide their immensely muscled bodies, or the fact that they were both carrying guns. Robert expected to see an icy cold stare in their granite like faces – but the extra dark sunglasses made it impossible to know for sure.

Robert smiled to himself as they walked down the hallway,

one bodyguard in front and one behind. With Joseph beside him he almost felt invisible, which he supposed was the idea. Despite Robert being almost five feet ten and a muscular two hundred twenty pounds, he felt incredibly small surrounded by these three men. Glancing at Joseph to his left he caught a glimpse of the handgun that he carried under his perfectly cut suit.

Nodding towards the handgun, Robert said, "maybe you should show me how to use one of those, so I don't shoot myself in the foot."

"Yes Sir, I have already made the arrangements. You start this afternoon."

"Is there anything else I should know Joseph?"

"Yes sir. We're going to have the security at the penthouse upgraded, and I have already started the work at the house in Cape May as well as the house on the Keys. I've also parked the Aston Martin for a while, from now on we take care of the driving."

Robert acted upset, but they both knew it was an act as he said, "you know how much I love driving that car! What did you get me instead, a tank?"

"I know sir, and I am sorry. Well, not quite a tank." But, as they stepped outside Robert saw he was almost right. Standing at the curb with engines running were twin GMC Yukon Denali's. Both were as black as the night with deeply tinted windows. As Robert approached the cars he saw two more bodyguards already sitting in the driver seats. As the doors swung open he could see they had been strengthened and tapping the glass he presumed they were bulletproof. "Not quite huh?"

Joseph grinned and got in beside Robert, closing the door quickly behind him. He could see one bodyguard get into the other Yukon as the second got in the front seat of their SUV. The driver already had the car in gear and no sooner did the doors close than they were moving. They slalomed through the Manhattan traffic with such ease that Robert had no doubt the drivers were true professionals. When he glanced back he saw that the second vehicle was directly behind them. Even as he thought that this was most likely overkill, Robert also knew that he had did feel safer. But, the thought jumped into his mind a little too easily – was the bombing really aimed at him? Who would want him dead, and why?

Chapter 4

As they pulled up to the front of the building, Robert saw several reporters waiting outside. He glanced at Joseph, who was already motioning to the driver, who quickly shot around to the garage entrance. The gate moved up before they even reached it, almost as if the guard was able to read their minds. But, the nod he gave the drivers as they drove past him let Robert know that he had been warned they were on their way. Had Robert looked back he would have seen the other SUV follow right behind them, and the steel security gate dropping back into place as quickly as it was raised.

The Yukon carrying Robert, pulled up in front of the elevator, blocking it from the street and at the same time, the second SUV pulled in so that no other cars could even get close to them. As Robert reached for the door handle, Joseph gently placed a hand on his arm holding him back. The bodyguard from the second SUV got out, looking all around. As he scanned the entire area he seemed to see everything all at once. After waiting an extra moment, the bodyguard from Robert's Yukon got out and also looked around before he opened the door. As he did, he pressed the button on the elevator which immediately slid silently open. "You have a personal elevator now, so use it... and only use this one." All Robert could do was smile as he quickly moved into the elevator. He was followed quickly by Joseph and the two bodyguards before the doors swiftly closed behind them. Robert was suddenly very glad that he did not have claustrophobia, and hoped that the four of them were under the weight limit.

As the elevator rode to the top of the building Robert thought about all this extra security. He wondered how Joseph had managed some of this since it was not like he owned the building. He might have leased the top two floors, but there were a lot of other companies in the building. Robert remembered back to when he had selected this space for his business and smiled. He had selected it because of it's locale – just off Wall Street – but also because of the way it looked. He remembered a lesson he had learned early in his career. That sometimes, the presentation was almost as important as the content.

As they climbed quickly to the top floor, Joseph spoke quietly into a hand held microphone. Robert grinned and said, "Secret Service school of spook?" As Joseph smiled and nodded in response, Robert began to wonder just who was in charge anymore. But, for more than just a fleeting moment he was glad that Joseph was indeed on his side. He accepted that Joseph was simply looking out for him, so he was going to make it as easy as possible for him to do just that. Quickly getting used to the idea and knowing in advance what the security would be like, he waited when the elevator doors opened. Not that Robert could have gotten past the human wall standing in front of him anyway, so he waited patiently.

The first of the bodyguards stepped out, looked around quickly then stepped to the right of the doors. He was quickly followed by the second bodyguard who immediately moved to his left. Joseph stepped out between them, glanced around as well, and then looking back he nodded briefly to Robert. When he finally stepped out, Robert looked around feeling as though he was seeing the lobby of his own company again for the first time.

Straight ahead was Sylvia's reception desk – everyone referred to it as her desk, because she ruled it like a kindergarten teacher with a new class. No one got into the Cutter offices without first getting past Sylvia. The half-oval walnut desk with the large Cutter & Co. logo behind it was more like the bridge of a battleship than the entrance to a Wall Street firm. The fact that there was another bodyguard standing behind the oversized desk did not help. It actually made the normally slight Sylvia seem even tinier than normal. But despite her silver hair and matronly look there was no doubt who ruled the waiting area. The bodyguard stood with his huge arms crossed across his massive chest, his eyes always moving but you could guess that he would still have to listen to her.

To Robert's right, the smoked glass doors and wall leading to the executive wing had been replaced by thick oak doors. Robert could see the new security access panel which had been added just to the right of the doors. He looked at Joseph who simply smiled and nodded, just as he had been doing all morning. The smoked glass doors and wall on the left side were still in place, but Robert could see a similar security panel just against the wall that had not been there before. And without looking Robert got the sense that there were also video cameras monitoring the entrance way.

The seating area for waiting clients was still to the left, and the two flat panel televisions were still in place. But, although they were usually programmed for either Bloomberg or Fox financial news, one was now tuned in to CNN. As he approached the doors to the executive wing, Robert heard the CNN announcer talking about the Philadelphia fires which had finally been put out. Now the police and firemen were trying to find out what was the cause of the fires. The announcer also mentioned briefly that there were some local people that had been moved to a church nearby and were using it as a shelter.

Sylvia smiled politely, as she always did, and greeted him the same as always, "good morning, Mr. Cutter, nice to see you," as if it was just another normal day. It was then that Robert noticed the uniformed policeman quietly waiting in one corner. As the policeman made a move toward them, Joseph addressed him, "give us a moment and we will be right with you, thanks." Although Joseph spoke politely it was obvious that he was not asking, but telling. The uniformed cop nodded and raised his cell phone, obviously to let his superiors know that Robert was back. The executive wing was cut in half by two hallways - one had various sized glass walled conference rooms running the length on both sides. The second hallway was where the executive offices were. Each of these offices was large and comfortably furnished. As Robert approached each office, the occupant would come to the door and say, "good morning," and Robert could feel them watching him walk down to his own office.

As he walked down the hallway he seemed to notice all of the furnishings, artwork, and plaques for the first time. As with the choice of the building, in this wing the presentation was definitely an important part of business. Clients that came into the office and met with the executives expected to see lavish offices, conferences rooms, and waiting areas. The clients were important and the staff did everything they could to make them feel that way.

Ahead of him he could see his administrative assistant, Jennifer, standing and waiting for him. Even from this distance he could see that her normal brick wall of an exterior had taken a beating over the past couple of days. And from the look in her eyes it was obvious that she had indeed been worried about him. They had been working together since before Cutter & Co, so when he approached her he was not surprised when she threw her arms around his neck and held him tightly.

After a moment she let go of his neck, and looked at him

before pulling back, and then she spoke hesitatingly, "I'm sorry, are you ok?" When she stepped back he could see the redness around the edges of her eyes and knew that she had been crying.

He smiled reassuringly, "Its ok, I'm fine, Jennifer. The doctor says it's just a concussion, so no coffee for a few days." Then taking her hand he gave it a brief squeeze and continued, "give me a few moments and then we can catch up."

Although she normally followed right behind him with the days messages, notes, and the few newspapers he read every morning, today she held back until he was ready. As she watched Joseph and Robert head into the office and close the door she looked as if she was going to cry again. But, seeing the bodyguard stop outside of his office she held herself in check. She also knew that the rest of the office would be watching to see her reaction.

As they stepped into the office, Robert headed behind his desk and stood, looking out of the floor to ceiling windows. "Did you replace these with bulletproof glass already?"

Robert could sense the smile forming on Joseph's lips behind him as he replied. "No, Sir, the height of the building requires that they are actually stronger than bulletproof would be." Joseph took a breath before continuing, "look, I know this is a lot of changes you have to deal with. But I won't take any chances anymore with your safety. Certainly not until we are sure that the explosion was not directly intended for you."

Robert looked around the office as he sat down in his custom leather chair and felt as though had been away for two months instead of two days. He glanced at the normally orderly walnut desk and saw the usual stacks of messages, notes, and reports that were always waiting for him in the morning. The two wing chairs facing the desk were high backed with the same soft glove-like leather, and comfortable enough to put anyone sitting in them, immediately at ease. To his left was a sitting area for more relaxed conversations. With its two couches and several comfortable chairs it could have been a seating area in any of the best hotels around the world. The LED flat panel TV on that side of the room was hidden behind sliding doors on one side, and a fully stocked bar on the other side. On the other side of the room was a conference table surrounded with high-backed leather chairs. Each seat always had a notepad and a pair of pens ready for any impromptu meetings. The flat panel TV on that side of the room was turned on with the volume lowered, but instead of Bloomberg it was also tuned to CNN. In each corner of the room were two twin doors - the one on the left side led into a private living area for Robert's use. The door on the other side of the room led to the main conference room, which was hidden on the other side, so that it could be used to "make an entrance" if needed.

The walls of the room were decorated with framed, Forbes, Money, Newsweek, and Time covers, each announcing one of his company's deals. As he looked around, Robert realized that there was not one personal photo or item decorating the entire office. In fact, other than his chair, either Jennifer, or the decorator of her choice had chosen everything. It was all top of line furniture and technology, but nothing was his. No mugs, photographs, cards, or hand panted signs. Nothing.

Robert tried to focus as he looked at the piles of messages on the right, the equally large pile of telegrams above it, and the daily management reports in the middle. Topping the pile of reports was his daily briefing report which summarized the status of all the company's ongoing projects, as well as the status of his various investment portfolios. On any day, reviewing the company's daily briefing report would usually bring a broad smile to his face. Today, he just wondered how he could possibly get through it all. His confidence had definitely been shaken since the explosion, something, he would have to do something about.

Robert shook his head to clear the cobwebs and spent the next several minutes focusing on the reports in front of him. It was time for him to get back to work and he was going to force himself to do so. When Jennifer knocked and entered, Joseph stepped outside, closing the door quietly behind him. The second bodyguard was now stationed outside the office door, and Joseph nodded to him as he walked away heading towards the kitchen to make himself a cup of english breakfast tea.

Inside the office, Jennifer was covering some of the more important items that needed Robert's immediate attention. Among them, his chief strategy officer needed to review an issue with the pending casino project. Also, his chief legal counsel needed to talk to him about several political issues that were also related to the same casino project. And it was imperative that one of the board members speak with him "as soon as possible". With Martin it was always urgent, and usually that meant Robert would have to spend valuable hours speaking with him and listening to his latest investment idea. Usually, one that Robert would totally disagree with and expect to be a total failure. Robert told her that he would see them later, and when he looked up he could see that she was looking at him differently.

"Are you sure you should be here, Mr. Cutter? Maybe you should have taken an extra day or so?"

Robert stood and walked around the desk and took her hands in his. "I'm sure. I'm fine, Jennifer. I need to get back to work and there are too many things for me to just let them go. One more thing, as long as we are in this office, just the two of us, please call me Robert."

Smiling politely she said, "Yes, Mr. Cutter. Whatever you say. Perhaps a nice cup of tea would help?"

Smiling a little more confidently, he said, "sure, a cup of tea would be great."

Jennifer started to say something, then turned and headed out of the office. As she did, he glanced over at CNN and saw something about the fires in Philadelphia. "One more thing, can you ask Roger to pull together whatever he can about the fires in Philadelphia?"

She looked back at him questioningly, but he smiled reassuringly again, so she turned back nodding and then left. Outside the closed door she glanced briefly at the bodyguard, and then moved to the kitchen to make the tea for him. Joseph was glancing through the newspaper, sipping his tea, when she walked in.

She stopped beside Joseph letting her hand fall to his shoulder, "he is ok right, Joseph?"

He reached up and patted her hand, "yes, he really is. I think perhaps his confidence is just a little bruised. I am sure he is just feeling a little off, but he will bounce back. We just need to keep an eye on him to be sure. Did something happen?"

"No. I am sure you are right. It was odd though, he asked me to have Roger investigate those fires in Philadelphia and put together a package for him." As she answered she moved to the counter to make the tea.

Smiling, Joseph answered her, "well, knowing Robert he is probably already starting to think about how he can make some money from the Philadelphia thing."

She nodded, still thinking about whether it was just that, or something more. "Joseph, do you think this security is really necessary? I mean, surely we are ok inside the offices?"

He smiled and said, "well, right now it's actually more for Robert than for us. Give it a couple of weeks and we can probably lose the guys. But the rest is here to stay."

Jennifer nodded and went back to her tea making, when it was ready she took it in to Robert's office and found him sitting at his desk just staring out the windows. "Is there anything else you need, Mr. Cutter?

Robert looked up at her. "No, thank you, Jennifer. You can let Lowell and Frank know that I will see them now." And then he took the file she was holding knowing that it was related to the casino project. As he glanced through first the summary then the detailed reports, everything seemed normal – at least on paper. He wondered what could be bothering the two normally unflappable chiefs of his. Lowell had helped him work through some pretty complex acquisitions before, maybe he thought this might be different because it was a casino. And Frank, well, he was probably just being a lawyer.

Robert looked up as they entered and smiled as they walked toward him. The two could be brothers in looks and yet he knew that each had a very different mind and way of approaching any challenges they might face. It was for this reason that he cherished and trusted their input as much, if not more, than any other executive on his staff. Both of them were about five feet seven inches and 180 pounds and both were even dressed alike wearing blue shirts, striped ties and navy blue pants. They both wore silver framed glasses and had thinning salt and pepper hair. The one difference between them was that occasionally you could see that Frank had a slight limp that seemed to come out even more in cold damp weather. When Robert had asked him about once he had answered simply that it was "from my past."

The two stood in front of his desk until Robert looked up, smiled and said, "Did I miss the dress code today?" Seeing the look on their faces he smiled and said, "I'm fine guys, sit down. Now, tell me what's going on with the project and what has got the two of you so worried. Is that senator from Nevada still hassling you for a sit down, Frank? What was his name?"

"His name is John Tower, and yes, his office has been trying to arrange a meeting with us since the deal for the Bellagio broke. But, we have other concerns as well. I have been hearing rumors that there is another private equity group looking to start a bidding war. As you know we are still within the window of opportunity for others to outbid us. It is even possible that the current management team is looking to take the company private with some backing."

Lowell leaned forward then looking at his fellow chief said, "Frank, rumor is a good word for it. And while we don't normally concern ourselves with rumors I have been hearing similar things. I already spoke to both Chase and Bank of America and they have assured me that when the time comes they will back us. So we will be able to move as quickly as we need to. But it wouldn't hurt to have Tower on our side." He glanced at Frank momentarily again, then back to Robert before he continued. "There is also a potential issue with the current ownership. It seems that there may be some additional background checks we need to do in case there are already private investors in place. It is possible that they would want to retain an ownership component, even if we were to go through with the deal."

Robert leaned back in his chair, "Ok, so what are you not saying out loud? Is there union trouble? Or something else?"

Frank shook his head and said, "we don't think it's the union members, but it could be something related. There may be a *connection* we were unaware of."

Robert looked from Lowell to Frank and back, the surprise evident on his face. "A *connection*? You mean you think there may be an organized crime connection?"

Lowell and Frank both looked at each other before Frank finally answered, "we are quite honestly not sure at this point. We are working to find out, and talking to people who may have an idea. But so far nothing. And in the meantime we are focused on finding out who the other private equity group might be."

"Ok, guys. Keep me in the loop on that. Anything else? How is the aircraft deal going?"

Lowell smiled and said, "as you expected that would be a piece of cake. It is basically already a done deal. But, because of the government contract we are still waiting for regulatory approvals. I don't see any real issue with this one, it should close in another month or so."

Robert stood. "Great! Good job, guys. And Frank, let's get in front of the Senator. Call Thompson from the political liaison group and have him set it up. Let's find a way for me to meet with him before he gets his panties in a bunch and becomes a real pain. Oh, and I asked Roger to work up a background package for me on a new project."

The two men nodded and left the office, as the door closed, Robert could see two men in suits standing in the hallway. Almost before the door closed, Jennifer buzzed him to say that the FBI and NYPD would like a few minutes. He told her that he needed a moment and then to send them in.

While he waited for them to come in, he saw that CNN was doing a story on the bombing. Turning up the volume he heard the reporter saying that there was still no word on who the target might be. Robert flinched when he saw the front of the building boarded up, and the burned cars at the curb – hopefully this was not a live shot. While the reporter continued to talk, they showed his motorcade as it had passed the office building quickly, and moved through to the garage. Then they flashed his photo, as well as that of several of the other high profile apartment owners, on the screen while discussing whom the potential target might be. When they showed footage of him being loaded into the ambulance, Simone on the gurney beside him he broke out in a sweat. Not because of seeing himself immobilized with the neck and back braces – which was bad enough. But it was the sight of the shrouded body on the ground nearby – blood already seeping through the cover.

Even though the doctor had told Robert he should stay away from alcohol, he made his way unsteadily over to the bar. His hands were shaking as he poured himself two fingers of his best scotch. He quickly downed it, then poured a second glass which he drank a little more slowly. The smooth burn he felt as he swallowed the scotch helped to reduce the shaking in his hands. But he could not seem to shake the overwhelming feelings of sadness, fear, and a growing lack of self-confidence. For most of his life he had been, "the boss". Now he was starting to feel as if someone else was pulling the strings. Before closing the door to the bar, he grabbed a couple of breath mints. He didn't need, nor want, the police to smell alcohol on his breath. He then walked over to the door and opened it himself, inviting the officers inside. As he stood in the doorway he got a look from Jennifer wondering what was wrong, since he never came to the door himself. Joseph also frowned and then nodded his head towards the bodyguard who was standing rigidly to attention. Joseph's look reminded Robert that he was not supposed to be opening doors any more.

As the two men followed him into the room, Robert offered a drink pointing over to the bar. He paused just before reaching the desk and instead turned back and walked over to the sitting area. As he sat on the couch and the officers each took a seat, Jennifer came in and offered drinks as she handed Robert another cup of tea.

The younger of the two smiled politely. "No thank you, Mr. Cutter. We would prefer to get right down to it, so we don't take up too much time out of your busy day. We have taken statements from the rest of the people at the scene and some of the other tenants. So here is the obvious question – do you have any reason to think that someone would want to kill you?"

Robert leaned forward and took a sip of the tea, "I want to help in any way I can, so, I will never be too busy for you, gentlemen." Then he frowned and took another sip of tea, "to answer your question, not that I can think of. But, to be honest I have not really thought about it. Certainly no-one obvious comes to mind. In the finance world we don't really go out and kill someone just because we lose a deal."

"So, nothing related to any of your pending deals? Perhaps the casino or even the aircraft company?"

Robert looked surprised "Agent...," he hesitated, trying to remember if he should know the man's name. "You are certainly well informed. But, no, I can't imagine that it could be that; or any other deal."

"Its Special Agent, Sam Simmons and this is Detective Jack Franklin. We would appreciate if you would give it some thought. And, if you think of anything - no matter how small, please let us know."

As they stood, each man handed Robert a business card, which he carefully looked over as he nodded. They could both see that his mind was moving quickly and already beginning to focus on other things. As they turned to leave though they were stopped by Robert. "Gentlemen, thank you again for coming to my office to see me. I appreciate your efforts so far in trying to find out what happened. If you wouldn't mind keeping me informed on any findings I would appreciate that also."

Both men turned back to face Robert, who was standing with his hand extended. This was different than what they were expecting based on their research of the ruthless man they thought they were meeting. They shook hands and then Robert handed each one his own personal card, with a comment to call any time they needed anything. Walking them to the door he noticed a distinctive black onyx ring on the FBI agent's right hand.

"That is a rather distinctive ring, Agent Simmons."

Simmons glanced down and said, "thank you, it was actually my father's. My grandfather gave it to him when he became a Philadelphia cop."

"Thanks again for coming by. I will definitely give it some consideration, and I will have my staff put the list together for you." As the door closed, Robert walked over to the windows and looking out he could still picture the agent's ring. As he closed his eyes, he did not see it on the agent's hand – instead he saw it on a bigger, older looking hand. He could not imagine why the ring looked so familiar, or why he felt like he had seen it before.

He turned back to his desk and sitting down, he forced himself to go through the messages and telegrams before focusing on the various reports. He started to make notes that he would need Jennifer and his staff to follow up on. For a while he quietly went about his business, focusing on the different projects and their individual issues. He was able to concentrate entirely on work for a while and started to feel as if things could start to get back to normal.

Chapter 5

*T*he boy opened his eyes, or at least he thought they were open. It was pitch dark in the room – he had never seen it so dark. So much so that he could not even see his hand until it touched his nose. For a few moments he did not know where he was. Then the almost forgotten dampness and musty smells came back to him and he knew. He was back at the old warehouse, lying on his damp mattress. He wondered why it was so dark. Maybe he should have stayed with Sam after all. But then he had never trusted any adult before so why should he start now?

Thinking of Sam reminded him of the flashlight he had given him. Reaching out with his right hand he found it and flicked the switch. The sudden blaze of light made him blink several times until his eyes could adjust. He was not even sure what day of the week it was or how long he had been sitting here. As he stood up, he realized that his clothes were damp so it couldn't have been that long.

The boy made his way carefully to the door on the far wall and opening it slightly found that it was night. Although, it was so dark that he could not see the moon or any stars. It was raining so hard that he could not tell where the sky ended and the building began. The boy wondered how it could be raining again – had it ever stopped? In just moments, even though he was standing partially behind the door he was getting drenched from the rain that was being blown in by the wind - which was getting stronger by the moment. He quickly closed the door and made his way back to his little shelter when he heard a large clap of thunder. In the empty warehouse the sound was amplified and seemed to shake every inch of the building right through his shoes to his toes. He couldn't help it – he looked up as if he were pleading for the storm to stop. Feeling rather vulnerable out in the middle of the warehouse he quickly made his way to the lean-to. He curled up in the corner and held the flashlight so tightly that his little knuckles went white as he silently prayed that the flashlight would not go out. He sat there curled into a tight ball shivering from the damp and cold as much as from the thunder crashing around him.

Suddenly, the door was blown wide open by a huge gust of wind and at the same moment several of the upper windows blew open sending shards of glass all over the warehouse floor. The boy pulled himself even tighter into a little ball, looking as though he was trying to crawl into the wall for safety. He looked at the drab pillows and bedding around him that were starting to get wet. Even amidst the noise of the thunder and creaking warehouse the little boy could be heard whimpering. His face was a ghostly white and the flashlight danced around the room as he hands shook.

As the wind continued to howl and shriek, the thunder crashed and boomed all around him. The lightning crashes, quickly became so constant that it was almost as if the night had turned into day. As several more windows exploded inward, littering glass all along the floor, the boy lifted his eyes to the sky and said a silent prayer that the storm would stop. By now, there were more broken windows and more glass on the floor than were left in the walls itself. In the next flash of lightning, the boy looked towards the main door and thought it looked odd from where he was sitting. The door looked almost like it was crooked – like a cartoon door.

He was more scared than he had ever been before. As his eyes roamed nervously around the warehouse he reached for a small wooden box beside his bed. It held the few meager possessions that he cared about and he pulled out a small silver medallion and chain, and clasped them in his tiny little hand. At the next flash of light he saw that indeed the main door was shifted more to one side than usual. He heard a deep rumbling sound that sounded just like the freight train that still went through the area from time to time. In his heart he knew it was not a train. Instinctively he knew that he had to get out, and at the next flash of lightening he began to make his way over to a side door that was closer to his shelter.

As the thunder and lightning continued to crash around him he started to run. The glass and rain made the floor slick and he slipped and fell, landing awkwardly on his ankle. He felt the glass on the floor cutting into his hands, but ignored it. He knew he had to get out so he quickly got to his feet and ran even harder for the door. He ran faster ignoring the pain in his ankle and leg, wiping his hands off on his jeans. The shrieking freight-train-sounds behind him were getting louder as was the thunder. He quickly reached the door and pushed against it, but it was stuck. He pushed harder, throwing all of his tiny forty-five pounds against it, as hard as he could.

Suddenly, there was a gust of air behind him and then he was sailing head over heels through the air. The heavy rains continued to drench what little bit of him was not already soaked. He felt something else pelting his little body as he landed heavily on the ground outside – it felt like heavy snow. He lay on his stomach where he had landed, trying to catch his breath. Then ignoring the pain he was feeling, picked himself up and started running again. He didn't stop running until he reached the end of the alley. When he turned around his eyes went wide and he gasped at the sight as he continued to walk backwards. The entire warehouse was gone, and where it had been standing there was nothing but a huge pile of rubble.

He stood there staring for several moments, his tears mixing with the rain. As he walked away it dawned on his that he had no place to go, no place to sleep, and certainly no place to get dry. The pain in his leg and ankle was getting worse with every step and had he looked he would have seen that the palms of his hands and his knees were bleeding. He could feel the scratches on his cheeks and chin but knew he had to keep moving. All he wanted was someplace dry where he could put his head down and rest for a few minutes. He saw a bus stop ahead and stepped into it, relishing the little shelter it gave him. The little boy sat on the bench and found that it was a little dry, even if the rain was still falling heavily around him. For the first time he realized that the thunder was now further off and the lightening was not right on top of him anymore.

He opened his left hand and looked down at the small medallion he was clutching so tightly. He closed his eyes to say a prayer but he was so tired that the moment his eyes were closed he began to fall asleep. He barely heard the voice talking to him, or the strong arms that lifted him up. The arms carried him over to a car and he felt as if he were floating through the air. He heard a car door open and could tell he had been laid down on the back seat and a blanket was being laid over him. The man noticed the medallion and box in his little hand and carefully placed it on the floor of the car. The boy felt the car shift as the man sat down in the front of the car, but he was falling asleep again as he heard the man speak.

"Central, this is P25. I have a young boy requiring medical attention. I am unsure of the extent of the injuries but there is a lot

of blood on him. Tell the emergency room that I am on my way. The boy has no identification so Social Services will have to be alerted. P25 Out." Had the boy still been awake he might have seen the policeman shake his head and mumble that he should have made the boy stay with him, but he had questioned whether he could even care for the boy.

***

The next few days were just like any other day for Robert – there were no car accidents, bombs, or other incidents and he started to fall back into his usual routine. Despite the extra security, everyone else also seemed to slip back into their regular work routine, coming in early and leaving the office late. The fact that he was living in a hotel didn't help him feel more at ease – but focusing on work seemed to help. The headaches he had been experiencing lately were becoming less frequent. Aside from some minor aches and pains to remind him of the bombing, he also found that he was paying a lot more attention to what was going on around him.

One morning he noticed that Jennifer had a new hairstyle, and he surprised her when he complimented her on it. He smiled when he saw her blush a deep crimson. Although he would not admit to anyone that he was feeling different, others had noticed that there was a change. He stopped to say hello more frequently and paid more attention to "normal" office things. No one more than Jennifer saw this change in him, but she was not going to admit to anyone that she liked this Robert Cutter, just a little more than the old one. Especially if he noticed her hair a little more.

On Friday morning, Jennifer came in as usual to go through his calendar with him and reminded him that he had a charity event that evening. She had already placed his tuxedo and clothes in the suite next to his office, and asked if he wanted a haircut later this afternoon. He had simply grinned – something he did a lot more these days – and said he would leave it to her discretion. To his surprise she blushed a bit and said that he looked just fine. Then just as quickly she asked if he needed a limousine to pick anyone up - he glanced sharply up, arched an eyebrow then quickly answered, "no need".

As Jennifer turned to leave he did not see her smiling to herself, when he asked, "who is the benefit for?"

She took a moment to gather herself, and then as she turned, she said, "it's for St. John's Hospital, a new department they are developing for head injury patients." She hesitated a moment, "but if you would rather not go…" She was suddenly at a loss for what to say. Quickly changing the subject, she said, "by the way, Frank and Lowell wanted me to let you know that Senator Tower was going to be there this evening."

"No, I definitely want to go tonight; besides it will do me good to get out. Make sure Joseph knows the details please. And if the check has not been prepared ask them to double it. Thanks, Jenn."

She did a 'double take' at the "Jenn," then said, "Yes Sir, I will find out about the check, and will make sure that Joseph has all the details. Is there anything else, Sir?"

"No that's all. Make sure that Thompson gets me the background package on Tower that I will need so I can review it on my over there." He flashed her an exasperated look. "And please, call me Robert when we are alone!"

"Yes, Sir." As she started to head out of the door, Roger handed her a file saying that Robert had asked for it. Before he could walk away, Robert called out for him to come in.

Roger stepped inside and as he walked towards the desk was already starting to talk. At just five and half feet tall, overweight, balding and with thick round glasses, Roger was the most unassuming person that Robert knew. He also suffered from a slight stutter which meant that most people never really understood just how intelligent he was. Robert had more than once called him his secret weapon. Despite being one of his top analysts, Roger would never advance any higher. He had more than once said that he was fine with that because he did not need all the added aggravation that seemed to come with a title. He also had the incredible ability to not only get to the root cause of any issue, but also to anticipate the various potential solutions just as quickly.

Roger always talked fast and with his stutter it was sometimes very hard to follow him. Robert asked for the short version and found that there was nothing much to tell about the Philadelphia fires. There were approximately three blocks that had been leveled by the fires leaving nothing behind but smoldering piles of burned wood and broken glass. The Philadelphia fire department was considering the fires to be suspicious and had already found the building which was the source of the fires. The three square blocks that had been burned were made up of warehouses, empty stores and about two dozen homes that had been occupied.

Robert was amazed that anyone could actually live in that neighborhood, given how run down the area was – from what he had learned, some of the city buses refused to stop there. What had made Robert stop reading for a moment was that these same people who had lived on the edge of complete poverty were now homeless and relying on help from a city that had until now completely ignored them. According to Roger the rumor was that a real estate company owning most of the warehouses and store properties had gotten tired of not getting any profitable rental income. The area had been slated for urban renewal but the loans and plans had never materialized. It was understood that either, no one saw any real potential for the neighborhood, or it was caught up in political red tape – or perhaps both.

Robert asked hopefully, "do you know which company owned the properties? And please tell me it is not one of ours?"

Roger looked relieved as well, and said, "no, Sir, it is not one of ours. The company that actually owns the properties is about a dozen layers deep, but it ends up in the hands of the GC Real Estate company. There is a detailed financial background package in the file."

Robert looked up from the report when he heard the hesitation in Roger's voice. "Ok... obviously there is something you want to add."

Roger hesitated for a moment "from what I can see of this company, they tend to focus on holdings that are low rent buildings - and they keep them that way. Their tenants are people who do not have a voice and generally have no choice, as they can't afford to move either. There have been public complaints filed before, but nothing illegal. From what I have found, even the city generally ignores the neighborhood. According to financial documents, they list the properties at their full potential value - which puts them at about fifty million. But the real value is probably less than half that. According to my contact at Chase, they owe at least that much, if not more on them."

"Thanks, Roger, good work. Is there contact information in the package for the real estate company, as well as the banks?"

"Yes, Sir, everything is in the executive summary."

As Roger made his way out of the office, Robert was already flipping through the file and picking up the phone to call his own contact at Chase. Since he was a much stronger customer with Chase he was not very concerned with being turned down when asking for the full financial package on the company. When he hung up the phone fifteen minutes later he already had an idea forming in his mind, and was grabbing pencil and paper to start putting things together.

Robert told Jennifer he did not want to be disturbed for the rest of the day, and then put together his own list. He knew there would be a lot to do, issues that would have to be overcome, and questions to be asked. The planning of this new project was going to take a lot of effort and focus from everyone involved. Robert also knew that some of those involved would not understand his motivation, but they would follow along regardless. He also had to admit that he felt invigorated with this project and that he had a real purpose behind his work - more than just making money. He double checked the list he had made, making sure that each of the people assigned were truly the best for their specific tasks. Finishing the list he turned to face the windows, leaned back in his chair and smiled. He could just imagine the reactions that this new project and list of assignments would generate. But, he also knew that he needed to shake the team up to accomplish this.

Robert spent the next hour writing a detailed business plan including both the financial projections, the roles of the major players, and a very lengthy and detailed management summary, explaining the purpose and benefits of the project. As best he could, he listed all of the potential issues they would be facing. As if to accentuate how important this new project was to Robert he finished it off with a personal note. He knew that the document itself would raise several eyebrows – just as he knew that sending this himself would show everyone just how serious he was.

Robert usually wrote his memos on paper, or made notes on reports for Jennifer to type for him as needed - even a lot of his emails were reviewed before he sent them out. His speeches, few and far between that they were, were normally written by his public relations group from ideas that he would draft for them. Today, he not only took the project from idea to plan, he wrote the document himself; something he had not done in quite a while. Then, when he was satisfied with it, he typed it himself and with a brief cover email, prepared to send it to the new team he had put together .

Robert stood looking out the windows as the dusk rolled across the city. He felt good about the project and confident it could be done. When he thought of those poor families out in the streets with no place to go, he felt a deep sadness that he had not felt in quite a while. Some of his staff would question whether this project was a result of the bombing. He would gladly admit that maybe it was. But, why not? Why not give something back to people who so obviously had no one else to turn to. He would be the first to admit that he had made a lot of money – certainly more than he could spend. As the day grew darker around him he looked at his reflection in the window. It seemed to smile back at him, as if giving approval for what he was trying to do. He knew that he had to do this, and that he had to be successful. And he was also quick to admit that it was as much for their sake, as for his own.

Turning back to his desk, he hit the send button and before the screen had even cleared he pressed the intercom to tell Jennifer that he was going to be getting ready for the benefit, and no matter what, he was not to be disturbed. She knew that he meant absolutely no interruptions, and she took that role of her job very seriously. Within minutes of hanging up the phone, Lowell and Frank were both standing in the doorway demanding to see him. Jennifer simply said that he had already left to get ready for the benefit and they would have to wait until Monday to talk to him.

Chapter 6

Robert stood in front of the full length mirror looking at the image in front of him. For a moment he felt like he didn't recognize the person looking back at him. The perfectly tailored designer tuxedo, Swiss made watch, bespoke shirt and matching cuff links were things that he was used to wearing. Somehow tonight felt different, almost as if he were wearing a costume and mask and that it didn't really belong. Almost as if he were a kid at Thanksgiving that had been invited to sit at the grown-up's table. Even as he stood there, Robert had to admit to himself that his life had changed. Literally, in a flash of light, his entire world had shifted and he would have to figure out this new existence – just as he had always done. He had always adjusted easily to changing situations in his life – but this was different.

There was a soft knock at the door and Robert opened it to find Joseph waiting for him. He was wearing a tuxedo as well, but Robert knew that he was going as security. And he did not need to see the earpiece to know that he would be by his side all night. The fact that there was going to be at least one senator there would surely add to his own heightened security. As they walked out of the office and down the hall Joseph handed him the invitation and the check that he had asked for earlier. The Yukon was waiting in the garage as usual and they drove to *The Pierre* without any trouble. When they got there they had to wait in a long line of

Limousines and Mercedes' before they could pull up to the front door. With the increased security and sitting in a car in the middle of unmoving traffic, Robert found himself fidgeting - something he had never done before. Sensing his discomfort, Joseph spoke quietly to the driver who quickly pulled out of the line of waiting cars and drove around to the rear entrance. Robert smiled and nodded as Joseph knowingly placed a reassuring hand on his arm.

They worked their way quickly through the kitchen heading to the ballroom with Robert sandwiched as usual between Joseph and one of the bodyguards. Approaching the ballroom they saw that there was a line of people waiting to get in. As Robert got in the security line he began to relax, smiling, nodding to others and shaking hands with people he knew socially. He was not sure if they were surprised to see him out in public again. Just as he was not sure if everyone happy to see him – the unasked question still floating around as to whether he had been the target of the bomb.

Robert suddenly felt a hand on his arm and turning saw that it belonged to Martin Anderson, one of his least favorite board members. Robert hoped that it didn't show on his face how much Martin could annoy him. It wasn't that Martin was a bad guy or anything, just sometimes his ideas could be a little difficult to put into action. And usually they would cost a lot of money and not bring the usual high level of return that his investors were used to. Plus, he always seemed to act like he was better than a lot of the other people around him.

"Good evening Robert. This will surely be a lovely event and such a good cause. Don't you think?"

"Hello Martin. Yes, the Pierre is a lovely venue and I am sure they did a great job. This is a wonderful cause as I don't believe that we know enough about concussion and head injuries."

"If you have a few moments Robert, I was actually hoping that we could discuss a new business venture. I think that with minimal investment we could turn around a struggling business. The owner is a good man, he just needs some help."

Robert fought the urge not to roll his eyes as he said "what kind of a business is it?"

"It's an art gallery that focuses on the alternate life style, and especially on the type of stuff of that book "Fifty Shades of Gray". But the owner – a good man – needs help with marketing, and perhaps new space. That kind of stuff."

"Martin, this really isn't the right time for that kind of an investment. But, if you would like to drop off a copy of the financial information I can have one of my analysts take a look."

"Sure, Robert. If all you can manage to spare is an analyst for me? But, I was quite honestly hoping for a little more. I would appreciate it if you would take the time to take this seriously and meet the owner at his store."

"Martin, I have quite a bit on my plate at the moment. Call Jennifer in the morning and she can try to arrange for a meeting. I make no promises, but I will try."

"Thank you Robert. That wasn't so bad." And then Martin turned away and walked over to another Wall Street investor that Robert knew.

As he stepped through the security gate and into the ballroom he paused to take in how beautifully it was decorated. Everywhere he looked there were fresh flowers and the tables were set with fine china and silverware. The round tables were spread around the middle of the room with a stage at the front of the room. Along both sides were two long bars staffed by several bartenders each. Throughout the room the waiters and waitresses moved about carrying trays of champagne glasses or appetizers. The men were, of course, all dressed sharply in tailored black tuxedos, while the women were dressed in a rainbow of colors. Standing and looking around the room, Robert felt as if someone had let a zoo-full of peacocks loose in the ballroom. As he stepped inside the vast room he felt a hand on his elbow and turned to find Lowell McDermott standing beside him.

"Good evening, Lowell. Beautiful room... don't you think?"

Lowell looked exasperated, "yes... beautiful. Can we discuss your email? There are several things I am concerned about that you may have overlooked."

Arching an eyebrow as he glanced at him, Robert replied. "Really? Well, that is why I want the team I chose, to figure out whatever I may have over looked. But not tonight. We will talk on Monday morning when the entire team has a chance to review the document. Oh, and Lowell – this is important to me - so maybe you should spend the rest of the weekend figuring how to tell me what we can do – instead of what we can't. Now, enjoy yourself."

As Lowell started to answer, Robert was distracted by a woman standing on the other side of the room. It was not just her natural beauty or her long luxurious red hair that seemed to attract Robert's eye. There was something else - something that looked familiar to him, he just couldn't place her. Considering the number of benefits he normally went to in a year, it was not surprising that she would look familiar. After all, most of these people all went to the same benefits. But, this woman did not look like the rest - she actually looked a little uneasy at all of the attention she was getting. She was surrounded by a group of men that seemed to hang on her every word. That may have just been because of the incredible black silk gown she wore, but Robert thought it had more to do with how she wore it.

Lowell was still talking and realizing that Robert was not paying attention placed a hand on his arm. "Robert... are you listening to me?"

Robert looked startled as he looked back at Lowell, obviously he had forgotten he was standing there. "Sorry. Do you see that woman across the room in the black dress? Long dark red hair, glasses. Do you know her?"

Obviously unhappy with this response he said, "no Robert I don't. Can we please..."

But Robert was already moving across the room, leaving Lowell standing with an uneasy look on his face. Robert did not know why he felt so attracted to this woman. He just knew that he needed to meet her – he could feel it deeply as if he was drawn to her. As he moved through the room he searched the faces around her looking for someone he knew. As he got closer the woman turned her head slightly in his direction, then smiled. Her smile caused Robert to pause a step. It was just a small smile and he had certainly had plenty of women smiling at him before. But there was something in that smile that seemed to light up her entire face. Not only that, but it also seemed to light up everyone else who was standing near her. Her smile moved easily from the edges of her lips to her bright green eyes, causing them to shimmer even if just for the moment that they connected with his.

At the same moment that he paused, he was jostled, by an apparently drunk guest who had been walking towards him. Something didn't quite seem right about the man as the white shirt he was wearing grew a red spot in the middle. And the red spot was getting bigger, engulfing his chest. His mouth had fallen open and his breath seemed to stop just as it was escaping his mouth. As the man fell into him, Robert tried to side step him then looked down at his own hands in slow motion. Robert was trying to understand what had spilled all over his hands that they were suddenly red and sticky. Obviously the man had been drinking red wine, and a little too much of it too early in the evening. In the moments it took for Robert to register that it was blood on his hands, he began to hear the screams forming around him. And in that same moment that the screams registered, he was being knocked to the floor. The weight on top of him was so heavy he felt as if he was being pushed through the floor. As Robert landed heavily his breath exploded from his chest. He tried to push the body off of him, but it was completely unmoving.

Then he heard the voice whisper in his ear, "Robert. It's Joseph. Just lie still for a moment while we make sure it's safe."

There were several more moments of them laying there and as Robert looked around he could see people running all around screaming or crying. When he finally looked up he realized that they had rolled under a table. Finally Joseph rolled off of him and checked that Robert was unharmed. As Joseph spoke into his microphone he motioned for Robert to wait a moment. As he waited Robert saw that there were several people kneeling over the fallen man trying to help him. Apparently he was already dead, as they finally pulled a cloth from a fallen table over him.

As Robert looked away he felt a heavy weight pressing down on his chest and found that he was having trouble catching his breath. He tried to call out to Joseph for help, but couldn't get his voice to react. He reached out for Joseph's arm and grasped it tightly, his fingers frantic to find a hold on the fabric of his jacket. Robert heard Joseph call out for a doctor to help him, as he effortlessly hurled the table out of the way and loosened Robert's tie and collar. Robert looked up at the ceiling and tried to understand how it could be moving, but it seemed to be moving further and further away from him. It seemed as if he were falling into a deep pit and he couldn't understand it, since he had been in a ballroom a moment ago. As his eyes began to flutter closed he became even more confused when he saw an angel appear above him. He felt her soft touch and just before he passed out thought he recognized the glimmer in the shinning green eyes.

***

Robert came awake, his eyes slowly fluttering open. As they came into focus he settled on Joseph who was kneeling beside him. "Welcome back, sir. How are you feeling?"

Robert's face was white and his eyes seemed to jump all around the room trying to understand what had happened. Then he whispered, "Ok, I guess. What happened?"

"According to the good doctor, you may have had an anxiety attack. But, she wants you to go to the hospital for some additional tests just to be safe."

"Doctor? She? What doctor?"

Joseph chuckled as he took Robert's elbow and helped him stand up. Waiting by his side as Robert steadied himself, Joseph's eyes continued to scan the room. "Yes – *she*. The doctor was the redheaded woman, green eyes, black dress. Perhaps you noticed her... since you were walking right towards her."

As they walked toward the exit, Robert saw the remaining guests looking his way. Some were trying to be less obvious about it and were sneaking a glance under down turned eyes, but some of the other guests looked directly at him, the obvious question in their eyes as to whether it was safe around him. At the door they were stopped by Detective Franklin and Agent Simmons – who were questioning all of the remaining guests. They briefly went through the evening and since Robert did not know anything more than anyone else they were allowed to leave.

As they drove to the hospital, Joseph explained that the man who had been killed was an aide to Senator Tower. Senator Tower had been standing just a few feet away and the man had been sent to ask Robert to join them. The detectives believed that a 9mm was used, but because no shots were heard also assumed a silencer was used. It had been mostly pure luck that Robert had not been hit. Joseph explained that they did not believe the aide was the target and the only reason the shooter missed was because Robert veered towards the doctor. It went without saying that if Robert had continued walking straight towards the doctor he would have been hit. Joseph left it unsaid that Robert had been mere inches away from being hit. Joseph further explained that they did not know who the intended target really was since the gunman had escaped during the bedlam that followed. However, Joseph was pretty sure that he had been aiming for Robert.

Robert turned quickly and stared at him, "how can you say that?"

Joseph hesitated, "because he fired a second time when he realized that he missed."

Robert's eyes were wide with concern, "you mean there was a second person killed? Who else was shot tonight?"

Joseph hesitated for a moment; glancing out the tinted windows as the streetlights moved past them, "let's just say that I will be forever in the debt of DuPont and Kevlar. Thankfully the shooter was far enough away that all it did was knock me over."

Robert stared out the tinted car window not seeing any further than the glass itself. He slowly wiped at the fine sheen of sweat that was had formed on his forehead. Joseph was trying to reassure him but realized that Robert was not listening. He was sure that the police and FBI were going to do everything they could to find out who was behind these acts. All Robert could do was shake his head and wonder – who could possibly want him dead this badly? It seemed obvious to Robert that he was indeed the target. He kept thinking over and over – what could he have done to warrant this? Or was it just some troubled soul who was hearing voices in his head.

***

They were in the hospital until almost dawn and by the time they pulled up at the Plaza Hotel, Robert was practically asleep. They were staying at the Plaza while his building was being renovated. As they arrived, Robert had to admit that he was never so glad to be greeted by the silence. For a city that never sleeps, this was a very quiet area of the city and a very quiet time of night. The fact that the hotel was right next to Central Park certainly helped with the quiet. Although his apartment had also looked out over the Park, this was a different view. Different, but just as peaceful and it was one of the reasons they had chosen the hotel.

The Plaza had gone to great lengths to make sure that he was comfortable until he could return to his own apartment. There were several guests that had been inconvenienced, and the entire staff had been given strict instructions about his privacy, plus there was a lot of additional security that everyone had to deal with. The guests were probably the most inconvenienced as some had been "asked" to change suites. The added security was not only an extra hassle for the guests on his floor, but was also the source of some embarrassment. Especially for the couple who had done a bit too much celebrating and had gotten off on the wrong floor. Unfortunately they thought the suite across from Robert's was theirs, and were quickly sobered when confronted by several body guards with guns drawn and pointed in their direction.

Robert spent the rest of the weekend trying to relax and find the peace that seemed to be just out of his reach. He had been having difficulty sleeping since the bombing, and the headaches were becoming more frequent again. He began to work out again, but as much as he loved jogging in the park Joseph had forbidden it. Besides, he guessed that neither of his bodyguards would be able to keep up with him. Robert had learned that there was no point in arguing with Joseph and he had to admit that he was feeling more secure with him as a shadow. Friday night's attack had just reinforced how important Joseph was to him. Robert had never questioned his personal security before. He was certainly not one of those rich guys that insisted on having an entourage follow him around everywhere. He drove his own car, and did his own shopping. But after the two attacks just in the past week he found the presence of the body guards and extra security help him regain some of his life's balance. He knew that he would need his confidence over the next week as his business decisions began to change and people would begin to question him.

On Sunday evening he set out his clothes like he always did so he would be ready for an early Monday morning start to the work week. He wanted to get to work extra early since he knew that his new team was going to be waiting for him. He was sure that Lowell was chomping at the bit to talk to him, especially since he had called his cell phone several times over the weekend. The hotel had been told to hold all calls to the room, and no one was allowed up under any circumstances. As he was going through his papers he found the invitation and the check for the St. John's charity. The check had gotten badly crumpled in his pocket, and the invitation was flecked with dried blood. He wondered how something as good as a hospital charity event had turned ugly so quickly. As he looked at the invitation he could picture the red headed woman with the sparkling green eyes and began to smile.

Holding the check in his hand he was determined to find out more about who she was and just knowing she was a doctor wasn't enough. It wasn't just that she had helped him , but she looked so familiar. Why did he feel so drawn to her? Something about her smile was pulling at him, like a cat playing with a ball of string. He was frustrated by the distant – and not so distant tug at his memory. It was right there and he just couldn't seem to put his finger on it.

As he slipped into bed he turned on the television and was flipping channels when he saw the corporate headquarters sign for GC Real Estate flash across the screen. He turned back to the station and turned up the volume to hear the reporter saying that the authorities in Philadelphia had determined that the fires were an accident. The company spokesperson said they were naturally pleased with the correct outcome by the fire and police departments. And that they had no immediate plans for rebuilding, but that could change at any time. As he drifted off to sleep, Robert smiled, wondering what the reaction would be once his plans were made public.

Chapter 7

Robert had set his alarm for five-thirty the next morning, but after tossing and turning most of the night, he was wide-awake an hour earlier. Usually a good sleeper, he found himself struggling to stay asleep through the night these days. After lying in bed for five minutes or so with his mind racing, he got out of bed. He did some easy stretches and was about to start doing his regimen of push-ups and sit-ups. Instead he grabbed a pair of gym shorts, t-shirt, socks and sneakers and quickly got dressed. He headed into Joseph's bedroom, turned on the lights and told him to get up since they were going for a run. Before Joseph could argue, he headed to the bar and reaching into the fridge pulled out two bottles of orange juice. Sensing that he was coming up behind him, Robert turned and quickly tossed a bottle of juice to Joseph. Robert chuckled as he saw the surprised look on his face, but could only grin more as he saw Joseph easily catch it.

"No arguments, Joseph, I need the fresh air. And at this time of the morning the most will we see is some rabbits."

Joseph nodded as they headed out of the room. He sensed some of Robert's old self was coming back and for the first time in a couple of weeks the missing self-confidence as well. After a slow and easy start to warm up, they ran a long hard circuit through the park, steadily picking up the pace until both men were sweating heavily. As they walked off the hard run during their cool down both men enjoyed the morning stillness as the city woke up. By the time they emerged from the park, cars were starting to move around the city streets. Executives and eager Wall Street types were all heading to their offices, hoping to make today's list of new millionaires. Even the hotel was waking up – the doorman sweeping away the overnight dirt that had gathered on the sidewalk out front. Inside, the hotel staff were dusting, polishing, mopping and vacuuming every visible area. Everything in the hotel gleamed like it was all brand new, and the staff worked incredibly hard every day to make it look that way. As they passed through the lobby, the fresh brewed smell of coffee filled the air all around them.

A short time later they were both showered, dressed and inside the pair of black SUV's sweeping through the heavily traveled streets that were starting to become more crowded with the normal Monday morning rush hour. As they arrived at his office building Robert nodded to security as he strode through the somewhat empty lobby to the elevators. He had insisted on going in through the main entrance this morning since he felt like he needed to try and get back to normal. As they rode the elevator in silence, Robert began making notes on the iPad that he always carried with him. The run earlier had cleared his head as he had hoped and that was evident by how easily his fingers flew across the keys. Joseph glanced over and saw that the notes were concise and clear – which he was glad to see as another sign that the old Robert was returning.

Despite the early hour there were already people working in their offices. Robert moved easily down the hallway towards his office. His stride full of purpose and confidence, and even Joseph noticed it more so than he had seen previously seen in Robert. The gleam was back in his eyes and the ever present smile was back on his lips. Indeed, this was the Robert he was used to seeing and dealing with. As usual Jennifer was in the office before anyone else, and Robert smiled at her as he approached. He had emailed his notes and asked her to type it and please bring it in when she was finished. As he spoke he caught her eye movement and tuned to find Lowell approaching rapidly.

"Robert, in your office!" He declared with authority.

Robert ignored him and turned back to Jennifer, "would you please bring me in a cup of coffee when you come in. I have some more things I will need taken care of and I want to get through the normal messages as quickly as possible. We have quite a bit of work to do." He started to turn away, then as an afterthought he turned back and said, "let Mr. McDermott know I will see him later."

Then he turned back to Lowell and without saying anything pointed to the wall beside his office door. There hung the original small wooden plaque from the company that read "Cutter and Company". Then with a raised eyebrow he shot one last look at Lowell, turned and walked into his office closing the door sharply behind him. He walked over to his desk, stood looking out the window at the city waking up below him. His hands were clasped behind his back as he felt the strength that had slipped away recently returning in a rush through him.

Then he turned and sat down, picking up the day's reports and messages that were all neatly laid out for him. Jennifer came in with his coffee and typed notes. After talking about his plans and what else he would need, he thanked her and she left the office. Alone again with his thoughts he began preparing for the meeting ahead. He reviewed the typed notes she had given him and continued to allow his mind to focus. Robert's competitors had learned about his focus and the impact it could have on a room full of people. This sharp edge often led him to be better prepared than anyone else for complications that they seemed to never consider. It was this attention to detail that had made Robert the winner on more than one occasion.

They were meeting in the executive conference room, and Jennifer had coffee, bagels, fresh fruit and various juices already arranged on the sideboard for them. Despite the room's size it was already crowded when he stepped inside and closed the door. There were people standing against the walls, so he told them bring in more chairs from the nearby offices. There were people from finance, real estate, legal, risk management, and marketing. Robert knew he was going to need and want input from all of these departments and especially from the leadership team. While there were executives in attendance, they were not necessarily going to be team leaders. He had purposely selected people that were not executives because he needed honest and direct answers.

The room quickly fell silent as Robert began to speak. "Good morning and thank you all for coming in early." This got some chuckles, since most people started their day before this 8.30 meeting. "I trust you all read through the memo I sent, but before we start I wanted to lay out some ground rules. First and foremost, you will see that there are people from many different departments and levels of the organization. For this project to succeed we are going to need direct, honest input from everyone. No one is expected to have all the answers, just the right questions. I know I do not have the answers which is why I need all of you. After today, some of you will no longer report to your immediate bosses. The new leadership team for this project will be your peers, and no one will be the boss. Well, almost no one." More chuckling, but still people waited cautiously.

"This is not like any project we have done before yet we have to do it better than any other project. I know we will make some mistakes and that is ok, I just need you to work as a strong team of my best and brightest to continually overcome and adapt. I know this sounds like the marines or something, but this is important - and not just to me, but to a lot of lost souls. I cannot promise you fortunes made on this project, but if we succeed you will hopefully feel like a million dollars. Now, let's get down to work on Project Firestorm."

As everyone opened folders and binders, Robert gave the group an overview of the project and what he expected from each of them. As he spoke he saw them all become more focused and begin to take notes. When he finished talking 30 minutes later, there was silence in the room. Robert took his first drink since he had begun talking and let the project settle into their minds. Then he reminded them that their questions, suggestions, and different ideas were going to be important for this to succeed. Slowly the questions and ideas began and he asked Roger to take notes for him. The more they talked, the more the ideas flowed and there were more challenges uncovered and discussed. There were also new solutions given which brought even more questions. Robert was somewhat surprised at how well and how quickly this team came together to bounce ideas off of each other and find potential solutions to some very difficult problems. It just served to give him more confidence as the meeting went on, and he was excited to realize that what started as an idea had quickly blossomed into a huge project. Looking around the room, he stepped back and let the team leaders take control of the meeting. As he watched, the team seemed to gel and come together even more. All around the conference room, white boards were being drawn on and whiteboard sized, sheets of paper were being stuck to the walls and windows.

The meeting took three more hours and when they were done Robert congratulated the team on a great start. He reminded them that there was still a lot of work to do, but based on today's results he was sure they would succeed. He waited by the door thanking each one of them as they left. The last person was Lowell and Robert stopped him before he could leave. He placed a hand on his shoulder and nodded toward his office door, then turned and walked through his private door. Inside Robert headed straight for the fridge and reached inside for a bottle of Vitamin Water. He offered one to Lowell who shook his head. Robert moved behind his desk and stood looking out the window as he took a long, deep pull from the bottle. When he turned back around, Lowell was standing stiffly as if he were at attention.

"Relax and sit down, Lowell. I'm not the principal, and I sure as hell am not going to fire you." Then he pressed the intercom and asked Jennifer to have Frank come down now for a follow up.

"Lowell, I know that we will not always agree, hell, that's one of the reasons I hired you to begin with. But I ask that you remember whose name is on the door when you decide to get authoritative with me. Especially when we are in public and I am standing right there. I expect you to pretend to trust my judgment even when you disagree with me. So far my judgment has not failed to make both you and me millionaires many times over. I know that you think you are being pushed aside, but I really need you to focus on the other projects. Plus, this may become a real public relations issue and I want the public to see the team as a group who rides the subway to work. Not someone who parks his brand new Mercedes in a reserved spot in an underground garage." As he spoke softly, Robert had walked around the desk and placed his hand on Lowell's shoulder.

Lowell looked down and said, "Yes, sir. I'm sorry I let my pride get the better of me." He took a deep breath as Robert walked back and sat in his chair, Lowell sat down and continued. "You really think this will be a public relations issue? It sounds like a fabulous way to give back to the community?"

"Yes, it may be a great way to give back. But, because of the scope of the project it is going to require a lot of politics and hand shaking to get it all to come together. That is also why I need you to appear to be un-involved. So the public perception is what we want it to be." Robert paused and then said, "Lowell – this project requires a wizard standing behind the curtain pulling the strings. For this project it can't be me since I will be out front. So, I need it to be you this time. I need you to be behind the curtain and not standing beside me. Can you do that for me?"

Lowell's face turned crimson and he could only glance at the floor as he realized what a complete fool he had been. Even as he began to nod there was a knock at the door and Frank came in. He took his seat, and Robert explained the more delicate parts of the project and what he was going to need from both of them. He especially laid out what he was going to need from them before the day was over. The two men had many questions, comments, and ideas, which they continued to discuss for several hours. During that time, Jennifer brought in drinks and sandwiches for them. They ate as they continued to work and finally Robert got up and stood in front of the windows looking at the reflection staring back at him. For the first time in several weeks and perhaps even months he smiled.

Without turning, he asked, "what do you guys think? Honestly?"

Frank spoke up first. "It is what you said Robert. It will all come down to GC and how they react. But, it sounds like you are going to make him an offer he can't refuse." They all chuckled at the obvious joke as Robert took his seat again.

Robert nodded, "well if I am right, it's not every day that he gets an offer of a legitimate way to get a 25 million dollar tax write off. Not to mention a five million dollar bonus just for answering a few questions. I guess it will be up to me to convince him to go along and answer me honestly."

"Yes," Lowell agreed. "Sorry there isn't more that we can do, but you said it – public and political opinion will matter a lot more than anything else. Fortunately given the city's lack of response so far the people should be somewhat on your side."

As they left his office, Jennifer came in with his Philadelphia hotel information. She also handed him the day's messages and end of day reports. She let him know that there was a bag packed for him in the suite and that Joseph was waiting for him. Just as she was about to leave, she placed a hand on his arm and asked him to please be careful. He gave her a reassuring grin, gave her hand a quick squeeze and promised that he would. As Jennifer turned to go, Robert was sure that he saw the glint of a tear in her eyes. Although, as she left, he wondered if he had made a promise that he had any control over anymore.

As he sat down at his desk he saw an email from one his board members. Martin was a bright man and had a good business mind, but sometimes he got lost in the details. His ideas sounded good at the highest levels, but often ended up costing more than he thought and made less money than he thought. Robert had learned to handle him with kid gloves, giving him the attention of a board member without spending too much time, effort, and money to disprove the business plan.

***

Joseph came in a little later and walked over to the suite to get Robert's bags and wait for him by the door. Robert was at his desk and began packing his laptop and briefcase with all of the files he was going to need. He and Joseph walked quickly to the SUV's waiting in the garage for them. They headed out of the city, hoping to avoid as much of the traffic as possible. They made good time getting to the tunnel and were quickly moving effortlessly down the turnpike to Philadelphia. Without looking back Robert knew that the other car would be right behind them.

He took this opportunity to rest his eyes, as he dozed it occurred to him that it felt good to be tired today. He took advantage of the two hour drive and slowly he drifted off.

Joseph woke him just as they were pulling up to the doors of the Park Hyatt Bellevue hotel. The hotel was situated on Broad Street just a few blocks from city hall. Robert knew that it would be useful to stay so close to where he expected so many of the necessary and the unnecessary meetings to take place. As they made their way to the check-in desk a man began to approach them carrying an envelope. He was quickly stopped by the two body guards, who glanced at Joseph. The man looked past them, seemingly unconcerned with their size. Without a word he handed the closest man the envelope which had *Cutter* written on the front. As he turned and walked away, Joseph took the envelope, carefully opening and inspecting it before handing it to Robert.

Robert opened the package and saw that Roger had once again come through. The file he had sent included as much background information as he could find on GC Real Estate, it's subsidiaries, and more importantly the owner of the company. It made for some interesting reading as Robert scanned the documents. More than a few times, he pointed to a segment and showed it to Joseph who simply shook his head.

Once they were upstairs in the suite, they changed into jeans and immediately headed back out to the waiting Yukon. Robert wanted to see the area as soon as possible and Joseph knew that there was no point in arguing with him, when Robert had made up his mind it was almost always unchangeable. They left one of the SUV's and the other bodyguards at the hotel. Robert had said he did not want an entourage, but agreed to have a driver and one bodyguard with them. As they drove towards their destination the neighborhood got visibly worse. Robert was shocked by how bad the area was – and not just from the devastation of the fires.

From what he had read, he knew that it was a poor section but he was not prepared for the despair which seemed to emanate from everywhere. As they approached a red light a woman crossed the street in front of their car. You could see the pain and years of hard work that creased her aged face. The entire world seemed to be pressing down on her shoulders and she was obviously struggling under the heavy weight.

The next block was where the fire had actually been and Robert began to see just how complete the destruction was. He sat up a little straighter in his seat as he realized that Mr. Lee's store was on the corner across the street – or it had been. Robert caught movement out of the corner of his eye and assumed it was a stray dog rummaging through the trash piled on the street. He was startled when he realized that it was not a dog, but a boy in dirty, ill-fitting clothes. Before Joseph could stop him, Robert had jumped out of the SUV and approached the young boy.

Robert tried to talk to the boy, but he could see the boy was afraid. Thinking about it, Robert realized there was probably nothing stranger for this boy than seeing a white man getting out of a shiny new SUV. Kneeling beside him Robert asked where he lived, and after several moments of hesitation and confusion, the boy pointed with his outstretched arm and a small bony finger toward an empty lot. Looking closer Robert saw a makeshift tent in one corner of the lot. Robert asked where his parents where, and in a small voice the boy said that his Mom was working.

The boy did not know where she worked, and only knew she would be home later, after it was dark. As Robert stood he gulped in air to hold back the tears from his eyes. Looking around he saw a small group of people approaching where he and Joseph stood. He saw Joseph reach under his coat where Robert knew his gun would be, but Robert put his hand on his arm. Instead they began to walk over to the group which was being led by a small middle aged man with a priest's collar and wire rimmed glasses.

"Good evening, gentlemen. Are you lost?" The priest asked pleasantly, as he glanced at the gleaming Yukon. From the look in his eyes it was obvious he did not trust many people – especially if they drove brand new cars.

"Not exactly, Father. Where does this boy live?" Robert asked hopefully, "certainly not in that tent?" As he posed the question Robert pointed to the lot across the street where there was a sheet draped across two sticks stuck into the dirt.

Warily, the priest asked, "are you a reporter?" Robert and Joseph both shook their heads, so he continued. "Probably. He spends his days with me. But, the church only has so much room and there is no other shelter in the area." The priest shrugged his shoulders and sighed, "those without a place to stay have had to make-do. Fortunately the weather has held up."

His voice cracking, Robert asked how many more people were without homes. And when the priest answered saying there were about thirty homeless families, Robert again had to look away. The city was apparently dragging their feet when it came to helping these poor people. Robert could hear Joseph talking quietly on his cell phone behind him. When Robert turned to face him, Joseph nodded and gave him a wink.

Robert was visibly shaken and working hard to hold himself together as he said, "Father, perhaps we can help. But, it will have to stay anonymous for now. It won't be a permanent solution, but we are already working on that also."

The priest looked at him through guarded, untrusting eyes. He then glanced at the two large men sitting in the front seats of the Yukon. It was clear from the priest's face that he did not trust these strangers. He wondered what Robert's angle might be and was obviously trying to protect his people from someone looking to take advantage. "My son," he said. "You should not get people's hopes up when they have been let down time and again. People are quick to help the downtrodden in far off countries, but often forget to look in their own back yard. Unless there is a political benefit... politics seems to bring out the best in some people."

Before Robert could answer, Joseph leaned forward and whispered in his ear. They spoke in hushed tones for several moments before he turned back to the priest. "Father, if you tell me where the church is I can have a proper dinner brought over. These people look like they could use a good meal. By the time we are done eating, I think we may have something a little more permanent for them to sleep in."

The priest looked back and forth between Robert and Joseph wondering if they were joking. He shrugged and gave them the address, which Joseph immediately repeated into the phone. Robert looked at the hard edged group of people standing around, then down for the little boy. He was hiding behind the priest holding tightly on to his pants leg. Robert knelt down to be eye level with the boy, then smiled and put out his hand to him. With just a moment's hesitation and a glance at the priest the boy walked over and took Robert's hand. As the group began to walk towards the church Joseph signaled the driver who moved slowly down the street behind them. The boy walked on one side of Robert, the priest spoke quietly to him on the other. The rest of people followed along with Joseph right behind them.

Several blocks later they approached a small clap-board building that was nothing more then four walls and a roof. If not for the faded wooden sign in front, you would never know it was a church. Inside, was just as barren as the outside was. There was nothing more then old wooden benches and a table, which served as the altar. In the sparse surroundings, the homeless group had found room to pile their belongings around the walls of the room.

As Robert and the priest stood in the doorway looking around, the group moved around to their individual piles of meager belongings. They moved towards the altar and continued talking in hushed tones. When Joseph turned to go outside, he looked back and smiled as he saw that the little boy was standing with them still holding Robert's hand.

Robert and the Priest sat talking quietly about the group of people living in the church and the little boy that had captured Robert's attention. As they talked the boy inched his way closer and closer. Robert was still amazed that they – the boy and his mother were living in that little tent in the lot. Finally the boy moved from sitting on a bench beside Robert to almost sitting in his lap.

He interrupted their discussion and stuck out his hand "my name is Mikhail. What is yours?"

Robert grinned and took his little hand in his "my name is Robert and it is very nice to meet you."

About thirty minutes later, Robert heard tires coming to a stop and car doors opening and closing. From the sound of it, there were several vehicles outside and by the looks of the headlights shining through the windows they were large vehicles too. As Joseph walked towards the door, he asked for help from several of the men. He also asked if they could make some room for tables by moving the benches. Joseph and about ten men walked outside, coming to a sudden stop at the top of the stairs. Robert and the priest followed the group and were amazed by what they saw in the middle of the street.

There were three National Guard trucks led by a camouflage painted Hummer stopped in the middle of the street. Joseph stood near the Hummer talking to the commanding officer. Joseph glanced at Robert and then climbed into the back seat and the two drove away. The Hummer left with the three trucks following closely behind, and as they pulled away three vans pulled up to the curb taking their place. Stenciled on the side of the vans were the words "Supreme Caterers." As soon as the vans pulled to a stop, the back doors popped open and several people in white uniforms climbed out. Before anyone could say a word, the men from the church group had moved to the vans and were grabbing boxes of food, drinks and supplies and taking them inside. Tables were also brought in from one of the vans and were set up as a work area. The women in the group began to help the cooks as the men continued bringing in more food and drinks. Even Mikhail found something he could carry – smiling as he was not wanting to be left out.

Once all the food had been prepared and laid out they gathered around the tables waiting patiently for the priest. He approached the table, said a quiet prayer then sat down to an incredible meal of fresh salad, chicken, potatoes, corn, stuffing and even a few deserts. They all sat together and talked over the hot meal, Robert listening to their stories of hardship and struggle. But through it all, he also heard stories of love and caring for family and friends, no matter what the cost. Robert looked around at the tired, worn faces of these people and wondered how they were able to manage day after day. As he looked at their smiles he realized this could possibly be the first real meal they had eaten in days, maybe even weeks.

Robert sat talking with them for a while longer until Joseph returned. He was followed by a dozen men and women wearing camouflage uniforms and army boots. As the new group got their dinners together, the families cleared their own plates making room for the new-comers. Joseph nodded at Robert and walked over to get himself a plate of food and took a seat with the rest of the national guardsmen.

Once they had finished eating, Robert stood and told the

group that their new home was ready, and once everyone had finished eating they could follow him. After cleaning the tables of the remaining plates and plastic wear, they hesitated for a moment waiting for approval from the priest. The priest walked over to Robert and then looking back at his group of followers nodded that they were ready.

It was almost 10pm when they started to walk back to the empty lot. The boy had fallen asleep so Robert effortlessly picked him up and carried him in his arms. Had Robert looked back at the crowd he would have seen Joseph standing at the back of the group smiling broadly. As they rounded the last corner the entire group stopped and gaped. The same Hummer and trucks that had pulled up in front of the church were now parked on the street in front of what was no longer an empty lot. The lot now had four circus sized tents set up in the four corners with the center area open. A generator had been brought in also and there were lights and power lines set up all over the compound. Each of the tents had several national guardsmen at the entrances and as they arrived the captain approached the group.

He came stiffly to attention in front of Robert and the priest and snapped out a salute. "Good evening, Sir. Captain Davis, Sir. We are ready for your group, Sir."

"Thank you, Captain. We appreciate your team coming out this evening and getting this done so quickly." Robert spoke for the group as he found that even the priest was speechless.

The captain then proceeded to lead the group to the center common area. From there they were able to see the entrance to each of the tents. The southeast corner housed the mess tent, complete with tables, benches, and a full kitchen. In fact, they could probably feed a small army from this kitchen. The southwest corner housed a storage tent which contained extra provisions and general supplies they would need during their stay. The northwest corner was furthest from the traffic area so they had chosen that tent to house the sleeping quarters. This main tent had been separated into smaller quarters so that some of the families could have some sense of privacy. The tent in the northeast corner was broken down into four areas for the men and women's showers and bathrooms.

After the captain had finished giving his tour the group headed back into the living quarters and began to select places to sleep and store their belongings. Robert, who was still carrying the boy found an empty cot and placed him gingerly on it. He slowly pulled a blanket up over the boy and tucked him in. As he turned to go he saw a woman talking to the priest with a worried look on her face before she walked over to Robert. She looked down at her sleeping boy, placing a hand softly on his head. She looked around before stopping at Robert, and with tears in her eyes she kissed him softly on his cheek mumbling… "Bless you." Robert could see the exhaustion seeping from her every pore. She lay down next to the boy stroking his thick hair. The boy immediately curled up next to the woman and they both promptly fell asleep.

Robert slowly made his way back towards the entrance of the tent. As he reached the entrance he turned back and looked at the rest of the people that were also making themselves as comfortable as possible. They all seemed to sense him looking and one by one stood, silently cheering for him. Robert could only wave at the group and smile before turning away. As he stepped outside the priest took his arm and led him aside. They began to talk and Joseph walked over and joined them.

The priest spoke softly, "I don't know how you managed to arrange all of this. First the dinner, then this. All I do know is that you just left an incredibly grateful group of people in there. Some day you will have to explain this to me."

Robert smiled, speaking as quietly as the priest, "I promise

Father, that one day very soon you will understand. But for now I ask you to just trust me."

As Robert and Joseph walked back to the waiting SUV, Robert looked at Joseph who simply winked and said, "let's just say that I know some people who were all too happy to help. But, for now I have ask you to just trust me." Then he smiled and climbed into the SUV which took them straight back to the hotel. They all drove in silence together, and even the driver seemed moved by the night's events. As they rode along the quiet streets Robert found himself thinking about the people he had just left. He couldn't imagine how they felt, but mostly he was amazed at their spirit. Not one person had given up – even in the face of desperation. Seemingly forgotten by a city and surrounded by devastation, they had all found a way to keep on living. As that very thought crossed his mind, he realized that these people were doing just that – living. His thoughts turned to the woman and that little boy. She had clearly been as exhausted as humanly possible, but the moment her eyes had fallen to the boy her entire face had lit up like the Christmas tree at Rockefeller center. Robert couldn't imagine a person with nothing in the world to speak of – yet that little boy was clearly all she needed to be happy.

Chapter 8

Despite how exhausted Robert felt from the long day he still found himself unable to fall asleep. He tossed and turned for a while, then got out of bed. He stood at the balcony doors, which did not open and looked out at the quiet evening. He slipped on a pair of jeans, a polo shirt and comfortable loafers then headed out of the suite. He took the elevator up to the XIX bar at the top of the hotel. He walked in and heading to the bar saw that there were only a few other patrons. It was well past midnight and although there were waiters sitting around, the round room was virtually empty. He walked through to the paneled bar and took a seat then ordered a scotch and began to make some notes on his ever present iPad. He could feel a pair of eyes looking at him and when he looked up he saw a beautiful woman at the end of the bar smiling at him. He smiled politely then turned back to his note taking. He was aware of her walking his way and hoped that she might be heading someplace else. As she placed a soft hand on his shoulder he caught the overpowering scent of her perfume.

"Can I buy you a drink?" She spoke softly in a breathy whisper that was designed to say more than just the words themselves.

He glanced at the bartender standing at the far end of the bar and replied, "No thank you, I really just came in for the one nightcap." Smiling, he left a twenty on the bar and turned and walked out. He could feel her eyes on his back as he strode out

– a part of him thinking about turning back. But just as quickly he dismissed the idea knowing in his heart that he was changing at his very core. He took the elevator back to his floor, but as the doors opened he changed his mind and went down to the lobby instead. As the elevator doors opened again he strode to the front entrance, but just as he was about to walk out saw Joseph standing against the wall. Robert nodded to him and they both continued through the doors.

The walked quietly to Walnut Street and turned the corner in step with each other. Robert was grateful for the company, but was glad that Joseph knew he just needed to walk quietly. As they walked along, Robert kept replaying the night's events in his mind, taking in each person's face, expressions and how much it had all meant to them. Not only that, but Robert recognized just how much it had meant to him. He would be the first to admit that until recently he would have never considered what he was about to do, unless of course he could find a way to make a buck out of it. It was not just Mikhail that had made him happy about what he was doing. As of a few days ago he had not really considered the true human impact the fires had on these people's lives. But, after tonight there was just no getting away from it. These people had very little to begin with, and after the fires they had even less. That the city could overlook them as if they just didn't matter amazed him even more, and he knew that his plans were going to bring it to the forefront of the news. Perhaps even more so than the fires themselves had.

Robert shook his head thinking again that tomorrow morning would be the start of big changes. Or at least he hoped so. After that he hoped that there would be a lot more people asking some of the same questions that he was. While he knew that he didn't have the answers, he did know that these people deserved a lot more than they were getting. Even in his own mind, he realized that what they deserved more than anything was to be treated as human. He hated to think it was all about politics. Even a politician had to look past the next election and see that this was the right thing to do. And he was sure that with a little direction, even the feds might help out.

Robert knew that he had had the benefit of opportunity more than anything else. And he wondered if, without that opportunity, his life might be different today. As he walked, he thought back to his past and knew that he could have been very different. He was becoming more aware that while it took a great deal of hard work to get where he was today, it could change very quickly. Robert had learned quickly that with one wrong move it could all be gone. As he walked, he hoped he could give these people the chance they deserved.

Robert was suddenly pulled from these thoughts by a tug on his arm. When he looked over he saw that Joseph was trying to direct him back into the hotel. When Robert looked at him, Joseph said that it was late and he was concerned that they had been walking farther than Robert had realized. Also, considering the next few days he wanted to make sure that Robert got plenty of rest – when he could. As they walked back through the lobby, Robert saw how quiet it was inside. Then he saw the clock on the wall and smiled when he realized they had actually been walking for almost an hour. Up in the room, he got into bed and while he didn't fall asleep immediately, it didn't take too long.

***

Early the next morning Robert was woken by the ringing of his cell phone. He glanced at the bedside clock and saw it was only a little after six. Picking up his cell phone he smiled, "good morning Frank."

"Sorry to wake you, boss. You have a breakfast meeting at seven-thirty with the chief executive of GC Real Estate. I sent the usual background package to your email. He is coming to your hotel and will be at the XIX café. From what I have learned, I suggest you be early as he is always prompt."

Yawning, Robert said, "Ok. I will take a look. In the meantime, give me the highlights."

Frank took a quick sip of his coffee, "you are meeting with Gino Caporelli. Before you ask - he is clean with no obvious connections to any organized crime family. Apparently, he has never even gotten a speeding ticket. But, according to our friends at the FBI he is still suspected to be involved somehow. The theory is that he stays clean so they can use him to hide their *less than legal* money. Even the FBI said that the only problem with this theory is that they can't seem to make the connection anywhere. The closest they have so far is that he grew up in Little Italy – but that could be said for a lot of the Italian Americans living in Philadelphia.

He files his taxes – both corporate and personal, on time and perfectly, without reproach. The company's financials are audited every year. He is incredibly smart and resourceful, and does not like to waste time or mince words. He also takes his security very seriously, although there are no reported issues. So far he seems to have the ability to make money at any project he takes on. He has done so on both the lower valued properties, as well as real estate investments like shopping malls and housing developments. Aside from Philadelphia, he has properties in New York City, Baltimore, Washington, and Boston. "

"Ok Frank… good job. So – now that you know him, do you think he will go for this?"

"He doesn't seem to have much to lose on the first part, so as smart as he is I think he will agree to the terms. I just don't know about the second part. And it could make him rethink the first – you know, wondering if you are working for the FBI or something."

Robert thought about what he had said, "Ok - anything else?"

"No... that should cover it. Although, he does have a soft spot for twenty-five year old McCallan's and Cuban cigars – Romeo y Juliet from what I hear."

Robert looked at the clock and saw they were running out of time. "Frank, are you in the office?"

"Yes, why?"

Robert got out of bed as he talked. "Good. Ask Jennifer to let you in to the suite. Next to the bar there is an unopened box of cigars as well as a bottle of McCallan's on one of the shelves. Get them and have someone get them here... but, Frank we need them before we are done with breakfast. So, you only have about an hour and a half. I suggest you get a move on buddy!"

Frank laughed and said "Great... so nothing to it." Then he paused for a moment, "hmmm, I have an idea that might work out better."

"Just get it here. I have a feeling it will go a long way to helping him make up his mind about us."

As Robert hung up his cell phone, he opened his laptop and began to read through the information package Frank had sent. He thought about waking Joseph when he heard him moving around in the other room. As he was about to open the door there was a knock and instead Joseph opened it and handed him a cup of coffee. As he sipped his coffee he brought Joseph up to speed on what Frank had said. Without having to ask, he knew that Joseph would begin getting his own background information on Caporelli. Joseph clearly had resources that Robert did not know about. After last night, he wondered just how far those resources really stretched.

A little later the plan fully formed in his mind, Robert sat back and wondered if he could be successful. At the end of the day though he knew that it was not up to him, and that it was not *his* success, which was important. Then Robert realized that might just be the answer – sell the man on his plan, not the money. As he continued to work through the events of yesterday and what would happen this morning, Joseph stuck his head in the doorway and pointed to his watch. Robert nodded and headed in to the shower.

Forty-five minutes later Robert sat waiting in the café at a table next to one of the small balconies, his back against the wall. The waiter arrived with a pot of fresh coffee and two menus. Robert asked him to leave the carafe and said he would let him know when they were ready to order. Joseph sat at a table across from the elevators and Robert knew it gave him a vantage point to see the whole room. Even though he was holding a menu, Robert knew that Joseph would be scanning the room constantly to ensure there was nothing out of the ordinary.

There was no doubt that it was Caporelli when he entered the café. While the sight of the two oversized bodyguards in front of him was the first sign, you could also tell by the way that he carried himself. Robert stood as Caporelli looked around the room and as he began to walk over, he motioned for his two bodyguards to wait by the door. Robert took in the man that he had been reading about all morning. His jet-black hair appeared to be freshly cut and perfectly styled - not a hair out of place, it was so dark that Robert wondered if it might have been dyed. Despite his oversized girth, the suit had been tailored to fit him perfectly. He wore a French cuff shirt with gold cuff links and matching tie tack. The suit he wore was navy blue with a thin white stripe running through it. The shirt was light blue with white cuffs and collar and the tie was silk navy blue and striped.

Robert extended his hand and smiled warmly. "Good morning, Mr. Caporelli. Robert Cutter. I appreciate you taking the time to meet with me this morning."

Shaking hands firmly and confidently, Caporelli looked into his serious eyes, "it is a pleasure to meet you Mr. Cutter. Please call me Gino. Your staff made it clear that I would be remiss in not taking this meeting." He spoke with an easy tone that gave the distinct impression that he had been well schooled. If Robert did not know better he would have thought either Harvard or Yale. Instead he knew that Caporelli's education was almost entirely from the streets.

"Please sit, Gino. And call me Robert." He offered coffee as he refilled his own cup. "Would you like to order right away or wait?"

Caporelli looked around at the nearly empty café "this must be important for you to have cleared your schedule. Let's order first, then we can talk - the food here is excellent, by the way."

The waiter appeared before being called, with a fresh carafe of coffee and took their orders. They couldn't have been more opposite in their order with Caporelli ordering a ham and cheese omelet, white toast, hash browns and both bacon and sausage. On the other hand, Robert ordered an egg white omelet, half of a cantaloupe, and a glass of orange juice.

Gino took a sip of coffee, and then looking over the rim of the cup grinned, "so, Robert… other than a good view, good food and polite conversation about the weather - what shall we talk about?"

Smiling Robert responded, "I have heard that you do not like to mince words and neither do I. I would like to buy your properties here in Philadelphia."

Caporelli paused, his coffee cup half way to his mouth and raised an eyebrow at Robert. "My properties here in Philadelphia? You mean the pile of rubble I own that was destroyed in the fires last week – perhaps you heard about that? And the apartment building which is down the street is not much better. Unless you mean the town house and condo development in King of Prussia or the outlet mall in Limerick?"

"Actually, I want both the apartment building, the pile of rubble – as you called it, and all of the other properties. My lawyers have already drafted the papers and, at my say so, the bank will transfer the money."

Caporelli chuckled, the sound rumbling deep from within his chest. "I had heard that you were a confident SOB. What makes you think that I want to sell at all? And how can you know the amount that I would accept or even consider?"

Robert smiled, "I was hoping to make you an offer you can't refuse."

They both laughed but before either could say anything the waiter arrived with their order. Then Caporelli stated, "I'm waiting."

As they began to eat, Robert spoke with complete confidence. "As I am sure you know, I don't make comments or take meetings without doing my research. I know that the properties are listed as having a value of fifty million dollars. I also know that between the fires and the way the apartments have been kept up, the true value is probably more like twenty-five million. You would need to spend ten more just on the apartments, never mind rebuilding the destroyed neighborhood. According to my sources the rent you do get barely covers the financing, which means any profits are slim. But, my people also tell me that is a benefit on your taxes towards your profitable properties for example – the Commons in King of Prussia.

I am offering you twenty-five million in cash, and my contact at Chase says they would be willing to accept that as payment in full. You would get a huge tax write off as well as getting rid of an even bigger headache, as from what I hear, the city is now considering inspecting the apartment building for safety issues."

Caporelli took a moment to have a couple of bites of his breakfast as he considered what Robert said. "And if you bought the building the city would reconsider the inspections? Funny... my research did not indicate that you did business that way."

Robert nodded, "I don't do business that way – you are right. I plan on doing my own inspections, then, either fixing, or just rebuilding it."

Caporelli just sat and stared at him for a moment. "Rebuilding? Fixing it all up?"

"Yes - new homes, a main street shopping area, a new apartment complex, and a park. Those kids need a place to play where there is at least some grass and trees."

Caporelli still had the look of complete shock on his face and it was obvious that he was not used to being shocked. He could not find the words for a moment, and took a drink of coffee instead. "Robert, you are an incredible investment banker who can turn a company in trouble into the new Apple or Google. But, you should leave the real estate business to those of us who know better. The city will drag its feet until your patience wears out and you move on. Plus, these people really can't afford what you are suggesting – new homes or new apartments. Hell, you are right – they can barely afford where they are living now. Unless you are doing all of this for the tax write off? But that won't help you with the city inspectors or licensing approvals. So tell me the truth... why do you really want this?"

This was the moment Robert knew would make or break the whole deal. Robert spoke in between bites of his own breakfast. "You're right, Gino. On paper, these people can't afford to feed themselves let alone buy a new home. But I met a group of people last night who have the desire and the will to find a way to have what we have – a home. And no, I am not being taken in by a group of bleeding hearts that can't do it for themselves so they suckered in a wealthy do-gooder. When someone is willing to work two jobs just to live in a crappy apartment, how much will they do to live in a real home? All we are going to ask is that they work for it. And as far as the city is concerned - once this goes public they are not going to have any choice but to move on it. I hadn't really considered the tax write-off until one of my own finance people mentioned it.

But, you asked me why? Well to be honest that's not as easy to answer. But, there is a little boy who doesn't have a father. And his mother works so hard to buy him used sneakers that he barely sees her either. Why? Because no one has given a damn about these people before or given them a chance. And if no one does now when they really need it then no one ever will. So, maybe the real question is – why not?"

Gino looked at him over his coffee cup trying to decide if he should believe him. "Hmmm... so why here? Why now?"

"Let's just say that I can relate. I never got a chance except when I gave myself one. And from what I hear you didn't exactly grow up with a silver spoon stuck in your mouth either, Gino."

Gino leaned back in chair, his plate empty. "Ok. Have your people send me the paperwork and I will have my staff look it over and maybe we can work something out."

"To be honest I was hoping to have an answer today." As he spoke, Robert reached down next to his chair for a thick envelope that contained copies of the paperwork. Holding the envelope out Robert said, "there is one more thing. I think you are right... I do need someone who has a good real estate background, and especially a local background. Someone who could consult with us on this project, probably for about a million a year for five years – after tax of course. And there could be another five million for a special bonus on a secondary issue."

Smiling, Caporelli said, "well, I am sure I can recommend a

good consultant to you." Then he turned serious again. "I do read the papers from time to time. So something tells me this second bonus is a little different."

"Yes it is. The bonus is not really related to our business but more of a personal nature. I want to know who has been trying to kill me and why?"

Caporelli blinked a couple of times, "And you think I might know something about that? I think you might have misjudged me, Robert. I am just a business man." Caporelli smiled broadly and spread his arms wide. "Or so my father always said."

Robert smiled in return, "I know. But, I also think that you might know someone who can answer me. I am not looking to bang heads, just see if we can't find a peaceful solution. Perhaps if I know who and why, we can take corrective action before this gets really out of hand."

Caporelli stood and extending his hand he took the envelope. "I will take a look at this and get back to you. No promises on the other thing, but I can ask a few people."

Robert stood as well, taking Caporelli's hand in his own. "I have already emailed the paperwork to both you and your attorney." Glancing at the doorway, Robert grinned as he saw a man approaching with a bag in his hand. "And if I am correct, here comes a little sign of my appreciation for taking the time to speak with me today."

The man was stopped by the bodyguards and then let through as Caporelli nodded to them. Robert smiled. "I hear that you are a man of particular tastes, Gino." Robert reached into the bag and lifted out the cigar box. Caporelli looked the box over, careful to note the seal around the edge of the box. Robert then handed him the bottle of scotch, which brought a low wolf whistle from Caporelli. Robert waited patiently then smiling said, "sorry, I couldn't find a McCallan's eighteen year old so I hope this works for you. It was the best we could do on short notice."

Chuckling with a booming barrel-chested laugh, Caporelli said, "Yes, I am sure I can make do with this twenty-five year old bottle – but only if you tell me where you got it. I think that a consultant making a million-five after tax would benefit from that information. And, I trust you will help me celebrate the deal with both a couple of fingers of the scotch as well as sharing one of these good cigars."

Robert smiled as they shook hands again, "I will be delighted to join you later when we are finalizing the deal and we sign the papers. Perhaps you will let me buy you dinner in celebration?"

Both men laughed and shook hands one last time. As Caporelli turned to go he handed the cigars and scotch to one of the bodyguards. As he walked out of the restaurant he turned back, "I will send you the details for dinner."

Chapter 9

Robert had returned to his room and worked on some of his other projects, trying to wait patiently for a response from Caporelli. He hoped that he had been able to appeal to both his wallet as well as his humanitarian side. But Robert had to admit that he was unable to get a read on the man. He had updated Frank about the meeting and they had thoroughly discussed the next steps. It had been about an hour when he heard the television in the other room; something the reporter was saying had caught his attention. A moment later Joseph was standing in the doorway motioning to him, when Robert walked over and looked at the TV his eyes went wide. The screen had the 'tent city' as a backdrop for the reporter stood in the foreground talking to the priest.

Robert listened intently as the priest explained that he only knew the mysterious man as "Robert" but nothing else. In fact, he admitted that he did not really know how the man had come to them or why. He did tell the reporter all about the incredible dinner and how wonderful and uplifting it had been to the entire group. The priest gave the reporter a tour of the tent city explaining as they walked that although it was all very good; they still needed something more permanent. Robert smiled as the reporter closed the piece by saying that so far they had been unable to locate the mysterious "Robert" and all they had gotten from the city was "no comment."

Another hour went by and Robert continued to try to focus on work, continuing to read and respond to emails and review the updates on his other projects. He kept thinking of the little boy and wondered how he was doing. He was glad that at least the weather was nice and dry so the little boy might at least be able to play outside for a while. Even as he thought it Robert wondered if anyone would watch over him while he played, or was he just left to himself. He found himself standing at the window looking out over a city hard at work, and knew that Mikhail just needed a chance. A chance at a regular life – as much as possible. And a chance to know that in fact someone did care about him. Robert could still feel the boy's energy and his positive outlook, which was almost overwhelming. Robert shook his head knowing that it was not just a will to survive that the boy possessed but also a dream of something better. He had that same feeling in himself all those years ago and knew he had to find a way for Mikhail's sake. He knew that he had to make this project successful – in fact he no longer thought of it as a project, but more of a vocation.

Robert turned at the knock on the outer door and tentatively walked to the bedroom door. He grinned to himself as he realized that for the first time in a long time he was nervous about a business deal. He knew that it had nothing to do with the money – not that it was a small amount, but because for the first time in his life he would have a chance to make a real difference. He waited as Joseph opened the envelope he had been handed. He saw Joseph smile to himself, and then he walked over and patted Robert on the shoulder. They shook hands as Joseph told him dinner reservations were made and the specifics he needed to know. Robert then turned and went back to his laptop, first reading an email with the proposed legal changes and then he reached for his phone. He typed "approved" on a reply email and hit send as Jennifer answered the phone.

He asked her to conference in Lowell and Frank and while he waited he began typing up a list of new challenges and things that would have to get done as quickly as possible. The next couple of days were going to be critical to the success of the project, and Robert had a feeling that they might not even get the couple of days they needed. When the two men got on the call he began to go through the list. As they discussed each item, more people from the project team joined the call until he could tell that the entire team had arrived. Each item on the list seemed to generate more ideas and new questions. They worked through it all taking new assignments and making the necessary plans. By the time the call had ended it was almost 4pm and there still was a lot to do before dinner.

Robert was supposed to meet Caporelli in his office at 6pm so they could go through the paper work one last time before signing. Frank was already on his way to Philadelphia, since Robert wanted him to be there also. Plus, Frank knew people in the city government that he would need to meet with in the morning. Robert had taken a long hot shower and slipped into a navy blue Armani suit, light gray shirt and polka-dot tie. Slipping into his favorite loafers he heard the outer door close and Frank's voice as he said hello to Joseph. Robert stepped out of the bedroom and they went through the paperwork again before leaving. Downstairs the SUV was waiting at the curb and they climbed quickly inside and made their way through rush hour traffic before arriving at Liberty Place.

They pulled up at the curb and Joseph immediately jumped out, looking around before opening the door. He escorted Robert and Frank in through the main entrance to the building noting by the clock on the wall that they were right on time. There was an assistant waiting in the lobby who took them in a private elevator to the penthouse suite of offices. As they stepped off the elevator

Robert saw that the entrance area was rather plain with a simple reception desk and a couple of chairs . By contrast, the entrance to Caporelli's inner offices comprised of two large elaborate and solid mahogany doors. Just as they reached the doors they were opened wide with Caporelli standing in the middle. He strode forward wearing another well-tailored charcoal gray suit, light blue shirt and matching silk tie. He grasped Robert's hand in his and leading him into his office asked the lawyers and assistants for ten minutes alone with Robert.

Caporelli closed the doors behind them and led him over to a sitting area. "Would you like a drink before we get started?" Robert shook his head so Caporelli sat down beside him on the couch.

"I saw an interesting news story earlier today about a mysterious man who arranged for a tent city to be built in just a couple of hours. Simply by snapping his fingers, or so it seemed. Then that same person also arranged for a first class catered dinner and to have the tent city completely stocked with food for at least a couple of weeks. But, you wouldn't know anything about that, huh?"

Robert smiled, "no sense in denying it. I felt that I was able to reach out and help some folks in a difficult situation, so I did."

"Are you sure you are not running for office? That was one of the most political sounding comments I have ever heard. Please don't use that line again no one will ever believe it. That being said, I am sure you are hoping that what happened will help with the press and the public opinion."

Robert chuckled and shrugged. "Gino, let's be honest. I can afford to do this, but I need your help and the public support to get it done. So I will do whatever it takes to make it happen."

Gino placed his big beefy hand on Robert's shoulder and said, "hey, don't get me wrong, I am doing this for the money first and foremost. But, I am willing to admit that even if I wanted to help – you have a much better chance of getting it done. So I will be happy to stand well behind you and help where ever I can. Just give me some time and a list and I will do my best."

"Thanks, Gino. I may be calling you sooner than you think. Is there anything else you wanted to discuss before we pull in the lawyers?"

Gino dropped his hand back into his lap, "well… on your second request – again, no promises. But I do know a guy who might know a guy. We will just have to take things a little slow… ok?"

"Thanks, I appreciate your efforts, and I will do whatever you need me to do on that front."

"One more thing, Robert. I did a little research and there is not a lot known about you in the public sector. The same could be said for me, but I like it that way and intend to keep it that way. Everything is going to change for you tomorrow and I just hope you are ready for it. I hope I can trust you when you say I will be left in the background, because if that can't honestly happen you need to tell me now. And that means the deal cannot happen. No matter how much you want this deal, I cannot be dragged into the public eye. The press will spend too much time looking for reasons why this is a scam if I'm in the forefront."

"Obviously I cannot promise what the reporters will or won't focus on. But I can promise that I will do my best to keep the spotlight out of your way."

Gino nodded thoughtfully, "I can't ask for any more than that. And based on what my sources tell me – and they are damn good – your promises definitely mean something. I still think there is something you are not telling me, but I don't think it is anything that will hurt me. So, why don't we get this done and enjoy a great dinner. But, someday I would like to hear the whole story."

Standing, Robert put out his hand to take Gino's in his and with a firm handshake said, "thank you, Gino. And if you don't get the full story on your own I will personally fill you in. You have earned that much."

Gino laughed, "yeah... well don't get all mushy on me. Kind of hard to pass up on all that cash you are throwing my way. Plus... well... doing the right thing is not always a bad thing."

Gino then walked over to the doors and opened them for the others to enter. He headed over to the desk where Robert was already waiting. Robert reached into his coat pocket and to the surprise of Caporelli and his people pulled out a plain Bic pen. Gino looked at him with his mouth hanging open, shrugged, then laughing said, "maybe you are a little crazy after all."

Robert laughed as well and said, "believe it or not this is the first pen I used when I signed my very first deal." Holding the pen in the air he said, "I could barely even afford this at the time of my first deal and I have used it ever since."

Gino smiled, "Robert, you continue to surprise me." Then they both signed their copies of the document with Frank and Gino's lawyers signing as witnesses. Once completed Frank handed Caporelli an envelope that had the confirmation from the bank of the wire transfers having been made. Caporelli found himself smiling yet again and shook Robert's hand.

Holding the envelope in his other hand he said, "thank you. I guess you were pretty sure of yourself."

Robert smiled, "to be honest I did have my doubts. But like you said twenty five million is hard for anyone to pass up. Especially for a pile of rubble."

They both laughed as Caporelli led him back over to the bar. "You did promise a toast with the scotch you gave me once we had finished. Shall we?" He took down two Waterford tumblers from the shelf and poured a finger of McCallan scotch in each glass. The two men then raised their glasses in a silent toast and downed the smooth scotch. They set their glasses down on the bar and made their way to the elevators. They rode to the street and chatted quietly, climbing in to the waiting SUV. As they rode to The Capital Grille for dinner Robert continued to lay out the detailed plans for the project.

As they entered the restaurant several patrons waiting by the bar nodded and smiled at Caporelli. Robert could not help but notice that they were looking him over wondering who this new friend might be. Caporelli slowed like a good politician and shook hands in greeting with several of the people, calling out to a few that he could not reach. The maître de spotted them and immediately rushed over, quickly taking Caporelli's hand in his and shaking it profusely as he led them inside.

"Mr. Caporelli, I was so pleased to see your name on our guest list tonight. It has been way too long since your last visit. I will let Chef Sean know you are here as I am sure he will want to prepare something special for you. And George will be pleased at another opportunity to serve you one of his fabulous wines."

The maître de was working so hard to make sure the Caporelli was taken care of completely, he barely noticed Robert walking on the other side of him. Despite the crowd waiting in the bar for their own tables they were immediately taken to what appeared to be the best table in the restaurant. Robert glanced at Caporelli who rolled his eyes, then grinned and winked. As they were seated, Robert hardly noticed the hundred dollar bill that Caporelli slipped the maître de. As soon as they were seated a waiter rushed forward with two glasses of scotch and placed them on the table.

Before the waiter could leave, Caporelli said, "please let Chef know that my guest and I will leave the dinner entirely in his more than capable hands."

Robert chuckled as the waiter left, "you continue to

surprise me, Gino. I would have never guessed you were such a restauranteur. Are there any other surprises for me this evening that you would like to warn me about in advance?"

Caporelli smiled and said, "Well, since you are obviously opposed to surprises. The gentleman over in the corner, gray thinning hair... that is the mayor having a working dinner with his deputy mayor and their aids. Sitting in the other corner is Assemblyman Franklin and Councilman Dell – two more, good people whose face's you may want to try and remember. Behind us is the editor of the Philadelphia Inquirer, the news director for the local ABC affiliate and the news anchor they just brought in to take over the nightly news. And yes – I brought you here tonight for a reason. Virtually every night there are people like this having dinner here and almost every one of these folks can help you accomplish your goals. Besides, I guarantee that while we enjoy an incredible dinner each and every one of these people will be trying to figure out who you are and why we are having dinner together."

Robert smiled, raised his glass, "tomorrow morning all of their questions will be answered. Now, is dinner going to be that good?"

Gino smiled, "Robert, if you trust me for nothing else, this I can virtually guarantee. Dinner will be one of the best that you have had, and I am sure that you have eaten at some of the best places in the country, if not the world."

Robert held up his glass, "if this scotch is anything to go by, I am sure the food will be excellent as well."

Their meal was truly a chef's creation starting with prosciutto wrapped mozzarella with vine ripe tomatoes, Japanese wagyu beef carpaccio, and Caesar salad. Robert had the porcini rubbed Delmonico steak with twelve-year aged balsamic and Caporelli had the dry aged porterhouse steak. For dessert Caporelli chose the cheesecake while Robert selected the key lime pie and both had a cappuccino. While they were waiting for the coffee the Chef came out of the kitchen and after stopping briefly to shake hands with several of the patrons walked over to their table. He was about to sit in a chair which seemed to have materialized out of thin air when both Robert and Gino rose and extended hands. As they all shook hands Robert and Chef were introduced and Robert thanked him for the incredible meal. They all sat and talked about restaurants that Robert had been to in New York and Chef made some recommendations for others. As they sat and talked, Robert could feel the room full of eyes looking their way.

When Chef rose to leave, so too did Robert and Caporelli, shaking hands and thanking him again for the meal. The dessert was indeed as good as the rest of the meal, and as the waiter brought the bill Robert chuckled when he handed it directly to Caporelli who dropped several hundred-dollar bills on the table. Robert thanked him for an amazing meal and promised to make it up to him when he next came to New York City.

As they walked out of the restaurant Robert stopped at the table with the news editor and anchor person and said, "in case you missed it – the last name is spelled C-U-T-T-E-R, first name is Robert from Wall Street. You may want to have some of your people out to the tent city tomorrow morning at 9am. But tell them to bring their own coffee, those folks don't have enough to share. Enjoy your evening folks."

He then turned and strode towards the exit where Caporelli was waiting. He was grinning as he caught up to him and Caporelli said, "so much for a low profile huh?"

Robert shrugged, "you know how it is - sometimes in business, when an opportunity presents itself you just have to take the bull by the horns. Besides, they were working so hard to hear my name before they almost fell out of the chairs."

Caporelli placed a hand on Robert's shoulder and offered a nightcap at the bar before leaving. Robert declined politely saying he had things to attend to, but would take a rain check. They left the restaurant together and stood for a moment shaking hands on the sidewalk. Both men climbed into their own SUV's waiting at the curb and Robert felt a rush of adrenaline like he hadn't felt about project in a long time. As they pulled away, Robert leaned forward and gave the driver instructions to go to the tent city. He was not surprised to see Joseph sitting in the front seat, nor that he had already directed him to go there. Robert noticed how much Joseph was smiling as they pulled into traffic and had he had a mirror he would have seen an even bigger smile on his own face.

As they drove, Robert changed out of his suit into jeans, a polo shirt and loafers. Looking into the back of the SUV Robert saw several bags from Home Depot. When they arrived at the tent city they were surprised to see several news vans parked on the street with the reporters and cameramen standing talking to each other, so without instruction the driver went around the block. They exited the SUV and Robert headed for the sleeping areas. Glancing at his watch he found himself hoping that Mikhail was not already asleep. He stopped in the doorway and smiled when he saw the little boy sitting on the floor in pajamas playing with puzzles. The boy looked up after a few moments and smiled back at Robert. Just then Robert heard the click from the cameras and the reflections of the flashes.

Robert turned to face the reporters and holding up his hands gave them his most charming smile. He said, "folks, these are private sleeping quarters and that is a little boy in his pajamas. How about we keep it that way?"

They hesitated briefly so Robert promised that each one would get a personal interview tomorrow morning as he escorted them back out of the tent area. After he saw them leave he turned back to the tents and went to find the boy again. He sat down on the floor with the boy helping him with the puzzles for several more minutes. Then he got several of the books that were nearby and taking the boy's hand led him over to a chair where he began to read to him. When Joseph looked in on them after a while he found both the boy and Robert were fast asleep in the chair. Joseph put the boy in his bed and then helped Robert into the SUV where he escorted him back to the hotel and then put him to bed also.

Chapter 10

After returning to the hotel, Robert had slept fitfully at best. He had tossed and turned for several hours, even sitting up and making notes on his iPad several times. He woke even earlier than normal and took a long hot shower. Over fresh coffee from room service he made some additional notes, and put the final touches on his remarks. Standing, looking out the window at Broad Street below he laughed thinking that he could not remember the last time he had been this nervous.

He heard Joseph behind him and turning said, "you know I have made multi-million dollar deals with the flick of a pen. I have spoken at conferences, professional dinners, and even in front of congress. But the thought of speaking in front of a group of reporters and answering their questions has my stomach in knots."

Joseph moved beside him and placing his hand on his shoulder and smiled, "I have known you for almost fifteen years and have seen you overcome great odds to get what you want. Whether it was that new Aston Martin in the garage, or the hotel in mid-Manhattan. When you wanted it you worked until you got it. What is that sign in your office – *if you think you can, you can*! You and I both know you can do this, and we know that you want this. This is nothing more than a deal and you are just meeting with a group of potential investors. At least they are like-minded, concerned citizens."

Robert smiled. "Thank you Joseph, I can always count on you can't I? Hopefully you are right and that's all this is."

Joseph shrugged, "you can always count on me. Now, perhaps you should get dressed. There is a little boy that you promised to have breakfast with, and I am sure he is waiting for you."

"Damn! I forgot about that. Get the car ready and I will down in fifteen minutes."

As Joseph turned he gathered Robert's laptop and iPad and headed out to the car. He had their driver bring the car to the front. True to his word Robert was down in fifteen minutes. They quickly pulled away and drove straight to the tent city, parking on the far side of the lot. As they parked Robert saw several TV crews already pulling up and starting to set up their equipment. He glanced at his watch and saw there was a good ninety minutes before he was going to speak to them. Robert looked in the living area for the boy and found him in the cafeteria, coloring, with a glass of milk in front of him.

To Robert's surprise when the boy saw him he jumped up and ran over grabbing his leg and giving it a tight hug. Robert was nearly overcome by emotion and it took him a moment to gather himself. He then picked the boy up and made his way to the kitchen, the boy's arms squeezed tightly around his neck. He sat the boy down on the counter and got eggs, milk, and cheese from the fridge. He also found some ready-made hash browns and put everything on the counter. As Robert prepared their breakfast, the boy told him all about his adventures as a pirate searching the tents looking for buried treasure. The smile brightening Robert's face could only have been matched by the flame of the stove.

Robert made them each a plate of food, poured glasses of orange juice and carried everything into the sitting area. The boy followed right behind him sitting down beside him on the bench. They talked about cartoons, puzzles, and the latest Disney movie the boy had watched on the communal TV. Robert couldn't tell if time had moved too quickly or just stood still, but when he saw Joseph in the doorway pointing to his watch he knew it was too soon. Robert wiped Mikhail's face and asked if he was ready to meet some people. The boy nodded and slipped his hand into Robert's, asking if he would be there too. Robert answered emphatically and then led him to the staging area at the front of the tents. Facing them were about twenty people including the reporters and camera crews. Robert stood for a moment holding the boy's hand as much for support as the boy was holding his. Then he looked down and saw the nervous look on the boy's face, he smiled and then stepped forward to the crowd. As he did the boy moved to stand just behind his leg, still holding tightly on to his pant's leg.

Robert looked out at the group as the flashbulbs started to pop and the video cameras began to whir. He began. "Good morning and thank you for coming. I have some opening remarks and then I will answer any questions. My name is Robert Cutter and I work on Wall Street. I am pleased to announce that effective 6pm last night the newly formed Cutter Foundation purchased the Philadelphia holdings of GC Real Estate." He had to pause as they began to shout questions at him. "Please, I will answer all questions when I am done. These holdings include the apartment house behind us, the six square blocks of burned out houses and stores, and this formerly, empty lot behind us." As Robert spoke he pointed to each of the areas so that there was no question about what he was referring to. As he saw a few reporters start to ask questions again, he held up his hand to stop them. He took a quick drink of water from a bottle Joseph handed him, then turned back to the reporters.

Once again, he held up his hands. "Please! Hold your questions, I promise I will answer them. About a week ago I saw the news reports of the huge fires that raced through this neighborhood destroying everything it touched. Like most people watching the news it appeared to be an unlived in area so I was not terribly concerned with it. A couple of days ago I became aware that there were in fact people living in this area and that they were now homeless. I spoke with Father O'Brien and found that since most of these folks could not afford anything else they would likely remain homeless. I asked an associate of mine for his help and he contacted Captain Davis of the National Guard. Captain Davis and his team," Robert paused to point to the National Guardsmen standing to one side, "spent several hours and built the tent city you see behind me. Before you ask, none of this is being paid for by the National Guard. The Foundation is paying for everything. This will give these people a place to live for a short while, but it is obviously not a long term solution.

The Cutter Foundation was formed with a focused idea – to give these folks a place to live. We could simply build houses over there, build a shopping area over there, and refurbish the apartments behind us." With each statement Robert again pointed to the specific area he was referring to. "While this is a good idea, we all know that these fine people could probably never afford to actually purchase the new houses. And probably not even afford to pay the rent for brand new apartments. So instead we opted to create a foundation, which will give us more freedom to do what we can to help these people rebuild their lives, not just their homes.

With the foundation overseeing this project we are going to bring in some of the best contractors to manage the various projects. Any of the people who have been made homeless by the fires who are willing and able will be asked to work with the contractors to learn and help with the rebuilding. For those who are not able to do the manual labor they will be asked to help with some of the administrative functions that will need to be done. Once the homes are completed each family will receive a fixed rate mortgage at the best current bank rates. This should make the homes more affordable for everyone involved.

While the homes are being built we will also have other contractors working on the business area to put in new stores. I have already contacted several franchise-oriented companies and they are more than willing to help people open stores in this area. And, if there is anyone within this group who wants to open their own business, we will work with them and make low interest loans available to them as well. Aside from giving the neighborhood residents a place to shop, it will also generate some much needed jobs. This is the second phase of the project.

Phase three will be to upgrade the apartment complex. From what I understand, running water, heat, consistent electricity, working elevators, and better safety features throughout will be projects we can start with. Painting, wallpaper, new lighting features and a lot of cleaning will also be part of the project and we are hoping that some of the tenants will also help where they can. For anyone who is willing to help they will be given a break on their monthly rent expense.

But the most exciting part of this project will be the last and that will be done right where we are standing. This will have to be the last phase of the projects because of the tents behind us. In place of the tents we are going to put in a park and playground area for the kids. Basketball courts, swings, jungle gyms, grass areas, and trees are all part of the plan. We will also be putting in plenty of lighting so that the area will stay safe for all of the kids. The key to this part of the project and all of the phases will be to gather input from the people who will be living here. They will be picking out colors, patterns for siding, carpets, and anything else that will be going in to their homes. We are hopeful that the upgrades and new jobs will also help to reduce crime."

After talking for the last ten minutes, Robert paused and took a quick drink before turning back to the crowd. Before he began to take their questions he looked out over the group and saw disbelief. He imagined they all thought he had lost it completely and that he would never be able to pull it off. At the same time several different reporters began to call out different questions. After a moment Robert pointed to one young lady who identified herself as a reporter from the local ABC affiliate.

She smiled then asked rather pointedly, "how much did you pay…"she paused and looked around, "pay for all this?"

Robert smiled his most charming smile, "sorry folks, GC is a private company and because of that all details of the deal are confidential. Anything else?"

She grinned and asked him rather bluntly. "Why? What's in this for you?"

Robert smiled since he had been expecting this question and took another drink before answering. He leaned down to his leg and after a couple of quiet words lifted the boy into his arms. He then smiled and said, "this is Mikhail - he used to live over there." Robert pointed to what was now a burned out pile of wood and glass. "His mother works two jobs just so that they could have their own house, and now she has to work two jobs just to find a tiny apartment with safety issues and not much else. Because Mikhail needs a proper home, a place where he can live and grow and play. He needs a place where he can color on the walls and get yelled at by his Mom. But mostly because Mikhail is six…"

Robert was interrupted when Mikhail whispered, "six and a half," into his ear.

They all laughed together, and Robert continued. "Because

Mikhail is six and a half and deserves to have the chance to grow up just like any other boy his age. So the question is not really why? Or what is it in for me? But… why not?"

Pointing to the next reporter who again asked, "so what do you get out of this? From our research, your firm is known as a buy and flip company. Your company has a history of making a lot of money for its investors regardless of the impact on the company it purchased or any of its employee's."

"The research that you did on my company is not quite accurate. Yes, we have certainly bought and broken up companies. But, in all cases we made sure that the employees were taken care of and we have kept an ownership interest in almost every company we purchased so that we can make sure management continues to do the right thing. But, that has nothing to do with what we are doing here. It's kind of funny that you asked what I hoped to get out of this project. The tents have been up for two days and as far as I know not one member of the city government has been by to visit, or even make sure that what we have done is appropriate – not that I would ever question the National Guard. I have had no conversations with anyone about what I will get out of this financially because there really is nothing financial to get out of it.

What I do hope to get out of this is the satisfaction of seeing these people," he paused and pointed to the rag tag group standing off to the side, smiling and living in a clean and safe environment. While my focus is on the kids, it is also about giving the adults a chance at a better lifestyle as well. I look forward to seeing the smile on this little face as he swings and plays with all of the other kids in the area. I have made a good living, so mostly it is about giving back to people who need our help."

Another reporter stepped forward and asked, "so, what happens when no one wants to help, or can't afford to stop working? What happens when winter comes and the houses are not finished?"

Robert put the boy down and slid his hand through his hair before answering. He then took a hammer that Joseph was holding out to him. "You are right. If no one wants to help rebuild these houses and businesses then we could end up with a very cold winter indeed. But, I also believe that if just one family, one person will step forward and work with us then I think the rest will fall into place. All they need to get started is for someone else to help them get started, and they will need a hammer." Robert lifted a new hammer high above his head and looked over at the group of people living in the tents.

"Remember, they will be using this hammer not to build a shack because that may be all they know how to do. Rather, they will be building a new house that they can begin to rebuild their lives in. Not only will they learn how to build these houses, but they will also learn how to fix and correct any issues that may come up. They will learn the proper way to build a deck on the back of their house, or simple repairs that we take for granted every day. So, all we need is just one person. One person who wants to build a home, build a new life and start over. With just one person we can get started and make a difference."

There was quiet all around with the some of the reporters looking over at the group of residents. Then, before they could ask any more questions, a man stepped forward. He was wearing torn jeans, a dirty t-shirt and work boots. He put one hand on Robert's shoulder and with his other hand he reached for the hammer still being held over his head. He smiled with a broken toothed grin and in poor English said, "I will learn to swing hammer if you give me a chance."

As the group of reporters started to shout questions in the man's direction, several more people began to step forward. All at once they said they too wanted to learn. As each person stepped forward Joseph moved to the group and handed each person a new hammer. There were men and women - some who had obviously seen the worst that the world could throw at them. Others were young enough to have not grown accustomed to being forgotten and left out. They ranged in age from their teens to their late 50's. Regardless of their actual age they all seemed older than whatever the number was that might be on their driver's license. As the camera crews continued to video the scene, one reporter could be heard saying that these people actually appeared to be standing just a little straighter than they had earlier.

Robert moved to the side with Joseph as the reporters began to call out questions to the group of tent city dwellers. As Robert moved, the boy stayed with him, holding tightly onto his pant leg. Mikhail was between Robert and Joseph and as Robert reached down and took the boy's hand in his, Joseph placed his hand on Robert's shoulder and gave it a squeeze. Robert took a long drink of water from the bottle in his hand and smiled.

Joseph smiled at him and said, "not a bad speech for someone who doesn't like being in the spotlight."

Nodding toward the group of people who were now surrounded by reporters Robert smiled, "it would appear that the focus is on the right group of people for a change."

As he took another swig of water Robert became aware of a woman standing to one side of the group. She looked uncertain and nervous, dressed in what appeared to be a maid's uniform. Even from where he was standing Robert recognized the uniform as the one he had seen at the Bellevue where he was staying. Her hair was pulled tightly into a bun, seeming to draw her face in as well. She wore no makeup and her face was deeply lined, she looked more tired than he had ever seen someone look before. Despite the dry cracked skin on her worn fingers and heavily lined face, Robert could tell that she was still an attractive young woman.

He smiled across the crowd at her and seeing him, she began to walk over to him. She stopped short when she saw the boy standing between Robert and Joseph and he immediately recognized the look of concern that crossed her eyes. When she realized that Robert and Mikhail were holding hands she scrutinized his eyes even further. Suddenly the boy looked up and saw her standing there. His face burst in to a huge smile and whispered, "mama," as he broke away from Robert and ran to her. She quickly lifted the boy and hugged him tightly to her chest, tears streaming down her cheeks.

After a moment the woman walked over to where Robert and Joseph stood standing. Robert smiled. "So, you are Mikhail's mother? He is an amazing young boy. My name is Robert." As he spoke he took her hand in his and patted it softly.

The woman hesitated for a moment then replied, "thank you, my name is Pearl. Mikhail has mentioned that he made a new friend here, but… you were not quite what I expected. Did you mean what you said about building houses for us?"

Robert smiled. "Well – I think he meant more to me. And yes, I absolutely did. If you are willing and able we would love to help you and Mikhail get back on your feet"

She looked around at the other people all holding up hammers and with a sad look in her eyes said "I don't think I can help build a house. Plus… well… I do have to keep working. And neither of my bosses will cut me any slack. I had to get someone to cover for me while I came over."

"I am aware that you are currently working two jobs and that means you know how to work hard. That is the first skill required for any good builder. If you would like to try to swing a hammer we will be happy to help you learn the skills. But, if you are not too proud I may be able to help with your job needs. I imagine that with just a little bit of training we could find something much more enjoyable for you. Something that would give you the time to enjoy watching this great little guy grow into the wonderful young man that I am sure he will be."

The tears began to slide down her cheeks again and holding Robert's hand in her own she asked, "why are you really doing this? You don't know us. I was at work cleaning guests' room when I saw the live coverage of your speech. I don't think you really want this exposure, and I doubt you are doing it for the money. So why are you really doing this?"

Robert paused and placed his hand on Mikhail's head, messing his hair even more. "The only way I ever got to do anything more with my life was with the chances that I gave myself. I decided to make my own opportunities and started off working hard. Like you I had two jobs also, and together they barely gave me a roof since I needed to wear clean clothes to work. Then luck came looking for me and I took it and ran. I have not stopped to look back in twenty years, until today." Robert paused to catch his breath. "I know you don't know me, but please take my offer to help. I promise that it is nothing more than that and all I want is to give you and Mikhail both a chance at a better future."

Pearl looked at Robert, smiling through her tears. She placed a hand on his cheek like a mother to a son. She leaned forward and kissing his cheek softly nodded her head. She whispered softly that she would only take his offer if he promised to let her find a way to pay him back some day. Before he could reply she pulled him into her and hugged him tightly, holding on for an extra moment until they heard Mikhail between them saying, "Mom, you are squishing me."

When Pearl stepped back from Robert she held his hand for a moment longer. Robert gave her a last smile then turned from the crowd. He took a swig from the bottle of water, holding it and his breath before swallowing it. Joseph stood behind him making sure that no one disturbed Robert for several moments. Joseph knew that what Robert said was the absolute truth and that he had never said any of that to anyone before. When Robert turned back to the group he had both physically and mentally pulled himself back together, ready to face whatever the world would throw his way. Nothing was going to stand in his way now. Nothing and no one.

Chapter 11

Robert spent most of the next day making arrangements for when the rest of his team would arrive and getting the appropriate contractors lined up. He also took a long walk around the neighborhood with the people who had lived there up until about a week ago. He also spent way too much time – in his mind – dealing with reporters. He had already told the reporters that they could tag along on his tour with the residents as long as they only observed and did not bother him with any more questions. For the most part they followed his wishes, most spending their time writing as quickly as they could in their pads. His biggest concern was how to get all of the debris cleared and where to put it. The city had been dragging their feet waiting for the fire department to publish their findings. That had been days ago, and from what he could see there were no immediate plans to start the clearing process.

As the group approached the tents, Joseph moved up beside Robert and placed a hand on his arm, pulling him back into the middle of the group. Robert gave Joseph a questioning look; Joseph turned and nodded towards the tents. When Robert glanced over he saw parked at the curb a shiny black Cadillac Escalade with darkly tinted windows. To his surprise two of the local residents also moved closer to Robert and stood in front of him. It was as if they too could sense that there might be trouble and that the car might be part of it. As they approached the car the rear passenger window slid slowly down. A distinguished looking man slid forward and motioned to Robert with his right hand. Robert could just make out the perfectly brushed silver hair which served to accentuate his deep rich tan. The perfectly manicured fingers were seen at the end of the french cuffs of what was surely a Thomas Pink shirt – one that he was pretty sure he owned also. He couldn't be sure but the cut of the suit jacket seemed to be similar to that of his one usual Brooks Brothers' suit.

Joseph moved quickly to the side of the car blocking the driver's door. Robert guessed that his hand was already resting on the gun on his hip. As Joseph continued to search the car for any possible threat, the man in the back seat kept his eyes on Robert. After several moments of looking around to make sure this was not a diversion Joseph nodded to Robert who stepped to the window.

The man leaned forward smiling and spoke in a firm, cultured voice. "You are doing good work here, Mr. Cutter. I hope you are acting as altruistically as you claim to be." He shrugged as much to himself as he did to Robert, then as he leaned back he handed Robert an embossed business card. The card was blank except for a phone number.

"If you need something call that number. We have interests in demolition, cartage, as well as construction. I also have several business associates who are very good at obtaining the necessary licenses and permits – especially when they appear to be stuck in political red tape."

Robert hesitated for a few moments then smiling said, "now that you mention it, there is a lot of debris that will need to be hauled away. And I know that the general contractors will be looking to hire skilled construction people."

The man smiled as well, then leaned forward to shake

Robert's hand. Holding his hand tightly in his own the man said, "consider it done. I will have the clean-up crews and equipment here tomorrow. We will consider this the start of a good, long working relationship. From what I have heard, Mr. Cutter, you are a man of your word, I am counting on that as much as these people are."

"Thank you, Mr. Salvatori. I am sure we will be able to rely on each other for a long time. You are right – these people are counting on us to take care of things and get the job done. I have promised them as much and don't intend to fail. Period." Robert smiled as he saw the surprise in the reputed mob boss' eyes. Had he asked, Robert would have said that as part of his research he had read about the local "suspected" mob boss.

Smiling, the man slid back into the plush leather seats and nodded as the window slowly slid closed. Joseph and Robert both stepped back from the car which immediately pulled away from the curb and drove off. They returned to the main tent and found that a list was already being put together by Pearl of people willing to help and what skills they had and that there were already quite a few names on the list. She smiled at Robert when he came in and he winked back. Walking over he patted her shoulder and then moved to a group of men sitting drinking coffee. He explained to the group about the crews that would show up tomorrow and told them if they wanted they could offer their help – he would make sure they were involved in the efforts.

The rest of the week Robert and his team spent moving from one meeting to the next. It seemed there were suddenly city council, county and state representatives that all wanted to be involved. All of them naturally seemed to be willing to do whatever he could to make it easier for Robert to get this great effort done. And to make sure, there were constantly reporters waiting for a "few words" from all of them. At the end of one meeting with two city councilmen, several directors, and even more aids and assistants they were all in such a rush to get in front of the cameras they almost knocked each other down. Robert thought of suggesting that they should probably decide who spoke first to the reporters before there was a stampede – but figured that might be counterproductive. Robert had glanced over at his team – consisting of just Lowell McDermott, Mark Thompson, and Pearl Franklin– and was pleased that he had only brought them. Anymore and he would have looked like the rest of the group in front of him – ineffectual.

He left any speeches needed to the politicians, instead he let his actions speak for himself. He was getting constant updates from the field and things were happening quite quickly. True to his word, Salvatori had a demolition crew on the scene tearing things down almost immediately. He had also arranged for what appeared to be a constant stream of dump trucks to carry the debris away. Plans for the new homes, the street mall, and the apartment building were all being ferried between the various architects and Robert. After several days he realized that it was not up to him to approve the designs so he decided to take them to the residents for their input as well.

By the time these daily laborious meetings with the politicians were over and he was tired of hearing the same thing said over and over – just different ways so the reporters got it right when it was mysteriously leaked – he would return to the tents. While he spent some time each night meeting with the residents talking about their day and what they thought of the progress, it was the time he spent with Mikhail that he enjoyed the most. Every night they had their own ritual of pouring glasses of milk, setting out a plate of Oreo cookies and reading. Several libraries in the area had brought over books, and several people had donated coloring books and other games and toys. The boy seemed to cherish this time each evening with Robert, almost as much as he did.

Robert had arranged for a new laptop to be delivered to Pearl so she could keep track of all the meeting notes and information for the project. She quickly learned the Microsoft Office programs and Robert watched as she taught herself while he and the boy sat and read. From the smile on her face he knew she was enjoying her role in the project. He also hoped a part of it was for him and the time he was spending with Mikhail. But mostly he hoped that she didn't mind his spending so much time with the little guy. Every morning that he woke up he felt even more refreshed. The fact that he was working twelve to fourteen hour days was normal and usually it took a toll on him. This week he felt like he could accomplish anything and never get tired.

By the end of the first week Robert and his team took a tour of the area. He was amazed at what had already been accomplished. Any of the burned out debris had already been carted away, and most of the remaining houses were in the middle of being demolished. The strip of stores was also being torn down, but because they were originally made with steel beams it was taking more time. Not surprisingly, Salvatori had known someone who could help with repurposing the steel beams. More and more Robert was finding that he was not just a man who could get anything done, but also that he was a man with connections everywhere.

Robert finally returned to his office in New York, not because he wanted to but because several of his other projects needed his focus. As they had driven back from Philadelphia, Joseph knew that Robert was still thinking of the little boy and wondering if there was a way he could help. Smiling – something rare for Joseph, he typed out an email to Pearl and hoped that would help. The ride was quick and uneventful and Robert was quickly behind his desk trying to catch up on all the messages that he had to take care of. He gave Jennifer, his administrative assistant, a list of responses for each and then turned to his emails. Even though he checked them constantly between his iPhone and iPad every night there were still well over a hundred that he had to respond to. Jennifer usually went through his emails and categorized them for him by project. He was more than a little surprised that the first email from Pearl was marked most urgent.

He opened up the email wondering what could be so urgent when he just left her a few hours earlier. For a moment he was irritated that she did not call him – if it was that urgent, she should have. He will have to remember to explain to her the use of 'most urgent'. He started to read the email and immediately his face brightened. Any person would have been able to tell that the irritation he had felt a moment ago was completely gone now. Pearl wanted to let him know that she had explained to Mikhail that Robert had gone back to New York, but that hopefully he would return soon for their nightly reading times. But – just in case, here was a video that Robert could use – if needed. When he clicked on the video he could see the boy's tiny smiling face looking into the camera of her laptop. The boy waved and then began to read from the last book they had been reading the night before.

Robert could not have imagined the effect seeing the boy would have on him and he quickly stood and turned to the windows. Behind him he could hear the little boy continue to read and as the tears began to form, the world outside became just a little fuzzy around the edges. When the email ended he lifted the phone and called Frank, his Chief Strategy Officer and second in command.

"Robert, you are back. I am glad. There are several things we need to discuss. Especially the Las Vegas project, which has taken a couple of more turns on us."

"Frank – we can talk about it now. Listen to me – there is nothing more important to this organization at the moment than the Philadelphia project. That project will not fail in any way, and we will not come up short. Is that understood?"

"Absolutely. I will be right down to your office. Is there something in particular you are concerned with?"

"Nothing specific. But, I don't want any politician to get in our way of this. No one is going to stop this. Come down and we can review the rest." Robert hung up and he could almost imagine Frank staring at the handset wondering what had gotten into him. Robert looked at the screen and saw the frozen face of Mikhail at the end of the video, and knew exactly what had gotten into him.

When Frank came in Robert was standing at the bar having a drink and offered one to Frank. "Sorry, if I bit your head off on the phone. I just want to make sure that everyone involved understands that I will not let this one go. It doesn't matter how much has already been invested, how much it will cost, and how we will not make any money. There is a six year old boy counting on us to get it right."

Frank nodded and sat down at the conference table with Robert. They reviewed the overall investments of the company and went through each of the projects currently under way. Frank was very good at summarizing the issues faced and generally had suggestions for solutions as well. They made several key decisions that required some additional analysis, and Robert had some changes for a few of the suggestions but overall they agreed on the next steps for the projects. All were progressing nicely and as Frank explained several should generate the cash flow to cover the Philadelphia project with ease.

The one project that was going to need Robert to be more involved in was the hotel in Las Vegas. Apparently there was a lot of red tape because it was a casino, and several of the unions were not sure about a change in ownership. They had only recently signed several new contracts for their employees and the unions were not sure how this would impact things. Robert shook his head as they reviewed all of the various licensing and government approval issues. He thought of Philadelphia and was amazed that this country managed to accomplish anything with all the miles and miles of red tape. As they reviewed the project Robert had visions of days spent in meetings with more politicians and more reporters.

Frank sensed that Robert was getting tired of that part of the business and even suggested that he could go in his place. Robert smiled at him and said, "thank you for offering, but you always tell me this is really what my job is. So why do I feel like more and more it is telling politicians how to run their own personal little backyards? Do they not understand that business is what drives the economy, not their own petty political needs?"

"Yes, they do know that. They also know that this is the closest some of them will ever come to having any kind of power. So, they make the most of it. The one guy in Las Vegas who thinks like us, and gets it, is the head of the Las Vegas city council and has already indicated that he is on our side and willing to help. He is a good guy and just wants to make things better. I would imagine that the Philadelphia Project will come up in conversation with him, so don't be too surprised. As for the rest of the people you will be meeting I have complete files on all of them. I would say good luck, but you and I both know it has nothing to do with luck. Unless there is something more today, I promised my wife dinner out?"

"No, thanks Frank. I will review this on the plane out there. Enjoy spending time with your wife. Do you have a reservation? Do you want Jennifer to make one?"

Frank laughed, "to be honest I already asked her to. It's been a while since we have been out and I wanted tonight to be a little special."

"Well, then get the hell out of here and don't keep her waiting. Have a good time and I will talk to you on Monday."

"Thanks Robert, have a safe flight."

When he left, Robert walked over to Jennifer and said, "you made his reservations for tonight?"

"Yes, I hope that was ok?"

"Of course it was. Call the restaurant and let them know I will take care of the bill completely. Also, arrange for a dozen roses and plenty of champagne to be waiting. Thanks."

Robert turned and walked back in to his office. As he gathered up his papers for the flight, he glanced again at the frozen smiling face on his screen and decided to call Mikhail later before bed. Jennifer came in and gave him all of the travel information and told him Joseph was waiting for him when he was ready. Because his apartment building was still not open, he had basically moved in to the suite off of his office. He packed a bag for the trip and within thirty minutes they were on their way to the airport.

Once onboard he and Joseph made their way to first class where Robert immediately got to work reviewing the background information Frank had given him. Joseph took care of getting their bags put away and took his seat behind Robert. They always booked the flight with extra seats so that Robert could have the extra room to work. Joseph had even asked him once about flying on a private jet, but Robert said he enjoyed flying this way better. Before they had even taken off the flight attendant brought Robert a glass of iced tea and tried giving him her best smile. She hoped that it was just work that had him distracted and nothing else. He realized she was looking at him and gave her his most charming smile and thanked her for the drink. Then he settled in for the flight and got back to his work.

He did a quick inventory of the people he was going to have to deal with and shook his head at the myriad of titles. Everyone seemed to be a director of this or a director of that. There were several commissioners, a few council members, and even the mayor wanted to meet him. Then there were the union members and presidents. He was amazed at how many different unions were involved in running the hotel and casino, but guessed that after getting screwed enough the staff felt this was better. He would have to see. He made a note to find out if it was even possible to run the hotel without the unions. As he continued down the list his eye caught the name of the primary union president in charge of all the casino employees – Anthony Salvatori, Jr. Was it even possible they were related? He quickly flipped through the bio's until he came to Salvatori's. He smiled when he saw that indeed he was from Philadelphia, and his team had even written that his father was the very same Anthony Salvatori, who owned Salvatori Construction, he had met earlier in the week. With no doubt in his mind he made a note to make the call as soon as they landed. He was going to have to call Frank also and let him know of the connection and to see if they could move up that meeting.

As the plane began to move he pushed the files aside and when it lifted off he closed his eyes. In a few minutes he looked out the window at the night skyline and could see how much closer and clearer the moon looked. He leaned back into the plush leather as the flight attendant brought him a glass of wine and took his dinner order. Looking at his reflection in the window he decided to close his eyes for a few moments.

***

The boy lay on his back on a small patch of grass looking up at the night sky. It was hard to see any of the stars clearly because of the all the lights from the tall city buildings. He should have been distracted by the sounds of the stray dogs scrounging for food in the trash cans, or the drunks that roamed the park at night looking for a place to crash. He had heard that at night the park was not all that safe because of the drug dealers and gang members roaming around. But he also figured that no one would bother with a six year old. He certainly was not buying any drugs and no matter how much money they offered he was not going to get involved. At his young age the boy had already seen the damage that drugs did to his "friends" here on the street. So instead he lay on a soft patch of grass and stared up at the stars.

He looked over to his left and just on the other side of the street he could see the now dark sign for Mr. Kim's. He was temporarily overcome with a sense of sadness and loss and once again wondered why anyone could be that mean to kill an old man just trying to earn a living. His thoughts were interrupted by a dog barking in response to the Franklin's fighting. It seemed like they were always fighting about something – especially when Mr. Franklin got paid, since he usually spent it on liquor. Or at least that is what Mrs. Franklin said. She was nice enough to the little boy, at least saying hello. The boy never let on that he did not have his own family – he didn't want to be let down again by someone who supposedly cared for him.

He closed his eyes again and blocked out all of the noise around him. He day dreamed of what it would be like to have a house with a backyard and his own personal patch of grass. He wondered if he did have his own house if it would be any easier to see the stars or the moon. As he slowly opened his eyes he saw an airplane lifting high into air. It looked so cool flying against the dark sky, its lights blinking on the end of each wing. The wings reflecting the light from the moon as it flew fast away from here. He wondered what it would be like to fly in such a big airplane and where those people were going. Were they dads and moms going home to see their own six year old boys? Were they going to a better city where there was no drug dealers, no bums fighting over yesterday's trash for their meal, no Franklin's fighting, and no dogs barking? He wondered what it would be like and if there were beautiful stewardesses helping the gentlemen to their seats – just like he had seen in that old movie? Would the pilot be nice and let him see where they drove the plane? He wondered mostly if he would ever have the chance to find out the answers to all of these questions.

As he lay there watching the plane fly out of his line of sight another vision took its place. He pictured himself stepping onto such a plane holding tightly onto the hand of his father. A man who was taking the boy home to see his mother – they had flown somewhere just to watch a ball game. And not on TV. No, his father would have flown him here to watch the Phillies play for real. He could almost picture himself sitting in a big seat just like all the other grown-ups on board. The hand that he had been holding was dissolved and he wondered if they would let him fly alone. He would probably have to find someplace to clean up before they would – can't fly on a big fancy airplane if you are dirty and smelly.

He felt the saltiness of the tear as it slid from his eye across his cheek and onto the edge of his lip. He licked it off but it was quickly followed by a second one. He wiped the tears away and standing up he made up his mind. He thought to himself I might be just six years old but I will fly on a plane someday. It was at that moment that he told himself he was never going to cry again. Crying was for babies and he had more important things to do then feel bad for himself. From that day on he swore to himself that he was never going to just wish that he was on a plane. No! From that day on he was going to find a way to get on that plane.

Had anyone else looked at him at that moment they might not have seen a six year old, they might have seen a thirty-six year old man named Robert who had accomplished all of that. A man who was determined to help another six year old boy find his own personal patch of grass. They would have seen the determination to do more than survive, but rather they would have seen a boy who was going to live. He had never stood taller nor straighter and he had never felt more determined. Now all he had to do was figure out how to start.

***

Robert had been so lost in his own memories that he did not feel a pair of eyes from across the aisle watching him. When he looked again at his reflection in the window he suddenly saw the second pair of eyes watching. Slowly he turned around to face the person and when he recognized the bright green eyes he smiled broadly.

"Dr. Adams, right? What are you doing here?"

Flustered that she had been caught staring at him she stammered, "Mr. Cutter? I'm sorry I didn't mean to stare before… but… oh… I am on my way to a conference? What are you doing here?"

"I have a business deal that needs my attention in Las Vegas. This is a pleasant surprise finding you here… I am sorry I didn't notice you earlier." He looked shyly over at the stack of folders on the seat beside him.

"Well, my conference is in Las Vegas also. But, you did seem engrossed in your thoughts so I didn't want to disturb you."

Pointing to the stack of papers on the tray in front of her he chuckled. "It seems like we both have homework to do on this flight. Care to trade?"

Her laugh was as full of life and even seemed to sparkle as much as her emerald green eyes. "I am sure that this would bore you, besides I am just as sure I couldn't follow one of your complex business deals."

He smiled broadly the happiness seeming to reach all the way to his own eyes. "So then you have been to one of my business meetings. Some days I am not sure I can follow them either. And other days I feel like I am doing nothing more than buying a used car."

"From what I have read, you must have quite a nice collection of used cars." She glanced at the pile of papers on the empty seat beside him. "I suppose I should let you get back to work."

Robert glanced at the sleeping traveler beside her and said, "why don't you sit over here? Then your light wouldn't bother anyone else."

She smiled and said "I wouldn't want to disturb you, Mr. Cutter."

"First of all, it is Robert. Second, you could never disturb me – distract, maybe. But definitely not disturb. Please, I insist."

She thought for a moment, then nodding, stood and gathered her things, placing them on the seat as she stood up. As she did he gathered his things and when he stood handed them back to Joseph. As he stood in the aisle to let her pass the plane hit a pocket of air. Suddenly they were in each other's arms and for a moment seemed alone as they stared into each other's eyes. For Robert the moment seemed to last forever while at the same time it was over too quickly. He had never seen eyes that were that green, or that seemed to sparkle and shine at every turn.

Quietly and shyly she mumbled her thanks and quickly took her seat. He wondered if she had felt the electricity as well. Considering the girls he usually dated, this woman was something special. Her eyes held the energy and excitement of a young woman, but also the intelligence of a woman who had learned a lot along life's road of lessons. He had always been so sure of himself with women, but with her he suddenly felt like a teenager on his prom night. The flight attendant smiled as she brought them both fresh glasses of white wine and then retreated to the quiet serving area behind the curtain.

"So, if you don't mind my asking – what business are you going to Las Vegas for?"

Smiling he responded, "If you promise to tell me the moment you get bored - there is a small hotel that my company is looking at buying. It seems that there may be some union issues so they asked me to come out for a visit. I sometimes think they drag me out of the office only when they need someone to look the part."

She laughed with that same twinkle in her eyes he had seen earlier, "you certainly don't seem like someone willing to just play a part. Besides – are there really any small hotels left in Las Vegas?

"Well… ok, it doesn't take that much to get me involved. After all, it is a lot of my own money. But enough about that. You said you were attending a conference? What is it about?"

She laughed and mimicking Robert said, "as long as you promise to tell me the moment you get bored." Chuckling he faked falling asleep and made snoring sounds. She lightly punched his shoulder as they both laughed. Turning suddenly serious she said, "it's a conference about concussions, especially focusing on the lingering effects, how to recognize them and treat them."

"Well… speaking after seeing you at work from first-hand experience, I am sure that you will be the hit of the conference."

She blushed, "thank you. I don't know. To be honest I am pretty nervous – I am giving the keynote speech this year and I am still trying to put the final touches on it."

"So I am keeping you from your work. I can let you go… if you want?" But from the look in his eyes anyone would know he wanted her to stay. Across the aisle would never be the same as right next to him. "So, how do you get picked to be a keynote speaker? Or do they always pick the smartest and most beautiful woman at the conference? Seriously… that sounds really impressive. I am sure that you had to work very hard to get there."

She blushed again, "thank you. Actually I got chosen because of a paper I had written earlier this year. There were some new ideas I had and based on some results I got from my patients that seemed to work."

"Well, I am sure that your other patients also appreciated how much care you take. I am sure the Mr. in your life is very proud of your accomplishments." He said with the real hope that there wasn't one.

"Actually, with my work schedule, conferences and papers there never seems to be enough time for that. But what about you? As I recall there was a beautiful young woman with you after your accident? Doesn't she travel with you?"

"She was just a friend actually. Unfortunately I don't really have time for that either. Seems like I have a lot of friends, but that is about it."

"So… do you have any brothers or sisters?" Robert's face suddenly went very still and the light in his eyes seemed to dim. She immediately sensed that he was uncomfortable and felt that she had overstepped her bounds. She placed her hand tenderly on his arm, "sorry, I didn't mean to pry."

"It's ok, nothing for you to apologize about. There is no way you could have known it was touchy for me. I am an orphan and don't know anything at all about my parents or if I have a family."

With her hand on his arm she looked into his eyes and he felt the sadness from a moment ago melt away. "I am sorry Robert that must have been very difficult for you growing up."

He paused for a moment, and then smiling said, "actually, it has made me the man I am today. I doubt that I would appreciate what I have today were it not for my growing up the way I did. I am also sure I learned how to work as hard as I do because I had to. And I can also tell you that I know I am not done."

She gave him that look again that seemed to melt right through him. "I read about your Philadelphia project... but to be honest I didn't put two and two together. I am sure your parents would be very proud of you."

"Thank you that is sweet of you to say. So what about you? I bet you have a big family... are you all very close?"

"I have a brother and sister, both of them are older. My father passed away about ten years ago, and my mom still lives in our childhood home. We try to stay in touch, but it is hard with our professional schedules so sometimes it might just be a random text."

Robert pretended as if he was looking into a crystal ball and smiling said, "let me guess. Your brother is a lawyer and your sister is an accountant. But, I don't see your mother as a housewife. Something more..."

They were both laughing again, the light in her eyes shone brightly. "Not really... my brother is an FBI agent and my sister is a high school math teacher. She took after my mother who teaches high school English."

He laughed, "if you think about it, I was kind of close." They were interrupted by the flight attendant serving their dinner of chicken, Yukon gold potatoes and string beans. All of this with a nice bottle of wine. Robert was always surprised at how good the food was for an airline. While they ate dinner they talked about colleges – she had gone to the University of Pennsylvania for both her under graduate and medical degrees. During her residency she had proven her quick wit and ability to adapt to different patient circumstances. She had also quickly shown that she truly cared about her patients and was willing to go against commonly accepted practices if she thought she could help her patients more. Much to the chagrin of her bosses, her ideas had proven more beneficial for the patients and she quickly became the head of the department.

Robert did not have parents to pay for school so he had worked his way through his under graduate degree at a state school and had gotten a job on Wall Street. While working there he had been mentored by one of the best deal brokers and quickly proven how adept he was at deal making. Very quickly he had built his own network of clients who were happy to invest in his ideas and trusted him implicitly. While working for the firm his client list became bigger and the bosses became more concerned with his accomplishments and how it made them look, than what it did for the clients. Before they had a chance to fire Robert he had packed up his things, moved to a one room office and taken most of his clients with him. He had to start from scratch but most of the clients were more than happy to loan him the start-up capital he needed. Within a year he had taken over the entire floor and had a staff helping to manage the company's assets.

She talked about her family while they enjoyed coffee and chocolate pie. Reminiscing about holidays and birthdays past, about vacations they had taken together. Mostly growing up they had gone to the Jersey shore, her father had been a police officer and did not make a lot of money. But he had been able to save enough to buy a small beach house, more like a kitchen with a couple of bedrooms but that was all they needed then. They still tried to get back there at least once over the summer but with her sister's growing family it was getting harder to have enough room. That and her brother had been relocated to the New York field office and since 9/11 it was harder for him to be able to get away. Despite their very busy lives they still managed to stay in touch via emails, or the occasional phone call. Shannon explained that a lot of it was because of her mother who insisted that the children stay in touch no matter how busy they were – "there is always time for a five minute email no matter what" - that is what her mother always told them.

Robert sat and listened to every word that she said, building an image of her family in his mind that was warm and comfortable. He felt as if he had known these people forever, even though this was their first real conversation. He couldn't explain what he was feeling he just knew that he didn't want her to stop talking. He wondered what might have been if he had grown up in such a friendly happy warm family, instead of moving from foster home to foster home. Would he still have grown up to be the person he was? Certainly everyone in her family learned the importance of being a professional and living a full life as a good person.

Her father had been a beat cop in Philadelphia and despite working in some of the toughest neighborhoods he had survived the job long enough to be able to retire. Shannon explained that the people in those neighborhoods had come to respect the man and the values because that was the way that he lived his life. He did not force those values on anyone, he simply asked them to act fairly towards their neighbors. Then one day after retiring he had come home from a fishing trip with another former cop and had not been feeling well. Shannon told him how he had sat down in his favorite chair to watch his beloved Phillies and dozed off. Her mother had come home later that afternoon and found him in his chair – he was already gone. The doctor's said that it was a massive heart attack and most likely he had not suffered at all, just simply slipped away. What helped them get through the next few days was that the night before he had made the effort to check in on each of his children, just to say how much he loved and respected them and how proud he was of them.

While Shannon talked he found himself wondering about his own mother and father. Did they ever live in a happy house like that? Were they wondering about Robert and if they knew would they be proud of him. Some days he had wondered if somewhere in the crowds of people he saw was his father or mother, perhaps even a long lost brother who was going to help him rebuild his past. Would it be possible for him to ever forgive his parents if they came to him now and showed who they were and explained their decisions? Maybe his mother had thought she was doing the right thing? Probably she never even knew who his father was. And at that moment he realized it didn't matter, they had made the decisions and he was the one who had paid the price. That was all there was to it.

Robert suddenly realized that Shannon had stopped talking and was looking at him. The sparkle in her eyes made him smile and the warmth melted his heart even more. "Did I say something wrong? Here I am rambling on about vacations and birthdays, when all you probably want is to get back to work. I'm sorry when I get nervous I seem to ramble on. You must be bored – no reason to be polite I can do my own reading."

He smiled as he tried to consider the possibility that she could ever say anything to upset him. How absolutely absurd the very idea was. "No, you could never say anything wrong or bore me, Shannon. Besides – what do you have to be nervous about?"

"Surely a successful business man like yourself does not want to hear about my family. Especially with your own background, and here I am prattling on like an old woman at the church picnic." He laughed heartily at the very notion of her prattling. "See, now you are just laughing at me."

"Shannon – I was not laughing at you, but rather the picture you just painted in my mind. I could not find anything more interesting at the moment than hearing about your family. You speak so endearingly about them I can almost picture them in my own mind. You are lucky to have such wonderful parents and siblings to have grown up with."

Before she had a chance to answer him, the pilot announced that they were in their final approach to Las Vegas' McCarron Airport and would be on the ground in moments. Robert offered a ride to her hotel which at first she declined. Then smiling he reminded her of the taxi line she would have to wait through, and he was sure his ride would be faster. She declined one more time before finally accepted his offer, on the condition that he would be her guest for dinner.

Still laughing as they gathered their bags and left the plane he told her she would have made a great business person. He picked up her briefcase and carried it along with his own, knowing that Joseph would grab his other bag. As soon as they left the security area of the airport, four linebacker-sized bodyguards moved in around them. Shannon gave Robert a sideways questioning glance who nodded towards Joseph as if that was explanation enough. As they walked through the airport the Friday evening crowds seemed to part in front of them. With the wall walking in front of them Robert felt like a rock star or famous athlete and the looks from the other travelers told him they were curious who he was.

As they stepped outside they were immediately struck by the still bright sunshine and the blazing heat of the desert. Both Robert and Shannon immediately slipped on their sunglasses taking both refuge as well as enjoyment from the heat and bright sunlight. There were two large black SUV's waiting for them at the curb, their windows dark as night. The lead bodyguard opened the door for them and they quickly slipped inside. Joseph moved to the SUV behind them and almost before all of the doors were closed they were moving. Shannon smiled as she looked at the now crowded front seat. There were only two men sitting up front but with their shoulders almost touching it was hard to see through the windshield.

Shannon did not want to tell Robert but this was her first trip to Las Vegas. She gazed out of the SUV windows astonished at the hotels and just how big they all were. It seemed as if one was bigger than the next, each with its own theme, and each theme even more dramatic than the one before. The pair of SUV's made their way through the busy Friday evening traffic and soon pulled up in front of Caesar's. The closest doorman moved quickly to the door but before he could open it the bodyguard had moved effortlessly to be in his way. After a moment's hesitation he opened the door and Shannon slid out. One of the other bodyguards had retrieved her bags from the second SUV and handed them off to the doorman.

Before she could walk away Robert slid down his window. "Oh Doctor. Don't forget our deal – you owe me a dinner." Shannon turned and slipped her sunglasses up revealing those warm green eyes, then smiling broadly winked and turned away. As Joseph climbed into the SUV next to him Robert watched her climbed the steps into the hotel. Despite the presence of Joseph sitting beside him, Robert was very much aware of how empty the car seemed without her there.

Moments later they pulled to a stop in front of the Bellagio and Robert waited for the body guard before exiting. Once again he was struck by the heat and bright sunshine. They were obviously waiting for him as there were several doormen to take his bags and before he reached the entrance the hotel manager was there. He handed Robert his card and assured him that if there was anything he needed to pick up the phone. Robert turned to Joseph who whispered that they thought he was a big gambler, nothing more. They were led to the top floor where his suite was one of the four on the floor. Clearly no expense had been spared as there was already a butler in the suite waiting to care of his every need. Robert thanked him but sent him on his way telling him they would manage quite well.

There were two levels to the suite, bedrooms upstairs and along with a living area on the first floor there was also a rather large office. Joseph placed his briefcase in the office area and then had one of the bodyguards take their suitcases upstairs to the bedrooms. Robert looked around as he walked over to one of the floor to ceiling windows. He had an amazing view of the strip below and hoped it would not distract him from his business here. As he settled in his cell phone rang and when he answered it was Frank telling him that Salvatori had agreed to move up the meeting to dinner later that evening. As Robert hung up he took a deep breath knowing that he had to get the next couple of days right or the entire deal could fall apart.

Robert spent the next couple of hours reviewing the casino's financials and other documents related to the company. He also studied the backgrounds of the board of directors so that if needed he could negotiate directly with them. He made several phone calls following up on the Philadelphia project as well. Things were moving along nicely, and he was very pleased with the progress. After that he had a nice salad lunch with fresh fruit and cottage cheese on the glassed in balcony. He sat for a while longer relaxing then got back to work.

This was the most important set of documents he had to review so he took his time making a long list of notes. These were the union agreements and given his meeting later today, he had to make sure that he understood them thoroughly. Frank, his Chief Legal Officer, had already gone through them and made his comments, but Robert knew he had to know every word or he would be at a severe disadvantage. He also knew that in negotiations like this he would have to be at the top of his game. Salvatori was sending a car for Robert at six for dinner, so Robert had some time. He glanced at his watch as he stood and stretched his back. Rubbing his tired eyes, Robert decided to take a walk and clear his head.

He looked around for Joseph before leaving, but as he stepped outside the suite was not surprised to see a bodyguard waiting for him. The two men headed to an elevator and took the quick ride downstairs. Stepping out into the noisy casino was not what Robert had hoped for so he quickly made his way outside. He paused long enough to slip on his sunglasses in the bright sunshine, and also to get his bearings. The bodyguard waited patiently as Robert turned and started to walk towards to the high level moving sidewalks that would take him out to the strip.

Robert paused briefly at the intersection to look up at the mini Eiffel Tower at the Paris Casino. As the light changed he crossed over and walking down the street he decided to stop for a cold drink. He found a seat facing the Bellagio and ordered drinks for himself and the bodyguard. They sat quietly watching passers-by in the bright sunlight, the Bellagio fountain show captivating even the most repetitive Las Vegas visitor. The sun seemed to help Robert's mind clear and soon he was typing away on his iPad. First making notes regarding what he had read in all of the documents from before, then his mind moving back to Philadelphia.

While he knew that things were progressing nicely he also knew there was still a lot to do. He went back through his emails answering them and asking more questions and requesting more information. He also made arrangements for several more meetings to be scheduled since the government there still seemed to be caught in red tape. Several of the prospective national businesses considering opening up nearby were having trouble and they all seemed to think Robert could pull the needed strings. Even mighty Wal-Mart had requested his assistance in getting permission to open a "small" store. Considering their pricing model, Robert was convinced that this would bring much needed jobs as well as cheaper goods for the families.

Apparently not everyone agreed and one council person had even gone so far as to say that it was not "beneficial to the overall community or the growth of small business that was the core of a strong community." It didn't take long for Robert to find out that the council member had large personal investments in competitors of Wal-Mart. As Robert sent the information to Frank for political handling, he simply shook his head.

Robert had been so engrossed in his work he did not notice the vans that had stopped at the curb until he felt the bodyguard's hand on his arm, "We need to move now!" was all he heard as he was suddenly pulled to his feet and manhandled into the nearby restaurant and straight through to the casino. Robert could hear the bodyguard speaking into a microphone and could also hear several people yelling at them as they were roughly pushed out of their way. In the reflection of the door Robert saw four or five men chasing after them, pushing just as many people out of the way, turning over tables as they did.

They walked quickly through the casino, cutting through between tables and even through roped off areas. A casino security person tried to stop them at one point but he was pushed out of the way by the linebacker sized bodyguard like he was a rag doll. The team chasing them was not giving up and Robert realized they were heading outside. He instinctively felt that would be a mistake so he grabbed the bodyguard and pulled him down a row of slot machines. It was hard to hide the big guy, but he got the idea and they ducked down as best they could. They paused and Robert saw ahead the elevators for the observation platform, at the same moment the doors opened. There was a long line of people waiting, but the bodyguard got the idea at the same time.

They both jogged over to the rope knocking it down and stepping into the elevator.

The attendant tried to stop them but he was pushed aside and when he saw the gun in the bodyguard's hand he moved back. The guard stepped in front of Robert as the doors closed. They could hear the shouts from the people waiting in line and they could see their pursuers catching up to them also. Thankfully the doors closed, but not before Robert saw one raise a gun and he heard several pops. The doors closed amid the screams from the waiting people and after a moment Robert reached out and hit the stop button making the elevator stop between floors.

He took a deep breath before he saw the bodyguard slump against the wall. He quickly moved to him and opening his coat saw that he had been hit by one bullet in the shoulder. Robert did his best to stop the bleeding with some guidance from the guard. He was finally able to call Joseph who said they were minutes away and trying to get through the growing crowd of onlookers and police that were now showing up en masse. Robert ignored the elevator phone ringing and sat with the bodyguard. As he held the man's coat against the wound Robert realized he didn't even know his name.

Finally his cell phone rang again and Joseph said they were bringing the elevator down and that the area had been cleared. Robert had lost track of time and didn't realize it had been about twenty minutes, taking that long to make sure it was safe and to get the police to understand the situation. There was also a gurney waiting and as the wall of new bodyguards closed around Robert he saw them load his protector onto the gurney. With the police leading the way, Robert was led through a maze of corridors before reaching the loading dock. They quickly got into the pair of SUVs and then drove around to the back of the Bellagio. Robert and Joseph quietly made their way back to the suite through the freight elevators.

Once inside, Robert went straight to the well-stocked bar and poured two fingers of scotch. He downed it quickly before pouring and drinking a second. Only then did he sit in the nearby arm chair and closed his eyes. He didn't know long he sat there quietly replaying the afternoon in his mind before he felt a hand on his arm. When he opened his eyes he was surprised to see Dr. Adams sitting in a chair in front of him. She wanted to make sure that he was ok, since sometimes concussion symptoms can be brought back on by mental trauma as much as physical.

They talked for a couple of minutes about how he felt and then even before he realized it Robert was telling her everything about the day. He was surprised at how much it had impacted him, especially the bodyguard being shot right in front of him. Dr. Adams did her best to help him work through his feelings, especially the helplessness that there was nothing he could do for the man. She called the hospital while he listened in, and found that the man was out of surgery and that thankfully the wound had not been too bad with no permanent damage.

After a while she apologized as she was giving her speech later that evening and had to finish preparing. When she left, Joseph sat down and they discussed the afternoon's events again. Joseph wanted more details about the attackers and the van, making notes of anything specific that Robert could remember. He explained that the police would want to speak with him as well and Robert promised he would do whatever it took to help find them. Robert also made sure that Joseph would have someone see to everything the bodyguard needed. He was surprised to learn that the bodyguard was married and immediately arranged for his wife to fly out to be with him.

Robert managed to pull himself together and got back to work, answering several emails and calls from people worried about him. Apparently he had made the news again and it had made it to New York as part of a breaking news update. They had rescheduled his dinner with Salvatori, so he worked until almost 8 o'clock that evening and only stopped when Joseph had room service deliver their dinner. After dinner Robert went back to work, deciding that life was indeed too short and he knew without a doubt that he needed to do things better to make a difference.

Once again, Joseph surprised him and had arranged for a video call with Mikhail. They talked about the new books that Mikhail was reading - with his mom's help of course, the games he was playing with his new school friends, and the latest superhero movie. Robert promised to take him to see the new Disney movie that had just come out once he returned to Philadelphia. Mikhail even held up several crayon drawings that he had done. As usual, Robert did not want to say good night but Mikhail's mother reminded him that it was getting late. This was punctuated with a lot of yawning and Mikhail's eyes eventually closing. It was his mom who picked him up and said good night before carrying him off to bed.

Robert himself went off to bed, stopping just long enough at Joseph's door to say good night. He tossed and turned in bed for quite a while, the events of the day firing through his mind like a 3D movie. Unfortunately, he knew that it was not a movie he was replaying. And at the end the director did not yell "cut", and the bodyguard did not walk away washing off fake blood. He truly hoped the man was ok and made a mental note to visit him after his meeting tomorrow. He further promised himself that he was going to find out who was behind this. Clearly these were not random events, but someone was determined to stop him. But, stop him from what? What could be so important that they were willing to kill him for?

Chapter 12

Robert woke early the next morning so he could get some work done before the meeting with Salvatori. He spent a couple of hours going through emails, reading through his daily briefing file, and making several phone calls to his staff to follow up on issues. He spent a full thirty minutes just talking to Pearl in Philadelphia who brought him up to date on several critical issues with the construction which seemed to be moving at a snail's pace. It still seemed that at every step there was some new bit of red tape that his team had to overcome. As he hung up he was incredibly frustrated and took an extra five minutes to draft an email to Lowell and Frank instructing them to come up with a strategy to put an end to this as quickly as possible. If they didn't resolve this quickly it would be winter with no homes built for these people.

As soon as he hit send Joseph knocked and came into the room carrying a fresh cup of coffee and a glass of orange juice. He told Robert that he had about twenty minutes to get ready before they would have to leave. Robert got showered and shaved and as he was starting to get dressed his phone rang. It was Roger letting him know that they had sent an updated package on Salvatori with some more current information. He also told Robert that Salvatori considered himself to be very much a blue collar guy, and Robert should keep that in mind.

Robert stood there in jockeys and an undershirt looking at his hand made Saville Row suit and starched handmade French cuff shirt. He smiled and instead went to the dresser and pulled out a pair of jeans and a polo shirt. They may not have been bought at Sears but they were also not hand made. He finished getting dressed, slipped on his favorite Omega Seamaster grabbed his wallet and left the room. Joseph looked at him with a cocked eyebrow and a smirk.

Robert laughed since he knew that Joseph had never seen him dressed for a meeting like this. "It's ok, Joseph, I haven't totally lost my mind. Roger told me that this guy is blue collar so I wanted him to feel comfortable and at ease." Joseph nodded still grinning and led Robert to the main door.

There were already two bodyguards waiting by the door for them and as Robert picked up his iPad one of the men stepped forward and shook his hand. "We're with you Sir, whenever you are ready." Robert nodded his thanks and the four of them left the room heading for the elevator. A guest in one of the other suites started to leave his room, but saw the group coming. One of the bodyguards quickly stopped Robert and Joseph while the other bodyguard moved to the man in the doorway and mumbled something. The man quickly stepped back into his room and closed the door. They waited for the door to click shut and then they quickly moved to the elevator. The elevator arrived and they paused again as the doors opened, the two bodyguards standing directly in front of Robert. The door opened and another bodyguard was waiting inside.

They all got in and rode to the main floor, Robert smiled and whispered, "I think the only danger right now is this thing not being able to carry all of our weight." They all chuckled and Robert was glad that everyone seemed able to relax a little. As the doors opened several people had to step back as the wall of men stepped from the elevator. Robert was sandwiched between the bodyguards and they moved as quickly as possible to the hotel's entrance. There were the usual pair of SUVs waiting and they quickly climbed inside, pulling away from the hotel immediately.

No sooner did Robert sit down when his phone rang. He looked down at the screen and groaned. It was Martin calling. He knew that Martin had been trying to schedule time with him and had been badgering Jennifer to set it up. Robert's calendar was always booked several months out, but he usually made time for the board members. But right now, even if he was interested in Martin's investment he just didn't have the bandwidth to manage another project.

"Good morning Martin."

"Good morning Robert. I know you are on your way to a meeting so I won't take up too much of your time. I have been trying to get Jennifer to schedule some time for that investment review and not having much luck. I really would appreciate it if you would speak with her."

"Martin, I am working on a couple of large and complex projects at the moment. As I said before I will let Jennifer schedule it. But, it could be a couple of months."

"In a couple of months it may be too late. I can't imagine that any project would whither if you gave up a few hours."

Robert sighed deeply "I will speak with her. Goodbye" And then he hung up quickly before he had to listen to any more of Martin's pleadings. He also made a note to mention to Jennifer that his travel plans should stay private from now on. Before he knew it Martin would be showing up here in Las Vegas for *just five minutes*. Especially since it would be "too late" – what nonsense.

At this time of the morning the strip was not too crowded, and they drove as quickly as they could out to the highway. Joseph leaned over and let Robert know they would have approximately a thirty minute ride. He settled back in his seat and started to review the project update he had received from Roger. He had a few more ideas about the Philadelphia project, and started making notes on his iPad. The SUV had tinted windows so the only sign of the early morning's bright desert sun was through the windshield.

They exited the highway and were on a secondary road when Robert suddenly noticed that there didn't seem to be much traffic. It didn't seem right considering there were stores on both sides of the streets and plenty of cars in the parking lots. Joseph seemed to notice that there weren't as many cars either and started to look around. They both looked at each other feeling as if something was wrong, but neither seemed to pinpoint it. Just as Robert was about to say something to Joseph there was a loud bang and the huge SUV rocked on it's wheels. Several of its windows exploded inwards and the men were thrown about in their seats. Before Robert could reach for Joseph he started to fade away and then there was just black.

***

It was what had become a typical Sunday for the boy and his friend Sam. They had gotten up and walked to the local donut shop where the boy was allowed to pick out two donuts and a drink. Sam always got the same thing - a large black cup of coffee and a bear claw. The boy always thought that was a funny name for a Danish, but what did he know. Today he chose his favorite - a chocolate donut with chocolate frosting. The manager must have expected them because he already had it ready, and today it was special because it also had chocolate sprinkles. For his second choice he pointed to one of the large cream filled donuts, it was huge and both Sam and the manager smiled at him.

Sam ruffled his hair as they took their purchases and walked back to the house. The house... It wasn't much really, just a couple of bedrooms and only one bathroom. But it sure beat an empty warehouse that leaked and was also home to rats and stray cats. They sat on the front porch and ate their breakfast while neighbors passed by smiling and waving to the two "men". Sam always called him "little man" and a lot of the neighbors had taken to calling him that also.

After a while they went inside and flipped on the television to watch the Phillies play. That guy Mike Schmidt was playing amazing and the announcers were saying he could be one of the greatest ever. The boy sure didn't know, but then he didn't really understand the game anyway. At least not like Sam did, he knew everything there was to know about baseball, the Phillies, and a lot of other things. Plus - he was the nicest man the boy had ever met. Most just wanted him out of their way, or to "run errands" for them - which the boy knew meant carry their drugs. After all, what cop would bust a kid his age?

Shortly after settling down to watch the game there was a knock at the door. Sam looked at the boy, shrugged and then went to answer it. At first, the boy thought it would be one of his cop friends or poker buddies. But instead he heard Sam arguing with someone at the door. At first, he was calm and spoke quietly and determinedly but quickly his voice rose. The boy didn't understand what they were talking about but Sam kept saying "it wasn't fair" and that "the home was no place for a boy to grow up". He didn't understand - this was a perfectly good home for him to grow up in. The argument seemed to end when the boy heard him say "I will tell him".

As soon as he saw Sam's face he knew something was wrong. He jumped up and ran past him quickly climbing the stairs to his bedroom. Sam knocked and after a moment came in. The boy was laying on his bed, his head under his pillow. It was HIS pillow and no one could make him give it up. Sam sat beside him and explained that the court had decided that Sam's house wasn't an appropriate place for a boy his age to grow up. Especially since Sam wasn't married and as a cop, was always in danger. They decided that the boy needed a "real family" to grow up with.

Sam scooped the boy up into his big arms and held him. The boy found himself crying at the same time that he felt tears on Sam's cheeks. "I'm sorry little man. I can't go against what the courts said, but I won't stop trying. And I sure won't stop looking after you. They say that this is a great family they have lined up for you, with a real yard and a boy your age to play with."

The boy leaned back, wiped away his tears and took a deep breath. "Ok Sam if you say so." But the look on his face told Sam the boy had been let down by another adult. And that Sam was just one more he couldn't trust. He helped him pack up his belongings and then took him downstairs to the woman on the porch. She led him out to her car and helped him into the back seat. As they started to pull away the boy looked back at the house and saw Sam standing watching. Sam gave him a short wave and the boy thought he saw tears glistening on his cheek. Sam had let him down just like every other man he knew, so he just sat back and folded his arms.

***

Robert opened his eyes slowly, but the blackness didn't clear. He held his hands up to eyes hoping it was just darkness, but he still couldn't see anything. Even when he touched his fingers to his face he could only feel them. He felt the bandages across his eyes and wondered what it all meant. He had so many questions but when he called out, no one answered. He was alone. Where was he and how had he gotten here?

A couple of minutes passed and then Robert heard a soft voice beside him. "Good morning, Sir, how do you feel?"

Robert's voice was dry and cracked as he answered. "I am not sure. What is wrong with my eyes? Where am I and why can't

I see?"

The voice answered softly. "This is the University Medical Center. In Las Vegas. You were in a car accident a few days ago and suffered some minor damage to your eyes. The bandages are to help with the healing, but I will let the doctor explain."

Robert out his hand and found her arm, "what about my friends? Are they ok?"

Had Robert seen the confused look on her face he might have been more concerned. She hesitated, and then said, "I am not sure. Sir, but I am also sure they will come around. Now try to rest."

A little later Robert woke up again and found a controller had been placed near his hand. He found a button and pushed it. Nothing happened, so he pushed it again. The soft voice was back and let him know that she would get the doctor. A few minutes passed and a man's voice told Robert he was the doctor. He also let him that all vitals were normal and if Robert was ready he wanted to remove the bandages and check on his eyes. Robert gave him an emphatic "yes" and closed his eyes as instructed.

After several minutes while the doctor removed the bandages Robert slowly opened his eyes, again. This time light slowly filtered in. The room was blurry and Robert could just make out some shapes and colors. The doctor told him it was ok to blink as long as he didn't feel any scratching or discomfort. There wasn't so Robert blinked several times and slowly the room came in to focus. He looked around and saw a nurse standing at the end of his bed, while the doctor stood to the side. He smiled broadly and said, "hey doc!" The doctor smiled as well and explained that he had been in a car accident and that there had been some glass in his eyes when he was found. He had suffered a concussion and Robert explained he had had one previously. The doctor told him about some of the things he already knew about, so Robert assured him he would check with his own doctor in New York.

Other than that and some minor scrapes and scratches he was fine and could leave as soon as he was ready.

While he waited for the paperwork, a police officer showed up and took Robert's statement. The police confirmed that there was only the one SUV left at the sight of the accident and that Robert was the only one in the car. The policeman wrote down his description of the three bodyguards and Joseph, and promised to let Robert know as soon as he found something. He didn't have his wallet or his cell phone, so the officer had him filling out additional paperwork for that also.

Robert was sure that Joseph would show up at any moment, even as the paper work was completed and he was dressed and ready to go. Robert walked down to the lobby and found a cab to take back to the hotel. Fortunately, he still had his room so getting a new key at the desk he went upstairs and called his office.

He reached Jennifer who couldn't stop crying and shouting when she heard his voice. Finally she calmed down and explained the situation. No one had any idea about Robert or Joseph and had feared the worst. The bodyguards had been found tied up in a deserted house by a real estate agent and perspective buyer that had shown up to view it. They had tried to fight off the attack, but were over powered quickly by more men and even more weapons. The attackers had dragged Joseph into a car after checking his wallet and taken the bodyguards to the house and left them.

Once the attackers had Joseph in the car they were content and never checked the car for anyone else. That was why Robert had been left behind. By the time the bodyguards were freed, Robert had been taken to the hospital and without ID they had been unable to trace him. Apparently there had also been a tour bus accident and his paperwork must have been mixed in with it. It had only been a few days and they had assumed the worst - that the attackers realized they had the wrong man and went back for

Robert, so they had them both. Or worse.

Robert had Jennifer arrange for new credit cards and identification to be overnighted. Then he hung up and immediately called Agent Simmons. He promised they were already doing everything they could since Jennifer had called them as soon as Robert and Joseph were thought to be missing. The FBI already had a few leads and were actively pursuing them. He hoped that they would have more in the next day or so and would be sure to keep Robert informed. As he hung up the phone Robert stared out of the full size windows in his suite and was overcome by a sense of sadness and loneliness. He couldn't imagine why they had taken Joseph and worried that he knew the answer to that. He must have taken Robert's wallet as soon as he realized what they were after and taken his place.

Robert sat at the desk and tried to work. First he sat and read his daily briefing report, but the words just ran together. He stood up and walked around the room, first heading to the bar where he got a bottle of water. Then he walked around the sitting area of couches and chairs. He walked back over to his desk and sitting down started to look at his emails. But after several tries the words on the screen ran together again and became black dots on the screen.

He stood up and walked over to the couch area flipping through the channels on the television. As he flipped through the channels he drank from the water bottle. Standing there praying for information, praying for a sign, praying that Joseph was alive. Finally he moved back to his desk and stood behind it staring out at the city beneath him. His arms hanging limp at his sides, the remaining water spilling from the bottle. Knowing that there was nothing he could do. He had so much, and yet there was nothing.

His phone rang and it was Agent Simmons and Robert quickly slide the answer button. "Yes! Is there anything new?"

"I'm sorry Mr. Cutter, we haven't found Joseph yet. But, we do believe that we know who has him. And if we are right then they likely just want money. We have an informant working with us now who is trying to contact the group. Acting as a broker if you will."

"Fine, tell me how much you need and I will get it."

"I understand how you must be feeling Mr. Cutter. I have an agent on his way to you now. He will be in street clothes acting as a business person there for a meeting. Just in case anyone is watching your suite. He will help you through this. Please follow what he asks of you, no matter what."

"Understood, Agent Simmons. Whatever you need I will do. Just please help me get him back."

"Yes sir. I am flying out to Las Vegas shortly, and will come straight to your suite as soon as I arrive. Thank you, Sir."

Moments later there was a knock at the door. When Robert answered it, he was surprised to see Joseph standing there. But before he could react two other men, both holding guns pushed him inside following quickly and double locking the door behind them. While one held a mean looking machine gun the other tied Joseph to a chair using police style flex cuffs. They secured both his wrists and ankles to the chair. Then they did the same to Robert. The look on Joseph's face said a lot, not to mention the bruising around his eyes and jaw.

"Ok, Cutter. You said being here in your suite would help since you needed your laptop. I suppose this is another of your lame bodyguards. He will prove as ineffective as the others. Maybe you will learn that firepower always trumps muscle power!" As the obvious leader and elder of the pair spoke to Joseph he kept his gun trained on Robert.

The man's cell phone rang and he barely glanced at the caller ID before answering it. "Yes, Sir, we are here now. No, Sir, not yet. Yes sir, I understand."

He hung up the phone looking a little less confident and sensing that they would take it as a sign of weakness turned and slapped Joseph hard. Robert wanted to look away, but was afraid of how the man would take it. As a bodyguard this shouldn't bother him. It certainly didn't seem to bother Joseph, who stuck out his jaw as if to say, "go ahead, give me your best shot." The man must have read his mind, because he hit Joseph again.

"I have had enough of your stalling!! You will get into your laptop and get me the information I need or things will get a lot worse! You don't need unbroken feet to work the laptop!" The man shouted in his face.

Joseph looked at him for a moment, then before he could answer there was a knock at the door. They all turned and looked. There was another knock and the older man started to move towards it, the gun leading the way. Joseph shot Robert a look who mouthed "fed" quickly. Joseph closed his eyes and opened them letting Robert know he understood. At the third knock, the man asked who it was.

"It's Mr. Simmons, Sir, from the Washington office. We have a meeting scheduled." The voice answered.

As the man was about to open the door, Joseph started to have a coughing fit. It was obviously faked, so the other man came over and hit him across the face. First on the right, then the left side. The loud slapping sounds were clear as firecrackers in the otherwise quiet room.

The elder man shot him a look, then said, "look Mr... uh... Simmons. I am not feeling well right now. Why don't you come back tomorrow?"

"Sure thing, Mr. Cutter. I'll just swing by tomorrow morning."

You could hear the footsteps in the hallway as the man walked away. Robert almost smiled knowing the agent got the message.

The older man didn't sound anything like what a man like Cutter would sound like. Forget the voice, it was in the confidence and demeanor. And based on the agent's response Robert knew that he understood. Even more, from the flash in Joseph's eyes Robert saw he knew it also.

The older man walked over to Joseph and with a quiet anger said, "Enough of this! You will get me what I want now, or he dies!" And as he said it he pointed the gun directly at Robert's chest.

Joseph hesitated only briefly then looked down and said, "Ok... no more. Untie me and I will do it."

The older man hesitated then stepping back, nodded to his partner. The man untied Joseph who shakily stood up and made his way over to the desk. He turned on the laptop and while it started up he started to list to one side, struggling to stay upright as if it was just too much for him. The man nearest him reached out to grab his arm, and as he did Joseph acted swiftly hitting him in the throat. As the man started to go down, Joseph grabbed the gun and shot the older man in shoulder holding his gun. It fell to the floor out of his now useless hand.

To everyone's surprise, as Joseph moved to kick the gun away, the hallway door burst open and another man stood there holding a gun. He shouted "FBI! No one move!" Joseph carefully placed his gun on the floor and kicked it to the side. Without knowing for sure, the FBI agent moved in and kicked the other gun away. Then he slowly looked around the room.

He looked at Robert, "Mr. Cutter I presume? I'm Agent Jones. Special Agent Simmons said you would get the reference if I used his name."

"Yes, Agent Jones. Your timing is excellent, but perhaps you can let Joseph help me out here?"

The agent nodded and at the same time moved to the older of

the two men. He quickly used his own flex cuffs and despite the obvious pain in the man's shoulder tied his wrists behind his back. Only then did he move to other unconscious man and tie his wrists as well. He pulled out his own phone and called the real Agent Simmons letting him know what happened. As he talked, several Las Vegas police officers entered the room. The agent flashed his badge to the officers as he hung up the phone.

It took another hour of taking the two men down to the police cars and taking statements from Robert and Joseph. The FBI agent told Robert that Agent Simmons had asked him to stay until he arrived with more support and the police also agreed to leave a man posted in the hallway. Robert and Joseph stepped into the bedroom to talk quietly.

"Are you ok, Joseph? I don't know if I should be mad as hell at you or so utterly thankful."

"Yes. Sir I'm OK. These guys just hit me a lot, but nothing that won't heal. And well, as far as the other... I know."

For the first time in years Robert found himself speechless. So with the words unable to be spoken he shook his hand. Then surprising them both Robert moved in and hugged him. They held each other for several moments then finally let go. For the first time for as long as he could remember, Robert felt a huge weight lifted off of him. Although he knew he owed Joseph his life, he also knew that he would never be alone again.

When they came back out the FBI agent was on the phone again speaking with Agent Simmons. Robert had told him about the phone call the older man had received and they were already trying to see if they could track the phone call. Hopefully they could do it before the real leader realized they had been caught. It might be a long shot, but aside from either of the men cooperating it was the best they could do. Besides, the two might not even know who the leader really was.

Robert and Joseph moved over to the desk, and it occurred to Robert something the older man had said. "Joseph, what information where they after?"

Joseph hesitated for a moment, "he kept asking me about a deal, code named 'Viper'. He wanted to make sure that not only could they access your information, but all related information. That's when I came up with the idea about the laptop."

"Good thinking by the way. Of course, having the FBI show up didn't hurt."

"Yeah, well I will be pissed later. Because I expected to see a hoard of body guards waiting for us, not you pacing the floor!"

"Yes, well... Sorry about that. I was upset that everyone was in harm's way because of me. So... Viper. Mmmm that's our project involving the private airplanes and helicopters. I can't imagine what is so special about that. It's really not a big deal at all."

"Well, it might be no big deal to you. But, clearly someone thinks it is."

Robert picked up his cellphone and called the office. First he updated Jennifer who almost couldn't stop crying that both were going to be ok. Then he talked to Lowell telling him to get someone to do a lot more research on the Viper project. As they talked it occurred to Robert that the kidnappers, or more likely the leader, knew it was known as "Project Viper". Robert paused in the conversation, then told Lowell he needed to also research anyone of his staff working on the project. He glanced at the FBI agent, then also asked what he would need to pull everyone's corporate cell phone records from the past few days.

As soon as the FBI agent was off the phone, Robert explained to him what he had asked for from Lowell. Then he gave the agent Lowell's direct number so they could communicate directly. As the agent walked away to call him, Robert tried to think of what could be so special about this deal. He was taking a mid-sized company private, knowing that management had a good handle on the operations, but also knowing that they needed some increased executive experience. It was his opinion that with the right executive the company could leap into the next tier of its competitors. Then with some additional capital investments he was sure they could grow the company, either through additional acquisitions or general business.

Robert walked over to his desk and pulled up the executive background on the company. There were a total of one hundred employees between two locations. The company had its headquarters in northern New Jersey and it's manufacturing facility was in New Mexico. The company's executives not only ran day to day operations but also got involved in some of the larger sales they got into it. While most of their sales where corporate based, they did also do some private business. Apparently for some companies and high end clients, having their private jet personally designed was important. The list of the companies they dealt with was above reproach.

Their client list was highly confidential, and that seemed to be as important to their clients as the actual designs. The company also paid their front office staff rather well to keep that list highly confidential. And as Robert knew from his sources, the company was being seriously considered for a contract with the justice department. Robert would have to look into that a little closer, to make sure the government had not found something. Between the justice department contract and the highly confidential client list there could be something hiding that Robert had not considered.

While the team in New York started to look into the company more as well as the people with access, he started to look more closely at some of their other projects. Robert spent the next several hours going through as much information as he could, Joseph wrote out everything he could think of for the police and

FBI. Robert also arranged for a doctor to come to the room to give Joseph the checkup he needed. Luckily the kidnappers only left bruises that would go away and nothing more. On top of all this, Salvatori called and still wanted to meet with Robert. At first, Robert had no interest in meeting with him, but then realized that he might be able to use his connections to get information. With this in mind, he made arrangements to meet him for dinner and got together some pictures of the kidnappers to take with him.

Later that evening, Robert was getting ready for his dinner when Joseph walked in to the room. The usual punctual Robert was already 10 minutes late. When Joseph walked in he was surprised at what he saw. Spread across the bed were two different pairs of jeans, several polo shirts, and a couple of long sleeve shirts on hangers were hanging on the closet doors. And to top it off, Robert was standing looking in the full length mirror in suit pants and a dress shirt with an untied tie around his neck.

"Robert... You ok? We need to get going."

Robert turned to face Joseph and opened his arms to show the mess. "Joseph, have you ever known me to not be decisive? No. How about non-decisive regarding clothes? Same answer. So how come all of a sudden I can't decide which knot to tie this tie. Or even if I should be wearing a tie."

Joseph shook his head and walked over to where Robert was standing. Then turning him back to face the mirror he said "Robert, we have both been through a lot. But the face looking back at me is the same face we have both been seeing for years. The same face who has made a ton of money by thinking of the best way to get something done, by looking at the worst and finding the best. The same face who looked at a pile of ash and found a little boy who needed a new home. So look at this position we now find ourselves in and find the right answer. Then chew them up and spit them out.

Now, as far as your wardrobe goes... skip the suit and tie. Throw on jeans and loafers and let's go have an enjoyable dinner. They say that Prime has the best damn food around. Come on... I don't know about you, but I am starving!"

Robert laughed and pushed Joseph out the door. Then he finished getting dressed in jeans and loafers as instructed and walked back out in to the sitting area. As he walked in he heard Joseph on the phone letting the restaurant know they would be down in 10 minutes. Robert smiled when he heard Joseph say that he hoped jeans would be fine. After hanging up, the two left the room and headed downstairs to the restaurant. With the four bodyguards front and back there was barely enough room in the elevator and at the several stops it made on the way they were met with stares from other waiting guests.

Robert and Joseph made their way through the busy casino and into the shops. With the body guards both in front and behind, people moved out of their way pretty quickly. They arrived at the restaurant and were quickly shown to the front room. It not only boasted a great view of the fountains, but tonight it was empty except for the two waiters and four servers. Robert moved to the two person table and arrived at the same time that Salvatori stood up. They both stretched out hands and shook.

Robert introduced himself "Robert Cutter, Mr. Salvatori thanks for meeting me here tonight. And I apologize for being late."

Salvatori waved him to sit, as he took the chair across from him. "Please, it's Anthony, and I understand. After the last few days I was surprised to hear that you still wanted to meet."

"Thank you, and its Robert then. I decided to meet to see if you could help me with my problem." He placed the pictures of the kidnappers on the table and Salvatori picked them up, studied them then slid them into his jacket pocket.

"I don't recognize them, but I still have a few old friends in this town. I will see what I can find out and let you know tomorrow." He paused as Robert nodded and the waiter came over. He quickly took their orders for drinks and dinner as a server poured water and placed bread on the table. After he stepped away, the sommelier stepped over to the table and made a few suggestions based on their dinner choices. They selected a good Californian Chardonnay with a pleasant "buttery feel that will give just a hint of the fruits while bringing out the flavor of their dinner even more" he explained.

Their drinks were delivered just as Robert started to explain his interests in the hotel. "We want to take it private and make it the hotel it used to be. A jewel in the crown of Las Vegas again. The Bellagio needs to not only keep up with the Venetian and the Wynn, but it needs to do more and be more. And it is our opinion that this will only happen if it is taken private. The company won't spend what the hotel really needs to take it to the next level, rather it will just keep it on par with what it is - a very nice hotel on a strip with a lot of very nice hotels."

"I see, and you think that you can not only afford to buy the hotel but also rejuvenate it? To make it - *the jewel of Las Vegas* again. I think perhaps you either under estimate the costs involved in such an endeavor or you over estimate your own worth. Either way, you will fail if that is your plan and then what will become of the Bellagio?"

"There are a couple of things you should know about me. First I don't take on a project if I think I might fail, it's just not what I do. Second, I employ some of the top people in a variety of specialties just so they can do both - overestimate the costs involved, and under estimate that capital available. Third, I do more research than anyone else in this business, and even more research than the company that owns this hotel will do.

And that means that I understand the nuances of owning a hotel and casino in Las Vegas. This isn't a wish list for me, or a check box to mark. I have already spoken at length with the owners of the Bellagio and they are actually pretty happy to let me have it. For about what they would have spent on refurbishing it, nothing more than a paint job and touch up really. So that means I get a really good deal on a great property and get to spend a ton of money changing it into one of the great hotels of the world - which is more than a nice hotel in Las Vegas.

The last piece of this puzzle for me, is whether you want to be a part of it. As I understand it, you have quite a bit of pull in the hotel with the unions. And also with several of the other unions in the city that we will be working with. In my opinion, we can work together as partners and all of your union members will be very happy."

Salvatori looked across the table at him and sat quietly while their salads were served. As soon as the wait staff moved away, he said, "well, my research was right. You certainly don't mince words. Except that I don't control the unions and it will be up to the members whether or not they want to work with you. I am not sure what your researchers told you, but we do things by the book here in Las Vegas. This is not the 60s or 70s anymore and the gangsters don't run the show. But, unlike then the unions do have a pretty strong hand here and the one thing they don't like is to have an outsider trying to give them an ultimatum."

"I think you misunderstand me. It isn't an ultimatum at all, simply a fact. All of the work that will need to be done, can be done by non-union people. And all of the supplies, equipment, and hotel staff can be non-union also. But this isn't about union or non-union. It's about paying too much for something and ending up with a hotel that no one can afford to build or operate. Because when that happens and they close the doors then everyone is out of a job. And you and I both know that is a bad thing for everyone."

"So what you are asking of the unions is that they all take sweeping cuts in prices and wages so that you can make an even bigger buck, and so you won't fail. Is that what you are saying?"

"Not at all. Actually just the opposite. What I am suggesting is that we all take pay cuts including myself. In fact I don't plan on taking any salary from the hotel for the top executives for the first year. But, when the hotel reopens on time and as planned then we will all be partners and stockholders. And when I take the new hotel public in five years everyone will make a lot more money than if they just took a higher payday today. And if you don't think I can accomplish that then I suggest you do a little more research."

Salvatori sat back in his chair, crossed his arms and then laughed. "No, I don't think I need to do any more research. You are a ruthless, no nonsense business man who believes in getting his way no matter what. Sorry about all that, but I had to make sure that my research was right and that you had the balls to take this on. And that you had done all of your homework as well as I had expected."

He paused and took a sip of his wine, then leaned forward. "Robert, I like you and my father told me that I can trust you. So, here is what I have to offer and it's the best I can do right now. I will arrange a meeting on Friday morning with the heads of the unions. You will have one shot, and trust me I know these guys, that is all you will get. Also, I wouldn't get tough with them as they don't take it well when people try to break up their unions. But, I will tell you that if you convince them, then the unions will be on your side the whole way."

Robert took a long slow drink of his wine, then turned and looked out the French doors as the fountains started their show. As he replaced his glass on the table, he leaned forward, smiling, "you just tell me when and where and I will be there. And I will expect a full list of everyone attending before the meeting."

"Now, seeing our dinners are on the way why don't we put business aside and enjoy ourselves. Or you can give me your opinions of what this grand hotel needs."

As Robert had said, the wait staff wheeled over their dinners - filet mignon for himself and a New York strip for Salvatori. The dinner was as good as expected and they both had desert and coffees afterwards. Throughout the dinner they discussed changes they thought should be made to the hotel, mostly around the rooms and developing more as suites. In addition they talked about the casino and some changes they could make there as well. Robert was scheduled to meet with the Vice President of casino operations in the morning, but agreed that they should take a walk around to get their own impressions.

As they walked around the casino, Joseph stayed just a step behind them with the bodyguards walking in pairs on either side. Not quite close enough to be crowded, but still close enough to react. For someone who never gambled in business, Robert was intrigued with several games and stopped by a craps table where Anthony was more than happy to explain the game. They both put down some money and after about twenty minutes had both won. They tried their hands at blackjack, and then roulette. By the end of their walk they had both made several thousand dollars in profit and had stopped outside of the poker room.

Robert looked around at its location and how crowded it appeared. Robert turned to Anthony. "I may not be a poker player, but this seems like more of an afterthought than anything else. Are all of the poker rooms like this? And what is that room inside for?"

"I agree and I am a poker player. It's crowded inside and the tables are almost right on top of each other. The problem is that the casinos don't make as much here as they do at the other games. And the room in the middle is for high stakes games."

"Well, I don't know much about casinos in practice but it seems to me that poker players come with friends, wives, or girlfriends who can't sit and look over their shoulders. Which means they would be out shopping or doing their own gambling. But, if the room is not comfortable then the poker players don't come. Do they?"

Anthony laughed and looked at Robert, "don't know much about casinos huh? Sounds like you already have a good sense of how they should operate. I would suggest going to a few of the other casinos - the Caesar's for sure, Venetian, Aria, and The Wynn. They all have good poker rooms and are considered to be in the class you want the Bellagio to get back to."

"Thanks, Anthony. We'll do just that. Now if you don't mind, I am going to head back to the room. I'm afraid I've been a little susceptible to headaches and the lights and noise are giving me one." As he spoke he turned and offered his hand. Turning back to Joseph he gave him a quick nod and they started back to the elevators. As they did the bodyguards moved back into place surrounding the two men. They quickly made their way to the elevators and back up to their room.

Once in the room Robert went into the bathroom, stripping off his clothes and taking a long hot shower. As the water cascaded over him he mentally reviewed the dinner and walk through they had done. The research on Salvatori was that he was smart and thought fast on his feet, and that little got past him. Robert had seen as much from him tonight and felt better about the entire project knowing that he might actually be on his side. And if he could help him get more information on the kidnappers all the better.

After the shower he sat at the desk with the lights dimmed

making notes of what he had seen and some of the ideas from Salvatori. Glancing at the clock he realized it was too late to call Mikhail. Instead, he recorded a quick video message promising to visit again as soon as he could and that they would find something fun to do together. As he emailed the video to Mikhail's mother, he found himself smiling. Just thinking about the boy always seemed to bring a smile to Robert's face. Then he sent an email to Jennifer asking her to arrange some time for him to be in Philadelphia and look into Phillies tickets - surely the boy would like that. Yawning deeply, he crawled into bed and quickly fell asleep.

The next morning Robert woke up with another headache. He was sure that it was related to the accident, and just hoped he didn't have another concussion. With that thought he suddenly remembered about missing the dinner with Dr. Adams and hoped she wasn't too mad. After getting showered and dressed he went into the living area of the suite and saw that Joseph had already been up. There was a coffee service and some croissants laid out already. Robert helped himself and sitting down at the desk began to work through his emails.

Jennifer had managed to secure a bunch of tickets for a Phillies' game against the Washington Nationals for next weekend. The seats were right behind home plate and given the standings it was sure to be a great game. Robert emailed her back a thank you note and asked her to get a glove for Mikhail and let his mom know also. As an afterthought Robert emailed Lowell and Frank and told them to invite the city councilman from Philadelphia... Certainly couldn't hurt.

He also asked her to find a way to get in touch with Dr. Adams and apologize for him. But not to go into too much detail. After twenty minutes more of emails he moved on to the reports, only getting up to fill his coffee cup a couple of times. He spent a good amount of time going through the information he had on the casino union bosses he would be meeting tomorrow. At twelve o'clock he had a conference call with the casino team in New York to update them on the prior evening and to ask for additional information. As Robert had learned quickly, it was all about information. He had also decided that he had to put on a show, so he had the team put it together for him and overnight it to him.

He was just about to take a break for lunch when a confidential and secure email came across. It was about the Project Viper requests he had made. What he read troubled him, since he knew the person. He tried to meet everyone that worked for him, but he had to admit that in the past year it had gotten a lot more difficult. The company had been growing by leaps and bounds, and some days he wondered if it wasn't getting to be too big. He was going to forward the email and have the man removed, but then decided on a different course of action. Perhaps they could use him to get to the person pulling the strings.

Just then Joseph came back in. For the first time Robert realized that he had been gone all morning. He laughed when he looked over and saw him carrying a bunch of bags from the nearby outlet stores. Joseph laugh and shrugged saying he got bored. Robert showed him the email and explained what he wanted to do. Joseph agreed with the plan and said that he would take care of it. Once again, Robert was reminded by how much Joseph did for him and how much he relied on him.

After a leisurely lunch, Robert rested in the dark bedroom hoping it would help his headache. Then he got back to work joining several conference calls. Afterwards he went back to answering his emails - some days he felt like that was all he did - and reading some of the additional information they had for him. As usual Joseph knew what he needed and had arranged for in an in-room massage. And indeed, it was just what the doctor ordered, sort of. He felt refreshed afterwards and instead of working like he normally would, he arranged to meet with the casino operations manager. They spent an hour or so walking around the casino and discussing issues and upgrades that might be needed. Robert was very surprised at how helpful the man was considering that it was not really public knowledge about his plans to buy the hotel. Then the manager told him that Mr. Salvatori had called him personally and asked for his help.

After the tour Robert and Joseph walked over to the Forum Shops for dinner at Joe's steak and crab shack. Calling Joe's a shack is funny and it is especially well known for its crabs and also the rest of its menu. This was a bit of a last minute decision so they ended up standing at the bar having a quiet drink. At least they hoped for it to be quiet, but because of the bodyguards nearby people seemed to think Robert was someone famous and kept asking for his autograph. Joseph leaned over to the bartender who nodded and then got the manager who quickly found a secluded spot for them. The bodyguards ate as well, sitting in the bar where they could keep an eye on them plus the entrances.

After dinner they took the SUVs down to The Wynn and walked around a while to see what some of the higher end furnishings and decorating efforts were that they had in place. They walked around for about an hour, then rode over to the Venetian. Unfortunately, without an invite there were limited areas they could see. This was more than just about the casino, so Robert made a mental note to stay there the next time he came back. Tired from the long day and all of the walking they headed back to the Bellagio and straight up to the room. In the room, he took a long hot shower and then practically fell into bed. He had a busy morning meeting tomorrow with the unions and he still had not heard where the meeting would be.

Robert woke up before the sun and had to smile when he saw his suit, shirt, and shoes laid out all ready for him. He stepped into the sitting area and saw a freshly delivered breakfast cart complete with croissants, coffee, and orange juice. Joseph was sitting quietly on the couch, reading the newspaper and drinking his own coffee.

"Good morning, Sir. Can I get you something?" He asked as he stood up.

"Joseph, after this past week what do you say you call me Robert. And you don't have to wait on me anymore."

"Yes, Sir." He said, grinning widely as he poured a cup of coffee, added the right amount of cream and handed it to Robert.

"Anything in there we need to worry about?" Robert pointed to the Wall Street Journal, Joseph had been reading.

"Actually, there is a rather interesting article in the business section. It seems that there is this big New York tycoon looking to make a name for himself in Las Vegas. Apparently, it has been leaked that he is considering purchasing an unnamed hotel and casino from a group that has grown bored with it."

Robert grinned. "Good, I was worried that they wouldn't actually print the story we leaked." When he saw the puzzled look on Joseph's face, he continued. "We felt that this would let the unions know that this was serious and that one way or another the hotel would be bought."

"Speaking of which, they delivered a rather hefty package for you this morning."

"Good. It's all part of the show we will need for this morning. Any word on where we are going?"

"Yes, Salvatori has arranged for the meeting to be at his house. He offered to have a car pick us up, but I declined saying we would use our own transportation. He understood, and suggested that we arrive at 10.30. He told the unions to be there at 11am and then after the meeting he will be serving a lunch. I did a little research and it's a pretty big property. I am also going to go ahead of you and the boys to check things out personally. Again, Salvatori understood and even seemed to welcome it. I don't think he wanted any trouble, certainly not at his place."

"Thanks, Joseph. As usual, you don't disappoint. Now, I think I better get some work done before I need to get going."

"Yes, Sir. Oh, and if I may suggest... The suit is fine, but I would forego the tie."

"Thanks again."

Robert took a fresh cup of coffee over to the desk and sat down to work. He started by quickly going through the most important of the emails before he started to review the electronic package the team had put together. Plus he had to teach himself how to use the technology they had sent over. After reading through the updated information, and the technology overview he took a hot shower and got dressed. As he was stepping out into the sitting room, one of the body guards came in.

"If you are ready, Sir."

"Yes thanks, let's go." Without being told Robert waited for the signal and then made sure that they were flanking him as they made their way to the elevator. The hotel had arranged for a bellhop to hold it on their floor and then take them direct to the service entrance. There they quickly made their way to the waiting SUV and drove out to Salvatori's house. It was indeed a beautiful home set well back from the road on a large property that appeared to be surrounded by a ten foot high solid stone wall.

The SUV turned off the main road through a ten foot high wrought iron gate. Robert saw a guard shack with a guard standing just outside of it, and assumed they had been alerted of his arrival. Had he glanced back he would have seen the huge gates swinging shut effortlessly. Inside the compound there was at least a 100 feet of open space on each side of the gravel driveway which was bordered by oversized evergreens as if they were standing guard over the drive itself.

When the driveway suddenly opened up even Robert found himself leaning forward to get a better look. The house was not at all what he expected, it was as if the house had been plucked from the French countryside. Granted, by a very wealthy French country farmer, it wasn't just big it was huge. The front of the house was at least three stories high with tall windows all across the front. As they turned into the circular driveway you could just see that there were two wings along each side that went back into the distance.

Already parked in the driveway were two Chevy Suburbans and a Ford heavy-duty pickup truck. Robert wondered if he was overdressed for this group until he realized that the pickup truck was as nice inside as any car he owned, with leather seats and probably every electronic toy available. As soon as the SUV slid to a stop, his door was pulled open and involuntarily Robert pulled back away from it. But, he had to smile when he saw Joseph standing there. He climbed down grabbing his bag as he did, and had to stop to look at the view. Because of where the SUV had stopped he hadn't been able to see it, but stretched out to the side of the house was obviously the desert and the Red Rock Canyon mountain range. It was truly breathtaking.

Salvatori came bounding down the steps with an outstretched hand. "Robert, thank you for coming. I trust the ride out was satisfactory? Not too far?"

"No, Anthony the ride was fine. I had no idea this view was so incredible, and your house is amazing."

"Thank you. We took a lot of time and effort to get the house right and to not look ridiculous with that view. My father thinks it was a waste of time and money, but every time he comes out he stays just a little longer. One of these days he may just forget he has a business in Philadelphia to run."

"Well I have a feeling if he did he would have a successor already chosen in his son."

Anthony nodded at the compliment and led Robert inside. The main hall was absolutely breathtaking, both in grandeur and in its simplicity. It was the full height of the house and the main chandelier had to be taken from a palace. There was artwork spread across the walls from all different periods and styles, but Robert found the photographs to be the most interesting. They all seemed so personal and private, yet professional in their simplicity.

"Anthony, you will have to tell me who the photographer is. I would love to get some of his work for my offices here in Las Vegas."

Anthony smiled at the obvious hint that Robert was coming no matter what. "Thank you, but I am afraid they are my wife's and she doesn't sell her work anymore."

Robert smiled politely as he recalled that his wife had died in a car accident a few years ago. He mumbled an apology and followed as Anthony led them into his study where the meeting would be. As he was leaving, Salvatori mentioned that a couple of the union men had come early and Robert asked if they would only come in once they were all here. After he stepped out closing the door, he and Joseph got to work setting up the laptop and special projector he had brought. He needed to get these guys on the first shot and he was hoping that this would help.

Like the rest of the house that he had seen so far, the study was a bit over the top. It was rounded at the back of the room and the ceiling was higher than a normal sized room by quite a bit. The back wall contained floor to ceiling shelves that were full of books, and even had a library ladder leaning against it. The wall to the right of the door had two tall windows on either side of an oversized gas fireplace. The opposite wall had two pairs of French doors which led out to an incredibly landscaped set of gardens, beyond which the view of the desert and canyon could be seen.

Promptly at 11am the study doors opened and a group of men and one woman followed behind Salvatori. Robert stood in front of the queen-Anne style desk, and smiled as they all found seats around the room. Behind the group a couple of waiters brought in a pair of trolleys which contained coffee pitchers, juice, muffins, and croissants. They quickly arranged the coffee mugs, glasses, and sweeteners then left closing the doors behind them.

Anthony stepped forward. "Good morning. I appreciate you all taking the time to listen to Mr. Cutter. He and I have already spoken and I think he is worth listening to. I won't give you my opinion until after you have heard him out. I will just ask you to listen to what he has to say before you decide."

"Thank you, Anthony. Good morning. As you know, my name is Robert Cutter, and yes - I am from New York. My company is known for buying companies and either helping to turn them around, or helping to get the most value for the shareholders. But sometimes, all we really want is to help turn the company around and keep it so that we can use the profits to build even stronger companies." Smiling broadly he continued "oh yeah, and make more money for the stakeholders.

We are here because I am not just *interested in* taking over the Bellagio, but I am planning on it. In fact I have already started negotiations with the current owners and quite honestly they are happy to make the deal. While I am going to take the hotel private I plan on having stakeholders instead of shareholders. The difference, as I am sure you know, is that the stakeholders will have more than a financial interest in the hotel. In fact, I plan on treating them more like partners than shareholders." Robert wanted to let this sink in so he took a break and walked over to the coffee taking his time to pour a cup. Not only did he want the coffee, but more importantly he wanted them to see the 3D image projected on the desk.

Robert was quite pleased when he saw everyone leaning forward to get a look at the model, and the best was yet to come. "Obviously we can't change the exterior of the hotel, other than refreshing it. But inside we can do a lot more. Keep in mind that these are just some ideas we came up with rather quickly so things can change." Robert paused and slid his fingers through the main entrance. The image shifted immediately to a 3D view of the lobby. "The lobby we will upgrade to include a lot more technology, and as you can see there is no check-in desk. Instead a team will have iPads and tablets which will make the guests feel more at home, instead of at a *hotel*. And continuing that theme, we will take a page from Disney where everyone is greeted with *welcome home*."

Robert pointed to a new area in the image and the scene changed and refocused. "This area will be for the high rollers and special guests, and again you can see that it is set up to be more inviting. I have also started to look into facial recognition technology, especially at the front entrance. The idea being that the system would immediately alert a greeter and they could meet the individual by name.

The casino will be the hard part of this project because we obviously don't want to interfere with play as we are going to remain open the whole time. But, the expansion will include an entirely revamped poker room with a lot more space and comfort. And again we want to make the high roller areas nicer and more comfortable as well. At the same time we won't focus just on poker and high rollers, but also make the *regular* gaming areas more hospitable. The bottom line is that the casino won't just be a place to gamble, but also a place to relax.

All of the rooms will get a refurbishing including painting, repairs, and technology upgrades. The TVs have to be better, and with the technology available we can even look at allowing people to access their own cable boxes at home to watch their shows. I know that we don't want people staying in their rooms, but let's face it - people don't eat and gamble 24/7 so let's make the rooms comfortable. We are also going to increase the concierge floors because guests will enjoy the feeling of being special. Even if we do charge them more for it.

Now, I am staying in a suite and it is quite large but I think we can do better. Not only do I want there to be several types of suites, but I want to create two floors that are the villa type suites. These suites will come with their own check in service, and for certain clientele they can even have butler service. These suites will also have the availability of not just *party hosting*, but in room food service with a personal chef. We want this to be more than just a hotel, this can be a place of refuge and even a home away from home."

Robert took a break at this point to give everyone a chance to soak up what he had said and think about it. He poured himself another cup of coffee, more to give them a chance without seeming like he was. Several of the group stood up and moved to the 3D image, moving their hands through and around to different areas he had not covered - the spa, pool, and shopping areas. A few moved over to get their own fills of coffee and juice. And then the questions started.

It started with several people all asking at the same time, but then they settled back down and the biggest question came out, "sounds like you are going to spend a lot of money on this?"

Robert smiled, "yes, we are planning on spending a lot of money. But honestly we are getting a good deal on the property and we are hoping that our new stakeholders will look at the project for its long term value rather than just getting what they can out of it."

A woman in the group spoke up "you keep saying stakeholders and talk about future value. You understand that any deals we make can and will impact us for a very long time. Every other property in Las Vegas will expect the same deals from us. You can't possibly think that this project will make up for all of that."

Before he could answer one of the others spoke up and added to it, "obviously you have done your homework, so what makes this project different from every other project in the city?"

Robert grinned and answered. "You are both right, I do my homework. Most of the properties in this city are part of huge companies that have several properties here in Las Vegas and all over the world. As a stand-alone we can negotiate freely without concern for any other properties. Plus, let's be honest. Do you think your members would take reduced hourly wages if they stood to retire sooner? I am not saying they will all be millionaires in a year, but this project can make money for people. People who bust their butts every day of their lives, this project can make them money well after they are done working on it and have moved on to another project. Also, I am not asking for free work. I still expect to pay you a fair wage, but we can get a lot more out of the hotel in the long run by paying a fair wage. And if the hotel is nicer, better, more welcoming, and more modern then more people will want to come and stay here. And that means more profits for us all."

"So, you are asking us to take pay cuts while the hotel stays open and you continue to make huge profits. We can do research also and the profit margins on properties like this are huge."

"Let me correct one part of that. The profits on a property like this *can be* huge. Right now they are just ok, and if something doesn't happen soon they will be less than ok. That is why the company wants out. Because the profits here have been slipping, because it is an expensive property to just maintain. We can change that together and by bringing it back to being a relevant hotel the profits will come back.

One other minor note since I know you see me as a New York Wall Street tycoon. This is not about the profits for me, it is about doing something special and leaving a mark, making a difference, changing the way business is done here in Las Vegas. Also, my salary for the first five years of this project will be the same as your most expensive person working on the project."

The questions continued for another hour, some more specific about the plans and ideas. Some still focused on the deals he was expecting, and the concept of stakeholders. It all seemed reasonable, but they wanted more specifics. Robert was prepared for most of the questions and answered them honestly and as straightforwardly as he could. He knew that if they sensed he was not being honest it would end quickly. And they could even make life really hard for him during the project.

Finally they broke up the meeting and Robert took the time to thank each person for coming one at a time, and by name. One even jokingly asked if he had already installed the facial recognition program for the meeting. Once everyone had gone Robert sat in one of the arm chairs and closed his eyes. Joseph handed him a glass of juice knowing how much these meetings could take a toll on him. As Robert opened his eyes Joseph also handed him two Excedrin.

Joseph packed up the laptop and projector and waited quietly for Robert. After several more minutes Robert quickly stood up and leaving the study they found Salvatori sitting on the patio with a chocolate lab at his feet. He had a cigar in one hand and a bottle of water on the table in front of him. He stood up as Robert approached.

"That was quite an amazing presentation you put together. I can tell you that group is not easily swayed, but you did a pretty good job. I can't say what their decisions will be, and I am sure the devil will be in the details. But, I think you made a lot of friends today and as you seem to know all too well, friends are important."

"Thank you for your hospitality today. And I appreciate your input and support. As I said, I think this can be quite a profitable venture for all of us. We don't need everyone's support, but it won't hurt."

They shook hands and Salvatori also promised to follow up on the photos that Robert had given him. Robert gave him his cell phone number and said he looked forward to hearing from him - on both of the topics. Salvatori walked with them to the front door and stood watching as they climbed back into the waiting SUV. The ride back to the hotel was just as uneventful as the one out to the house. It was only two o'clock but with his head pounding Robert closed the drapes darkening the bedroom as much as possible and laid down. Joseph had arranged for them to fly home later that night so Robert had the time. Besides he wanted to be fresh and relaxed when they got to Philadelphia.

Chapter 13

The red eye flight to Philadelphia was quiet and uneventful which was just was Robert needed. He spent the flight resting and woke up refreshed and ready to get back to work. Joseph had arranged for the SUVs to be brought down from New York along with the bodyguards, so they were waiting at the airport for them. Somehow he had also arranged to be met at the gate by the group along with a police officer. For a change Robert was glad it was early in the morning because it looked like quite an entourage with the bodyguards, a police officer, and he and Joseph.

They rode directly to the hotel and checked in with no delay. After a quick shower and a change of clothes Robert went straight to the tent city. He had hoped to catch Mikhail before he went to school, but he had already left. Robert sat with Pearl for a while going through the status of the demolitions, the building which was more than ready to begin, and even her discussions with some businesses to occupy the refurbished properties. Robert was both pleased with the progress the project was making, and also with how well Pearl had adapted to her new role. He was also not too surprised to learn that the New York team had taken Pearl under their wing and was training her on the computer systems and processes they all used.

What did upset Robert was hearing that the city council members were still bouncing back and forth and slowing progress in any way they could. Robert shook his head as Pearl explained that several councilmen had come by the site, but had still dug in their heels when it came to approving any of the new housing plans. Surely they could see the increased tax revenue as a bonus, plus a whole new group of voters that would certainly vote for them with just a little help.

Robert called his New York office and talked to Thompson who told him that the man to talk to was Tom Dell, who seemed to carry some weight in the council. Robert got his office number and a quick rundown on the man. He called the office and after some discussion with his secretary found out that there was an opening for 15 minutes at 1230 before the councilman went to a luncheon. Robert arranged to be there, but then called back to New York and got an invite to the luncheon as well.

Robert arrived at the Councilman's office five minutes early and waited ten minutes for the man. He was led into a rather ornate office with an oversized desk, a large leather chair behind it, and two small simple chairs facing the desk. Clearly this office was designed to show the guests who was in charge, and that they wouldn't be staying long. Robert strode in with his usual confidence and thrust his hand forward to shake hands. Dell was shorter than Robert but it was immediately clear that everything about him said he was in charge, or thought he was. Robert disliked the lifelong bureaucrat almost immediately.

He didn't get up but spoke to Robert without even looking up from his computer. "Yes, Sir. My secretary said this was important. What can I do for you?"

"I want to discuss the issues and delays with the tent city area so we can get the folks into proper housing as soon as possible."

Dell barely glanced at him as he responded, "that is Philadelphia council business. And since you are from New York we don't have anything to discuss. Thank you for stopping by."

Robert stared at the man and considered his options for just slapping the man. Instead, he responded. "I understand how you might think that, *Sir*. But, as I am a businessman who has just invested a great deal of money in the city and as someone who is working hard to bring tax dollars and jobs to the city I think you should reconsider your stance."

Again with barely a glance at Robert, he said, "I'm sorry I am late for an important meeting, you can try to schedule more time with my secretary. Thank you." The dismissal was as clear in his tone as if he had waved his hand at Robert.

Had he looked up he would have seen Robert smiling as he left the office. Robert went back out to the SUV and rode straight to the luncheon, which was being held at The Capitol Grille. He arrived well before the councilman and spent the time meeting with the other businessmen already there. After just a few minutes of meeting people a group had formed around Robert. This was a luncheon with bankers and finance people so Robert was not only right at home with them, but also had a reputation among them. Most of these young professionals, and even some of the older people were thrilled to meet him.

When the councilman walked in and saw Robert he shook his head. As he tried to move through the crowd and shake hands with his fellow citizens - as he liked to call them - they all mentioned Robert in some way. "What a treat to have him here." and "can you believe what he is trying to do here." And other similar comments. Finally Dell came face to face with Robert and given the crowd was forced to shake hands with him.

Robert smiled broadly and said, "why Mr. Councilman, what a pleasure it is to meet you. I understand that you are quite the initiative taker here in the city, and insist on being very involved in the cities biggest projects. I look forward to meeting with you after lunch as we planned, to discuss my plans in detail and how we can overcome some of the obstacles we seem to be struggling with." Much better than actually slapping the man, Robert thought.

He was painted into a corner and it was clear that Dell had no choice but to go along with him. "Mr. Cutter, I have been looking forward to our meeting this afternoon as well. What time do we have it scheduled for?"

Robert grinned, "I believe it was immediately after lunch. But seeing this fine group of people here gave me an idea. Why don't we all head over to the tent city and after a tour of the area and a discussion of the plans we can meet in your office to finalize things."

Dell just nodded and was saved from having to say anything else as lunch was about to be served. Robert found himself at a table with a group of young bankers who seemed to hang on his every word. At first Robert was not sure how to handle this group, but then he found himself listening to their ideas and questions just as much as they were to his answers. He would have to make a note of who these people were as he might want to work with them later in the project.

After lunch Robert and Dell rode in the same SUV and discussed some of the issues that the project was facing. By the time they reached the tent Robert realized that what it really came down to was that he hadn't talked to anyone - they had simply gotten the tents put up. And that made both the city and the council look bad. Robert had never been very good at politics and found himself apologizing, but explained that once he saw the church they had been living in he just reacted. And he was sure that when the councilman saw it he would be moved as well.

"Tom, I know that these are not the voters you usually think of. Hell, I am sure most of them don't even vote. But most of them also work damn hard just to put a roof over their heads, even if it did leak all the time. And now they have nothing. As I see it, we can toss them aside and let them join the throngs of welfare recipients or we can help them become the citizens you want them to be. All they want is a fair chance, and all I want is to give it to them."

"You make a strong case for these people and clearly you speak better than they do for themselves. Of course, it is easy for you when you don't live here and won't have to live with it when the area goes bad again. We have tried time and time again to renew the area and somehow the bad always finds a way to win. But if you want to throw your money at it, and it makes you feel good then go ahead. I won't stand in your way but don't ever expect a thank you card."

"Did you ever think that the bad moves in because people have lost hope in the good? Or that it is easier to follow the badness because no one ever gives them a chance. The people I met aren't bad people, they are just lost. You are going to meet people who only ask for one thing - not a handout, but an opportunity. Believe it or not that is what life is about - opportunity. Sometimes it is thrust at you and you are ready for it, and other times you have to ask for it. But just asking isn't enough, you still have to be ready to accept it and work at it. Opportunity doesn't create success, people create success."

Before Dell could respond, the SUV pulled up at the tents along with a half dozen cars full of people from the luncheon. They all climbed out and standing at the curb Robert proceeded to point around at the now empty housing lots and the run-down apartment building, and explained what the plans where. With the demolition mostly under way, and almost all of the debris gone, the area looked ready for rebuilding. Pearl strode out and joined the group, expanding on what Robert had explained, pointing out specific plots where families were waiting to build. Not only that but the color choices and styles they wanted to use in their new homes.

You could tell that the councilman was taken with Pearl and treated her as if she was one of Robert's executives that had come from New York. "Miss, I must say you don't sound like you have a New York accent at all. Is that where you are originally from."

Pearl smiled politely and glanced at Robert who was grinning. "I am not from New York at all Mr. Dell. Actually I used to live in a house right over on that corner. I worked two jobs a day and an extra one on the weekends just to make ends meet. And they barely did most weeks. When the fire came through we lost everything we had, so I had still had to work two jobs but no way to even consider rebuilding anything. Then Mr. Cutter gave me an opportunity and with some help from his team I have been able to help out here."

Robert slid an arm around her shoulders, "don't let her fool you, Mr. Dell. If it weren't for Pearl a lot of these people would have no idea where to start. She has helped them with design and style, even helped with documentation for the city zoning and building requirements. If not for Pearl I would have had to move a small office in to accomplish what she does."

Dell turned from Pearl to Robert and shook his head. It was obvious that he didn't know what to say. Instead he shook Robert's hand and nodded. He turned looking around him and then turned to Robert, "there is a council meeting on Monday morning, it starts at 9am. Be there at 8:30 so I can introduce you to a few people. Your project will be the first item on the agenda so be prepared to answer anything that gets thrown at you. I know you have a team in New York, so I would bring as many of them as appropriate." Then he turned and walked towards a waiting car and driver that took him back to his office.

Robert spent another thirty minutes talking to the bankers and finance people from the luncheon. By the time he was done he knew he would have no trouble getting whatever financing was needed. And more than a few people were going to reach out to their corporate partners about getting businesses investing in the area as well. After everyone had gone he and Pearl had a conference call with the New York team so that they could be prepared for Monday. Just when Robert thought the day couldn't get any better, Mikhail arrived from school and ran straight to his mom for a hug, then turned to Robert and shook his hand. But they were both laughing as Robert picked him up and headed into the kitchen for milk and cookies.

After they had their snack and Mikhail showed Robert how good he was getting at reading, they played on the playground for a while. Then Robert had to get back to work, but promised he would say goodnight before he left. As they were walking back from the swings Mikhail slipped his hand into Robert's and smiling up at him said that he was glad that he was back. Robert reached down and scooped the boy into his arms carrying him back to the tent. As they did Robert reminded the boy that he had a big surprise for him on Sunday.

Mikhail smiled excitedly, "are we going to the beach? I have never been to the beach before?"

Robert looked at the little boy and stopped walking. "You know something, that isn't the surprise for this weekend. But that is great idea for another day, we will have to see if your Mom is ok with it. Maybe she will even come with us."

Grinning broadly Mikhail hugged his neck "we better ask Joseph too. He always looks so serious I bet he could use a day off!"

Robert had to laugh, "well he has a very serious job, he makes sure that I am safe. Something that lately seems to be getting harder and harder."

"Well then we definitely have to make sure he comes with us.

I bet he doesn't even have a bathing suit!"

As they reached the tents Robert glanced back at Joseph, who as usual seemed to be on the phone. The bodyguards were there milling around but not surrounding them as usual. This was the one time when they gave him some space since Robert didn't want Mikhail to worry. Robert had to smile at the young boy's honesty and then realized that he didn't have a bathing suit himself. And being perfectly honest wasn't sure if he could recall ever having gone to the beach himself, even if he did own a beach house.

Mikhail gave Robert a big hug at the SUV and then he headed back to the hotel. He had a lot of work to do for Monday morning and he already knew just who he wanted there with him. He spent a great deal of the ride to the hotel speaking with Mark Thompson, his political guru, to get his take on what he planned for Monday at the city council meeting. Several members of the team had already arrived at the hotel and settled in. They had already convened in Robert's suite and arranged to have a conference table brought in so they could all work together.

They had brought several whiteboards and didn't wait for Robert to join them as they started to put together a presentation. Not one that Robert would use to show to at the council meeting, but they would have it bound and delivered to the council members on Sunday morning. They had a very tight schedule and they were more than happy to work as hard as needed. When Joseph saw that they had taken over the suite he worked with management to get another room that Robert could use for sleeping.

They arranged for dinner to be delivered to the room at 9pm and knowing he wouldn't make it back to the tent city, Robert arranged for a Skype call with Mikhail to say goodnight. He made the call in the privacy of his bedroom and had to take several minutes afterwards to gather his thoughts. As he rejoined the group he wrote a note on a slip of paper and handed it to Joseph.

He glanced at it questioningly, then smiled and nodded saying he would arrange something soon.

The team worked late into the night before Robert said that they had to get to sleep. It was close to two in the morning when they broke up, and as Robert went to his new room he had to smile. While the group had full run of the suite the guys immediately moved to the couches and chairs leaving the bedrooms to the ladies. As he tiredly walked down the hall to the room he made a mental note to give these guys more than just a bonus. He would have to give them vacations.

Robert fell onto the bed just as exhausted as the rest of the team, and was sound asleep even before Joseph could turn out the lights. What seemed like not nearly long enough later Robert was awoken by the sun shining through the windows. Glancing at the clock he got undressed, took a quick shower and slipped into jeans and a polo shirt. Joseph was already awake and waiting with fresh coffee. He handed Robert a mug and together they walked back to the suite.

"Mr. Cutter, we need to leave for the game by ten-thirty so we can pick up Mikhail and Pearl. There are some special treats that we have arranged that I think you will both enjoy. Which is why we need to pick him early. I have also spoken with Mr. Dell and he will be meeting us at the game."

"Thanks again, Joseph. I am sure whatever you have planned will be very enjoyable. For both of us."

Back in his suite, Robert found that the team was already back to work. The smell of strong coffee, fresh Danish and bagels filled the room over riding the distinct smell of tiredness. "Team, you folks have been amazing. I am going to leave my company credit card with Mark and I demand that you all go out for dinner. I have arranged for a Chef's table at LaCroix at the Rittenhouse for 9pm. I understand that jackets are required, so I suggest you all get showered with plenty of time before dinner. They have an excellent bar and wine cellar so I also expect to see a very high bar bill. And this is not optional. Now, where were we?"

Amid the murmurs and mumbled "thank you's" they quickly brought Robert up to speed. Who, with a quick look at Joseph saw that he was already on the phone. They spent the next several hours totally immersed in the presentation for Monday and then Robert had to leave. The body guards followed him down to the main lobby and quickly moved out the doors to the entrance. For the first time since they had been staying there, Robert was glad that the entrance was in a private alley.

They quickly drove to the tent city with a second SUV following. They had already agreed that Joseph would ride with a driver with Robert, Mikhail, and Pearl with the remaining team riding in the second car. Joseph assured Robert that aside from their individual seats the row behind had also been purchased for the bodyguards. Mikhail came running out to the SUV to meet Robert and jumped into his arms. He was babbling away as he hugged him and it was Pearl who finally had to explain that this was their first game.

As usual Joseph came fully prepared and going around to the back opened the SUV where he produced a brand new Hamels t-shirt for Mikhail and a matching one for Robert. Even though he wouldn't need it he had also bought the boy a glove, and matching hats for both for them. Robert joked that he hoped his New York clients wouldn't be upset that he was supporting a Philadelphia team. One of the arrangements that Joseph had made was for parking in the private owner's area, so they had complete privacy as they entered.

They were greeted at the entrance by a member of the Phillies' management team who offered a tour of the stadium including the dugout and the locker rooms. Inside the locker room they were introduced to the manager and several of the coaches. Then to his surprise, several of the ball players who were already at the field for early practice signed autographs on a baseball the team supplied. Cole Hamels, Dominic Brown, and several other players were more than happy to sign the ball for Mikhail. The boy could not stop smiling the entire time and he even got to go out on the field and play catch with one of the outfielders.

During all of this the team photographer kept taking pictures and promised to share them with Robert regardless of what was printed or used. But, he was really surprised when he found out that they wanted him to throw out the first pitch. They got him an official jersey to wear over the t-shirt and after a couple of practice tosses he threw out the pitch. It was given to him as a souvenir and even Robert found himself smiling ear to ear. The first few innings were amazing and the Phillies took a quick lead in the second inning when Dominic Brown hit a deep home run driving in two other runs.

Joseph was sitting at the end of the row with Robert next to him, and Mikhail sitting between Robert and his mom. So Robert was a little surprised when Joseph stood up and even more surprised when he stepped aside to reveal Dr. Adams standing there. He jumped to his feet and then realizing they were blocking people they both sat down. Joseph took a seat in the row behind them and leaning forward asked everyone if they wanted some food. As if reading his mind, a waitress appeared and took their orders.

Robert felt like a high school freshman being asked to the senior prom by the most popular girl in the school. Shannon was wearing jeans, sneakers, and a Phillie's jersey. Her long red hair was pulled back in a braided pony tail and she was wearing Oakley sunglasses. She had very little makeup on and Robert thought that no matter how hard she tried to look like a regular girl she would always look amazing to him.

"Mr. Cutter, I didn't know you were a Phillies fan. And to be honest I didn't have you pegged as a sports fan."

He laughed and said, "well, honestly I am not a Phillies fan or even much of a sports fan. Although I think I have an ownership share in a basketball team. But this little guy sitting next to me is a huge sports fan. I think he can tell you everything there is to know about the game. But, what are you doing here?"

"One of the local hospitals is recruiting me and I guess they decided that coming here would be a good idea. I am a Phillies fan since I grew up here, my dad used to bring us to games all the time. Of course we never got to sit down here."

Robert actually looked pained for a moment. "Oh, then I suppose you have to go sit with the other doctors?"

She smiled and for a brief moment the air around her seemed to sizzle. "Actually I was supposed to come with my brother, but he got called away on a case. But instead I came with a girlfriend. I guess I should go."

Robert glanced back at Joseph and smiling said, "you know there is plenty of room in that row, why don't you ask her to move down here with us? If you want to of course."

"That would be a great idea!"

She called her friend who was all too happy to join them. They caught up on what had happened in Las Vegas since Robert had promised her a dinner. And when she heard about the accident, she went into doctor mode and they talked about his headaches. She told him that even without testing she was sure he had another concussion and that he really had to find a way to take it easy. He nodded the whole time and while it looked like he was just patronizing her, he admitted to himself that he wanted to please her. They also agreed that once he was back in New York he should come to her office for a visit.

While they ate hot dogs and popcorn they enjoyed a cold beer, and each other's company. For Robert it was like being on the airplane again, he felt incredibly at ease with her. After a couple of innings Tom Dell showed up and Pearl moved over so he could sit closer to Robert. She tried to get Mikhail to move over as well, but he was having no part of it. Despite Robert and Shannon talking, Mikhail still found ways to continue to give Robert a play by play of the game.

Robert introduced Tom to Mikhail who then proceeded to share the play by play with him also. As it turned out, Dell was as much of a baseball fan as Mikhail so they quickly fell into place together. Suddenly, between innings Robert heard Mikhail say to Dell, "Mr. Dell, are you the man that is going to give me back my house?"

Before Robert could respond, Tom Dell looked at the little boy and said, "well young man, it is actually Mr. Cutter who is working to give you back your house. But, I am going to do what I can to help him."

Mikhail just nodded then looked over at Robert and smiled. Then he leaned in close to Robert and in as close to a whisper as a six year old could manage he said, "he seems kind of nice. But I like her a lot more."

Shannon laughed and leaning in whispered, "I am glad, because I like you too!" Then she winked at Robert, "he's cute... did you tell him to say that?"

Robert shook his head innocently and they all chuckled, even Mikhail who was not quite sure what the joke was. The rest of the game was fairly uneventful and the Phillies won. Afterwards they waited for the crowds to clear out and Shannon and her friend were nice enough to wait with them. While they were waiting Robert was going to invite them all to dinner, but Mikhail climbed up into his lap and after a few moments fell asleep. Everyone chuckled when they noticed it, but it also meant they were all heading home.

As they were leaving Robert was approached by the Phillie's marketing executive. He asked if Robert would join him in the team office for a quick meeting. Robert looked at Joseph who nodded, then he handed Mikhail over to one of the bodyguards. He and Joseph walked together to the office where they first met the general manager, and then the manager of the team.

The general manager invited Robert into the locker room, and opened the door. As Robert and Joseph stepped in, the room went quiet and all of the players turned and stood up. They all moved closer thinking the manager had something to say then they saw Robert. Questioning looks moved around the room and then the general manager began to speak.

"Gentlemen, this is Robert Cutter. He is the person you may have heard about lately. He is from New York and is working to rebuild the neighborhood that was consumed by fires. Mr. Cutter, we invited you down here because both as a team and as individuals we would like to help. We will have to schedule it between games, but you can count on us to show up when it makes sense. We want to give both money and our time and with that in mind we would like you to accept this check for one million dollars. We are counting on you to spend it wisely."

Robert looked around the room in awe as he accepted the check from the general manager. "We do have a foundation set up, so we will find a way to put it to good use. I know that there are a lot of kids who will appreciate having a new park and playground to play in. Thank you from the bottom of my heart, I am sure these folks will want to thank you as well." Then he walked around the room shaking hands individually with each of the players one at a time. He and Joseph were led back to the rest of the group and climbed into the waiting SUVs.

Back at the hotel the team had already left for dinner and Robert was suddenly very aware of being alone. He wandered around the suite looking at what the team had been working on, then looking quickly at his emails. He was having trouble focusing when suddenly Joseph walked over to him and handed him the phone.

"Call, please. Maybe she hasn't had dinner yet and would also like some company."

Robert grinned and took the phone from him shaking his head. He dialed her cell phone and would have hung up like a scared teenager, except that she answered. He quickly invited her to dinner and when she accepted he smiled broadly. They made plans to meet at a small Italian place near her mother's house in an hour. After he hung up Robert went into the bedroom and started to pull out different outfits. Joseph stood in the doorway watching these antics and had to work to keep a straight face.

When Robert saw him he said, "these clothes are sweaty and smell from the game. I can't possibly wear them out to dinner."

"Yes, and I am sure the fact that she is a beautiful woman has nothing to do with it."

Robert started to answer but then even he had to admit he was a bit nervous. While he had certainly been out to dinner or to parties and events with plenty of women, this felt different and he knew it. She was smart, probably smarter than him. And Joseph was right - she was amazingly beautiful. He imagined that she could wear a potato sack covered in oil and feathers and still look amazing.

The SUVs pulled up to a building that looked like a neighborhood house and if not for the small sign in the doorway they wouldn't have seen it. Two of the bodyguards climbed out and after a moment spoke to Joseph through a slightly open window. He promptly stepped out and looked around as well, then waved to Robert who stepped out. As he closed the car door behind him, he glanced towards where the bodyguards were watching and saw and equally large man leaning against a white Lincoln Town Car. Robert smiled recognizing the car as he hustled inside through the front door. He expected to see a small matronly woman with an apron waiting to greet him, but instead was met by a beautiful woman wearing an elegant black dress standing next to a pedestal.

She smiled and with a distinctly Italian accent wished him good evening and then led Robert through what could only be described as a former living room, into the first of the rooms arranged as a dining area. The inside of the house was longer and wider than it looked from the outside, and Robert realized that they must have combined two houses. The front of the house had a small bar area and Joseph made himself comfortable at the bar. The bodyguards moved outside and waited by the SUVs standing just as the other man was.

The girl led Robert to a table where clearly the most beautiful woman in the restaurant was seated. Shannon had pulled her hair back into a pony tail, which seemed to accentuate her shining emerald eyes and soft skin. She smiled as Robert approached and offered a cheek as he leaned in to kiss her. He was right, she would look exquisite no matter what she wore and the jeans, heels, and loose silk blouse did nothing to dampen her beauty. Robert was glad that he had also decided on jeans and a button down dress shirt.

Suddenly Robert felt a hand on his shoulder, "my friend, I was wondering who was lucky enough to be meeting this lovely woman. I had no idea you were back in town."

Robert turned smiling "Gino! It's good to see you again." They shook hands quickly and then Robert turned back, "Dr. Shannon Adams may I introduce Gino Caporelli, a partner of mine here in Philadelphia."

Gino took her hand gently in his large hand then lifted it to his lips kissing it briefly. "*Buona sera mia caro.* It is a pleasure to meet you. You must be from the area to know of our little gem?"

She smiled brightly at him, "yes, I grew up not far from here. My mother still lives in the neighborhood."

"Well I will let you two lovely people enjoy an absolutely fabulous meal. But Robert I insist that you let me suggest a bottle of wine for you."

Robert nodded, "thank you Gino, as always you are too kind."

Robert and Shannon sat down and Robert explained how he and Gino were working on the tent city together. Shannon seemed very interested and Robert ended up spending more time than usual talking about one of his projects. Where they were in the process and what Tom Dell had ended up doing for him and what he hoped would happen on Monday. They had an excellent calamari as an appetizer, then Robert had the special which was pasta with shrimp in an Alfredo sauce. Shannon had the veal with mushrooms, grilled asparagus, and a side of fresh pasta. Everything was either made fresh at the restaurant or purchased fresh that morning.

The food and the wine were excellent, but Robert barely noticed it as he was so taken with Shannon. Over desert and cappuccinos Robert admitted that he had been nervous about dinner. Shannon looked surprised and admitted that she had been just as nervous. They both laughed at the ideas that two such highly accomplished professionals could be nervous over a simple dinner. But as Robert reached across the table and took her hand they both seemed to realize it was more than a simple dinner.

The restaurant was closing and the waiter politely dropped off their check, but not intending to rush them. Outside they stood on the steps, both seemingly unsure of the next step. When Shannon said she could walk to her mother's house Robert immediately offered to walk her. He stepped over to the SUV and told Joseph who was waiting by the door. He smiled and nodded and as Robert and Shannon set off, Joseph and the SUV followed at a discreet distance.

They talked quietly as they walked along the quiet small south Philadelphia streets, nothing but the sounds of nearby traffic around them. As they approached the house, Robert took her hand in his and stopped walking. He looked up at the star filled sky, seeing the almost full moon shining brightly. Then looked at Shannon and lost in her smile for a moment, found himself speechless.

"When you are back in New York we should do this again. If you think you could find the time of course."

She smiled brightly, "I would like that very much Robert. I think I needed this more than I realized."

"I can tell you that I definitely needed it, Shannon. I am so glad that you were being recruited so that we could run into each other. Again. Although if you were to take the job I would have fewer opportunities to see you. And of course – have to find a new doctor."

She laughed and despite the only light coming from the moon he was sure she blushed also. "If it's all the same Robert, I would prefer to see you socially from now on."

He laughed and softly placed a hand against her cheek, "nothing would give me more pleasure." Just as he was about to lean in and kiss her a police car, siren screaming went by on the next block. They both started and then the porch light came on in the house. Robert laughed again, "guess that still means we have to go." But, he still leaned in quickly and softly kissed her on the mouth. Shannon responded to his kiss, but broke it off when they heard the lock turn at the front door.

Shannon laughed and bounded up the steps, the turning back

said, "yes, I will go to the prom with you!"

Robert laughed and waved then after watching her go inside turned and climbed into the SUV. They waited for a moment before the porch light went out and as they pulled away he laughed. Had he looked he would have seen Joseph smiling as well. They drove back to the hotel and Robert was thrilled to see that the team had not returned to work. He got changed and climbed into bed, but found that he was too distracted thinking of Shannon to fall asleep. Finally he did doze off and didn't wake up until he heard the sounds of coffee and breakfast noises from the team.

Robert got dressed in jeans and a polo shirt after a quick shower and then stepped into the main room. The team was seated around the table and all stopped talking as he approached. Robert looked around the table at all of the young faces staring up at him, and he recalled how hard he used to work. And also how much he used to look up to his boss for leadership.

"Folks, what you have done is nothing short of amazing. Both here in this room as well as for the project. But, it's not fair of me to ask you to stay here on a Sunday and away from your families. Send me what you have so far and I will finish it up. Mark, I'm sorry, but if you don't mind staying with me I would appreciate it."

Everyone sat quietly for several moments until Mark stood up. He had been unofficially named the leader of this little group, so they looked to him for guidance. He turned and shook Robert's hand. "It will be my pleasure to stay and work through this with you. Folks, I couldn't agree with Mr. Cutter any more. You have been a great team to work with over the past month, and I look forward to working with you all every day."

One at a time the group all stood and shook their hands then they started to gather their things. Both their work things as well as their clothes, which a few were suddenly embarrassed to realize they were somewhat strewn about the room. Robert suggested that he and Mark take a walk while they cleared the room. Joseph left with them and leaving the hotel they walked down Chestnut Street until they came to a coffee shop. They turned in and ordered pastries and coffees which they ate at an outside table. While they ate the two men talked about the strategy Robert wanted to use during the council meeting. He also made sure that Mark understood that there was no telling if Tom Dell was really on his side or just setting him up. After they finished eating they got refills of the coffee then walked to nearby Rittenhouse Square where there happened to be a local artist's show. Stalls were set up all around the park and for the first time Robert felt like he could truly relax.

The three of them wandered around for a bit, before Mark headed back to the hotel for a little downtime. As Robert and Joseph walked around Robert pointed out several pieces of local art - mostly photographs - that he thought would look good in either his apartment or office. He suddenly found himself looking at scarves and trying to find one that would match Shannon's hair or eyes and that is when he saw Joseph looking at him with a big grin.

"Oh stop it! I just thought she might like a little something." But all this did was get Joseph smiling even more.

"Yes, Sir, Mr. Cutter, Sir. Would you like me to slip her a note after math class?"

Before Robert could answer a couple standing nearby turned and the man said, "excuse me, are you Robert Cutter from New York? Working on that neighborhood that burned down?"

"Uh, yes I am... I guess." Robert looked perplexed since he knew he didn't know the couple.

The man reached out and took Robert's hand in his. "Let me be the first to thank you. This city's government is acting like a large horse's ass in not acting faster, and they should be helping you not standing in the way!"

Robert shook the man's hand then with a puzzled look said, "thank you for that, Sir. I am sorry, but you have me at a loss. How did you know about any of this?"

The woman standing there smiled and said, "there was an interview with Tom Dell and he was talking about what great work you are doing. To be honest, it sounded a little over the top to us but there were pictures of the tents." She then handed Robert a paper she had been holding which was folded over. Opening to the page Robert was shocked to see the pictures of the tents and several of the families. He handed it to Joseph who simply smiled. Then before anyone could react the woman leaned in and hugged Robert. "You are a special man and the woman getting that scarf is very lucky."

Robert felt himself blush, and then blushed even more as the woman kissed his cheek. "Come on dear, let's leave the poor man alone." And before they could say another word they turned and walked away.

Robert stared at Joseph for a moment, then just as he was turning away he remembered the scarf in his hand. He reached into his pocket and handed the woman a $20 bill and said thanks. Then they quickly walked back to the hotel where they found Mark already reading the article while at the same time scouring the Internet for blogs and posting responses to it. There was a local talk show on TV and they too were talking about it. Then as they watched, Dell was introduced as he walked out and they spent the next 15 minutes interviewing him about the tent city. To Robert's surprise the man made sure to mention him several times throughout and gave him all the credit. Robert was astounded and made a point to call him and thank him later in the day. The rest of the day they spent relaxing after a couple of hours working on the presentation, and going through emails. Finally after a nice dinner at XIX they all went back to their respective rooms for a good rest.

Chapter 14

The next morning Robert was up early and the night before had arranged for an early room service of coffee and croissants. He took a hot shower and came out to find that the barber had arrived and moving back into the bathroom had his hair trimmed, plus got a close shave with a straight razor. After the barber left he dressed in his best suit, perfectly starched French cuff white shirt, silk tie and shoes that had been freshly polished. When Robert stepped out of the bedroom he paused at the full length mirror again and straightened his tie one last time. Joseph looked him over and with a smile, nodded.

Mark was also waiting with Joseph and if asked probably would have admitted that Robert looked better than he had ever seen him. The ultimate professional was standing before him and looked like he could conquer the world with a word. Mark was dressed for a meeting and looked good as well, but standing next to Robert felt like an old pair of shoes. Which was fine with him since this was Robert's show. And truth be told, he was quite happy being in the background. As much as he understood politics he never wanted to be on the front lines, maybe he just understood it too well.

The three of them left the suite to find three bodyguards waiting in the hallway. Once again there was one more waiting at the elevator holding it for them, so that when they arrived they would be ready to go. Just as they were approaching the elevators a woman stepped out of the room ahead of them. She hesitated for a moment, before Robert motioned for her to go ahead. He looked at Joseph who nodded and then they all climbed on the elevator together. Robert really didn't have to worry. Aside from the woman being an incredibly petite five foot nothing, she couldn't have ever seen around the bodyguards let alone move inside the elevator.

When the elevator arrived in the lobby, the bodyguards exited first and then as the woman stepped off Robert apologized to her. She simply turned and smiled then continued through the small lobby out in to the alley way where a taxi was waiting for her. The bodyguards held Robert up until after she left and the SUVs were able to pull up to the door. They all climbed in to the two SUVs which promptly pulled away. Joseph had arranged for them to enter through the normally reserved garage under city hall and security helped them take the elevator that was usually reserved for the mayor and his chiefs.

The meeting was scheduled to start at 9am and Robert had purposely arrived early so that he could say hello to Dell and then hopefully get to meet a few of the other council members. To his surprise there was already quite a crowd gathered in the chambers, and looking around he also saw quite a few reporters and photographers getting their equipment ready. As soon as they recognized him they started taking pictures and several reporters moved over to call out questions. Robert was surprised to see the woman from the elevator there and even more surprised when he saw from the badge she wore that she was the local ABC reporter.

"Mr. Cutter, care to give us a preview of what you are going to say to the council this morning?"

He smiled back at her. "You will just have to be patient like the rest of the council members."

With that Joseph moved him away from the group and over to where Dell was speaking with a couple of other reporters. Clearly he was using his fifteen minutes of fame to make sure that they all knew his name. But as they approached Robert realized that he was still talking about the tent city project and how much it would mean both to the residents as well as the city.

He finished his remarks by saying that, "nothing but good things could come from giving people real homes to live in, safe places for the kids to play, and local stores to help grow their business." Then he turned to Robert and after shaking hands he introduced him to several of the other council members. Robert took a seat in the front row facing the council and noticed that Joseph and Mark had both taken seats behind him. The rest of the council members came into the room and after some private discussions between themselves they took their seats.

The council president called the meeting to order and they spent the next sixty minutes going through some existing business and protocol. After a short break they opened the floor up to new business, of which there was an agenda of items. Despite Dell's hopes to get Robert moved to the top of the list there were several other matters ahead of his. When Dell motioned for him Robert simply shook his head. After another thirty minutes of business the council took one more break before he was given a chance to speak.

He moved to the podium holding just a bottle of water. He took a quick drink, and pulled a sheaf of papers from inside his jacket. He started to open them then thinking twice put them all back. He looked around the room, slowly catching each of the members eyes one at a time. It was as if Robert was making sure that they were finally ready to pay attention to him. Their regular business out of the way, now it was time for the big decisions to be made. Even if they were seemingly easy decisions. But, of course that was his job - to make the hard decisions seem like easy decisions.

"Ladies and gentlemen, let me start by apologizing and thanking you. First I would like to apologize for not coming in to speak with you sooner. Unfortunately since I am from out of town, I am used to doing things a little differently. And quite honestly I usually have a staff to do this for me. But this time I felt that I needed to be here, especially since this is such an important project.

"And along the same lines I would like to thank you for allowing me to come in and speak with you. I understand that, as we saw earlier, it is common for citizens to speak before the council. However, as we also know I am not a citizen. At least not a citizen of Philadelphia. As you know I am a citizen of Manhattan and the state of New York. But, I don't come to you as a New Yorker or as even a potential Philadelphia citizen. Rather I come before you today as a citizen of the United States.

"I was going to plead my case here as a business person trying to improve the situation in the tent city area. And I was going to also talk to you today about the potential businesses which have already expressed an interest in opening stores in the neighborhood. But that is only part of the story, the truth is that we all know improving the neighborhood will improve the tax situation, the voting situation, and the economy for not just the area but all around it. As a businessman I honestly find myself in a bit of a quandary and in fact I have had a lot of questions about the business side of this project. The banks and other investors that are helping to fund this are all asking about the potential profits and the return on investment. They have trusted me before with their money, but now are asking some very serious questions.

"And to each of them I have said the same thing that the money will come. But this is a long-term project and that honestly we may never see the profits people are used to on my other projects. And yet, despite this, they have all chosen to keep their money in the project. You might be wondering if I pulled some strings, or told them I would drop them as clients or as a banker if they didn't stay. I will tell you that I had many private discussions with all of my investors in this project, but not once did I mention anything like that. The purpose of those discussions was not to twist arms, but rather to explain the real intentions of the project. Besides, the bank will be paid back according to the terms of that agreement if not sooner. And the investors are giving products and services that their companies already provide, not cash.

"I will tell you the same thing I told them. This is not a project about money, about profits, or about a return on investment. No ladies and gentlemen, this project is about doing what is right. It's not about anything more than giving people a chance that want to succeed. It's about giving people a chance who don't usually get one. It's about giving people a chance when they seem to have been forgotten. It's about people who work two or three jobs and still can't afford proper housing, proper clothing, and in some cases a proper meal. This project is about letting people help themselves and being respected for doing so.

"But, I have to be honest, this project is also about a little boy. His name is Mikhail and he is almost seven years old. Most days if you ask him he will tell you just exactly how many days and hours until his birthday. And it is a birthday that he will celebrate for the first time in his life wearing clean clothes that fit, with his mother who won't be working her third job that day, and surrounded by his friends. You might be wondering why I am so focused on this one boy and I will tell you... Because he is almost seven! That is why and nothing more and nothing less.

"I don't expect you to focus on this boy and give the project the approvals it deserves, just on my say so. I was going to invite all of the families to come over here today so that you could meet them. But all of them have jobs and couldn't come in anyway. I can simplify this project down to one simple idea. What if this was you... how would you pick up the pieces if your home and neighborhood were totally destroyed? You would have insurance and families and friends who would rally around you and support you. You would have good paying jobs that would allow you to bounce back quickly. But these families, these people don't have any of that. So, when you go back to your office and deliberate approving this project I want you to think about one simple question... What would you do if this was your seven year old son or daughter? Wouldn't you do everything you could for them?

"Thank you again ladies and gentlemen for allowing me the opportunity to speak before you."

The room, which had been totally silent as Robert spoke, suddenly burst into a rousing applause. As Robert turned to take his seat he saw that everyone in the room was not only clapping and cheering, but they were also all standing up. All Robert could do was wave around the room and sitting down take a long drink of cold water.

The council president stood up, and after asking if there was anyone else with business before the council adjourned, thanked Robert for taking the time to speak before the council. "We will take the project under careful advisement and will let you know of our decision." With that the council left the room returning to their private conference room where it was known that they could deliberate new business that had been presented. As they were leaving, Tom Dell caught Robert's eye and gave him a quick nod.

As they were leaving the room they were once again inundated by reporters' questions, but Joseph took his arm and led Robert from the room. They quickly made their way down to the basement parking garage and climbed back into the waiting

SUVs. As they pulled away Robert took his phone out of pocket and saw that he had several texts from several of the executives as well as one surprising one.

Dr. Adams had still been in Philadelphia and had watched a broadcast of the meeting on a local channel while waiting for a meeting. Apparently the channel had broadcast his speech live and the timing was right for her to be able to catch it. She had been impressed more with his heart felt passion than anything. He answered quickly asking if she would be in town for dinner, perhaps they could meet again. As Robert waited for the response he rested his head and closed his eyes. Had he opened them he would have seen Joseph watching him carefully making sure that he was feeling okay.

Unfortunately Dr. Adams had to hurry straight back to New York for a shift she had later that evening. But promised to catch up again when he was back in New York. Robert found himself both sad and happy at the same time. Sad that he would have to wait to see her again, but happy that she wanted to see him again. He had certainly had his share of girlfriends, but somehow with Shannon he felt more relaxed and at ease than he had ever had before.

Unfortunately, this distraction was short lived as he saw an email come across that would require his immediate attention in Las Vegas. He responded to the email quickly and was hoping that it would not mean a return trip. After his last trip there he was in no hurry to return, but at the same time he knew he would have to meet with the union presidents again. His chief legal officer had good news about their decision, since several had asked for clarifications instead of amendments to the agreements. But, he also said that it looked like Robert would need to go out for another face to face just to finalize their deal. And then hopefully on the same trip close the deal for the actual hotel itself.

They arrived back at the tent city and the families that were there all came out to meet him. They sat down and over coffee and a quick snack, Robert brought Pearl up to speed on what had happened. She surprised him with a quick hug and said that it was ok.

"You did the best you could Mr. Cutter, and no one could ask for any more than that." Robert wasn't sure how to respond considering if he failed she would be homeless in no time at all.

Robert found a quiet place where he could work on his emails and reviewing the documents for the Bellagio project. Before he knew it the afternoon had flown by and as he leaned back to rest his tired eyes he saw Joseph moving in to the doorway. He asked if everything was ok and if Joseph had any Tylenol. Joseph reached into his pocket, pulled out a bottle and shook out two pills for him. Robert swallowed them quickly with a pull from his water bottle and then looked up Joseph questioningly.

"Sir, perhaps you should take a break? Besides if you have a moment there is a visitor that would like some of your time."

"Joseph, I don't know if that is a good idea..."he started to say, but stopped when he saw his face. "Why didn't you say so?" Robert got up and walked out of the makeshift office to find Mikhail sitting at a table coloring with a huge pile of crayons. When Mikhail saw him he jumped up and ran over to Robert launching himself into Robert's arms who leaned down just in time to catch him. Mikhail hugged his neck tightly and then asked if Robert wanted to have milk and cookies with him. The two went straight into the kitchen and by the time they came back out Robert's headache was gone, and his smile had returned.

Much later Robert returned to the hotel, and after a little more work went to bed. But as much as he tried he couldn't fall asleep, his mind filled with questions. What else could he have done at the council meeting so they would have made the decision immediately? What will happen if they say no? Will Mikhail and Pearl ever really have an opportunity for a good full life or is he fooling himself? And worse, is he fooling them also?

Robert woke to a loud knocking at the door and when he opened his door he saw Joseph standing there with a cell phone in his hand. He walked over to Robert and handed it to him. It was Mark and it took Robert a couple of moments to realize that it was already after 8am. Robert listened to Mark talk, the smile growing on his face and when he looked Joseph was already getting out jeans and a polo shirt for him to wear.

Robert hung up the phone, put it on the bed beside him and sat there staring into the distance. Joseph walked over and put it his hand on Robert's shoulder, looking down at him. "Robert, you have done an amazing thing and there are going to be a lot of very happy people. It makes me especially proud to work for you today!"

Robert looked at him for a moment and nodded. "Thank you Joseph, but you don't work *for* me. You work with me and it makes me happy to have you by my side. Now... what do you say we go spread the word?"

Smiling Joseph flipped on the television in the room and the screen was immediately filled with photographs and video of Robert. As he turned up the volume he heard the reporter explaining the decision by the city council to grant all zoning permits paving the way for all of their plans. The TV screen was then filled with live video of the tent city where several city inspectors could be seen with design drawings under one arm and clipboards in the other. At the same time Robert saw several trucks also pulling up across the street at the first of the empty lots. As the reporter went on, Robert could see a large truck from the lumber yard pull up and as quickly as that, it was being unloaded.

The next few days were packed with planning meetings,

design meetings, business meetings, emails, preparing, reading, and rereading documents. Robert was awake and at his desk by 7am every morning and worked until 11pm every night. Dinner was delivered to his room every night, and except for an hour he spent with Mikhail the only break he took was to eat. He was running out of time in Las Vegas and didn't want to leave any part of either project to chance.

On Thursday morning he and Joseph boarded the first flight out to Las Vegas and already had meetings planned within an hour of their arrival. As they took their seats, Robert looked across the aisle at the empty seat thinking about Shannon and wondering when he would get the chance to see her again. A soon as the plane was off the ground he had his laptop open, but before he started working again he sent her an email. He explained about work and hoped that the next time he was in New York they could get together for dinner.

As soon as the plane landed they hustled outside where a pair of SUVs were waiting. They drove directly out to Salvatori's house and spent the next hour reviewing several of the agreements with him. Salvatori had become a great source of insight into the unions and was also the intermediary they needed between the two groups. After a couple of hours spent updating the various documents they both felt that they had a deal that was agreeable to both Robert as well as the various unions.

Of course before he could finalize any deals with the unions he had to actually purchase the property. So with that in mind they left Salvatori and rode to the hotel. As before a suite had been arranged and they were quickly ushered through the check-in and in no time Robert was back at the desk working. As much as he looked and hoped, he still didn't see an email from Shannon. Hopefully she was just working hard. Both Lowell and Frank arrived later at the end of the afternoon and after checking in to their rooms came to the suite. They had arranged for dinner with the executive team of the hotel and Robert wanted to make sure that everything was ready.

Promptly at 6.30 the four of them left the suite and without a single bodyguard and quickly made their way to the elevator and down to the lobby. Robert wanted to make a statement and that meant leaving the bodyguards behind. Joseph seemed to understand and had agreed to go along with the plan. But to be sure he had hired a few guys he could trust to stay nearby without being obvious. They arrived at Prime promptly at 6.45 and were quickly escorted to a private room facing the fountains.

The room had been closed to the public again, and they were the first to arrive. They ordered drinks, Robert a single malt scotch and both Lowell and Frank ordered martinis. They stood looking out at the fountains and Robert was scanning his emails, when his phone rang. He didn't recognize the number so he stepped outside to answer it and got quite the surprise.

"I hope I am not interrupting an important meeting, Mr. Cutter, but I wanted to check on one of my favorite patients before I finished my shift for the evening."

His smile grew larger and answered, "good evening, Dr. Adams. I do appreciate the personal attention you big city New York doctors give us little people. I am just fine thank you."

"Don't kid yourself, Sir. I am just in it for the money. My clinic needs a new MRI and I was hoping you had an extra ten million sitting around you would care to donate."

That got Robert laughing loudly, "if that's what I have to do to get you to go out with me again it will be a bargain."

"Well it certainly sounds like you got your sense of humor back. I guess convincing an entire city you were right will do that to a person. But I have to tell you a little secret... I will go out to dinner with you whether you give us a donation or not."

"Really? Careful you don't make promises you can't keep. Are you working tomorrow night?"

"No, actually I am not. I have the whole weekend off. I think they are being extra nice to me once they heard that Philly was looking to steal me away. What time will you pick me up?"

Robert thought about it for several minutes then smiled "I will have to catch a flight, but is 9.30 too late?"

"Actually, my shift ends at 8 so 9.30 should be perfect."

"Fantastic! I will pick you up then."

"Great, I'm looking forward to it."

As much as he hated to, Robert had to go. "Now I am really sorry, but I see my business guests have arrived and I have to save Joseph before he starts to frisk them."

Shannon laughed, "it was nice talking to you again and I am looking forward to dinner."

He could feel her smile through the phone and held it to his ear even after she hung up as if he could feel her next to him. Robert had never felt this way about anyone before, and he had a feeling he might never feel this way again. He hung up the phone and stepped into the room apologizing for the distraction. The staff had already set up a large round table and after introductions they all took seats. Robert sat with the CEO on one side and the COO on the other.

It ended up being a very lengthy but interesting dinner during which they discussed the future of the hotel and the how Robert was going to buy it. The executives were quite impressed with what he had managed to do in Philadelphia and said, "if you can pull that off in a city like that then there is no telling what you can do here in Las Vegas."

Before the night was over they were celebrating over champagne at what they all agreed was an exceptional deal. And the CEO promised that he would speak to the board of directors first thing in the morning. They had all been given advance notice of the discussions, so they should be prepared to make a quick decision. Everyone knew it was the right thing, and with the backing of the unions they also knew it wouldn't - or shouldn't fail.

When they returned to the suite, Lowell emailed the notes to his team in New York and assured Robert the documents would be completed and emailed back first thing in the morning. Then he and Frank returned to their rooms while Robert wandered around the suite. Joseph knew that it was a combination of things making him restless so he got two of the bodyguards to accompany him and Robert downstairs for a walk. First they walked around the Bellagio and then they walked over to Caesar's to see what the competition did. From there they had an SUV drive them down to the Wynn and finally much later back to the Bellagio.

Robert went to sleep and for the first time in several days fell soundly asleep. He felt at ease as if things were coming together nicely. The Philadelphia project was finally on its way and now nothing could stand in his way. He had no doubts there would be setbacks, but nothing that couldn't be overcome. This project was also working out just the way he wanted and if all went well, by close of business he would be the new owner of a Las Vegas casino. But most of all he was going to see Shannon again, and no matter how much he tried to downplay it, it thrilled him. She was truly a special woman and he was amazed by her every time that he spoke to her.

The next morning Robert woke early and immediately went to work. True to Lowell's word, the revised documents had already been emailed to all of them. As he was starting to review it both Lowell and Frank came in, with their own marked up copies. Clearly they had been up longer than he had been. They moved over to the sitting area, getting fresh coffee as they sat down. They spent the next thirty minutes making final updates and corrections, then Robert emailed the final document to the executive team for their review. They called a board meeting for 1pm and planned to present a set of signed final documents for immediate board approval.

Robert had suggested attending the meeting as well to make his case, but the executive team had recommended against it. They felt that Robert showing up might be too forceful and they might insist on getting other bids. Even though there were no other bids or interested buyers, opening it up to public scrutiny could mean a lot of different things not the least of which was losing the unions. Instead, the three of them worked on some of the specifics needed for the Philadelphia project. Robert was amazed at how finally getting approvals had not just meant the project could move forward, but also a lot more planning.

Robert was so confident that this deal would go through and as much as he wanted a private dinner tonight with Shannon, he had arranged for a dinner party at the Chef's table at Bobby Flay's restaurant Bar American. He smiled at the idea of the celebration dinner, but knew that his real joy was at seeing Shannon again. He always made a point of celebrating with the team after closing a deal, but rarely did it include personal guests.

After waiting an hour for a call from the executive team Robert decided he couldn't sit still anymore. He stood up and taking Joseph and a bodyguard went for a walk around the hotel. iPad in hand, Robert roamed around the hotel making notes and comments as they came into his mind. They walked through the casino and around past the various restaurants heading to the pool. He was standing there when his cell phone rang and he first glanced at the screen, then at Joseph.

"Hello, this is Robert." He stopped walking as he answered and Joseph stopped beside him. "Thank you for calling me. I will come by your offices to sign the documents shortly." Another pause. "Thank you, Sir, I hope you are pleased in knowing you have made the right decision. Good day, Sir."

Robert hung up the phone and stood staring at it for several moments before turning to Joseph. "It seems I have a hotel to buy! Care to join me?" And smiling broadly the two men shook hands. Then Robert called the suite to give them the good news and let them know he was on his way to sign the documents. Hotel security met them at the elevator and they waited for Lowell and Frank to arrive, then took the private elevator to the mezzanine where the operating offices were located.

They were met at the elevators by a lovely woman who escorted them to a conference room. Already waiting were the executives they had met for dinner as well as the chairman of the board. On the conference line was the chairman of MGM Resorts International who quickly congratulated Robert on the deal and then apologized as he had to get back to a meeting. They took turns signing the documents including a witness for each of the companies. Afterwards the same woman brought in a bottle of champagne and glasses, carefully pouring it out and handing each of them a glass.

They quickly toasted the deal, and after several minutes of small talk, Robert and Joseph left for the suite leaving Frank and Lowell to make the final arrangements for handover. The actual transfer of ownership would take another couple of weeks, but that was a formality. As soon as they arrived back at the suite Robert called Salvatori and told him the deal was final. They then arranged for the union leaders to meet in the suite to complete their deals. Robert hoped that would not take long as he was looking forward to spending time with Shannon.

They had several hours to kill waiting for the union leaders and Salvatori to arrive so Robert went to work on his emails. Just once, he thought, I will have to do only one deal at a time so when it closes I can actually relax. But, he knew that wasn't true - for some of his deals the easy part was closing it. The hard work came afterwards in actually making it work. Amongst his worries today was that he would miss the flight home and have to cancel dinner then he remembered he had bought a casino. And this casino owned a private jet for their high dollar gamblers. Robert had to laugh since considering the deal he had just made, he had quickly become their highest dollar gambler.

The union leaders arrived at 1pm and they had already heard that the deal had been closed. Aside from the group in the room, Robert had arranged to have a video call with his team in New York. Robert wanted them to meet the project leader who would be their primary contact after today. A few of them seemed concerned that it was not going to be Robert but he assured them that the project leader was quite capable to handle the day to day issues. They signed the contracts with each of the unions and it took a lot more time than Robert had hoped.

Joseph had already packed everything so they were ready to go. He had even settled the hotel bill so all they had to do was leave. Frank and Lowell were also packed and ready to go, so as soon as the unions left, Robert did as well. The SUVs were waiting outside the hotel and they quickly made their way to the private airfield, after a quick security check the group climbed aboard and the plane took off. One of the luxuries aboard was a very good Wi-Fi as well as a satellite phone system. Robert got back to work as a few issues had come up in Philadelphia that needed his attention. Weather was good and the flight landed at Long Island's MacArthur airport in good time. It was only 45 miles outside of Manhattan, but at this time of day Robert knew traffic would be a challenge. There were two SUVs waiting for them and the group made their way as quickly as they could into the city.

Traffic was typically slow for a Friday evening, so Robert called and had a car pick up Shannon. He hoped she would not be mad at being kept waiting. But he also knew that the others on his team would enjoy the chance to get to meet her. It seemed like the closer they got to the restaurant the worse traffic got, to the point where they were a full hour late for the party. Luckily Robert had booked the upstairs room for the night so there was no real rush to get there, other than wanting to spend as much time as possible with Shannon.

When they got there they found that they had started without him. Drinks and appetizers had been served and when he walked in got a round of applause. He made his way through the group of twenty or twenty-five associates, greeting each by name before finally getting to Shannon. To his surprise she planted a very friendly kiss on his lips, to which he responded immediately. He had the bartender and wait staff serve champagne around and then took a place towards the center of the group.

"Good evening and thank you for coming." He paused while the group all laughed and clapped. "It really is my pleasure to host this party, since you have all been working so hard to make this happen. We have certainly worked together on many other projects, but this was definitely the biggest gamble." Again he paused through the laughter. "While some of you may have thought I was more interested in the Philadelphia project, this project was never far from the top of my mind. Thank you all for your hard work to date, and now we can start the next phase of the project. Several of you will be asked to take a very large, hands on role, as we move forward and I thank you in advance for your ongoing support." Robert raised his glass in toasting the group and everyone raised theirs as well. "It might be my name on the door, but it is you who make us all so successful."

After that, they all took seats at the tables and the conversations covered everything from what the Kardashians were doing next to what the latest political scandal meant. Through it all Robert joined in several of the conversations, but he found it just as entertaining to watch as Shannon easily moved from one conversation to the next. Clearly as informed about each topic as the next one. Several people engaged her even more by finding out about her specialty and some of the work she did with child athletes. At one point in the evening he sat watching her intently as she spoke with a woman sitting beside her. Blushing deeply when Shannon looked at him and smiled, that same smile he had seen at the benefit that drew him to her. The same smile that lit up her entire face, radiating from her warm lips through her emerald eyes as if it was only meant for him.

He had arranged for everyone to be driven home so they did not have to worry about drinking. Shannon was happy to ride with him and he had the driver take them on a route through Central Park. Shannon raised a questioning eyebrow at him since she lived in the opposite direction. He just grinned like a high school boy at his first dance, and said he didn't want the evening to end. She looked at him and smiled again and just as he was about to kiss her, the driver announced they were at her apartment.

Robert walked her up to the door and they made arrangements to meet at the MoMA for lunch and then a stroll through the museum. As they stood there awkwardly, Robert took her hands and leaning in kissed her softly on the mouth. She responded to him and wrapped her arms around his neck. They stood like that for several minutes knowing neither of them wanted it to end. As she stepped back and got her keys out, Robert looked at her and smiling simply said "I know". Then with one more quick kiss he went down the steps from her brownstone and got back into the SUV. They waited for her to go inside and lock the door before pulling away, and Robert sat back against the seat, contented.

On the ride back to the hotel, Robert stared out the windows. Only in New York City could a person ride through the crowded streets at night and see almost as many people walking as during the day. Looking over at Joseph he asked for an update on his own apartment. Joseph said he would find out, and promised to move things along. They arrived at the hotel and headed straight for the suite. Robert tossed and turned for a quite a while before finally falling asleep.

He woke early in the morning as usual and with a cup of coffee from the room Keurig moved to his desk and began reviewing his emails. There were several that required his immediate attention, but there were several others that were updates on the existing projects. All of them were good news - both in Philadelphia and in Las Vegas. He was always amazed at how quickly things were moving along in both projects. In Philadelphia the cement contractors were already laying the foundations for several of the new houses. And several other houses already had walls, roofs, windows, and siding in place. He also learned that a local lumber yard had arranged for all of the supplies to be made readily available, and for easy shipping to the location. And several small businesses had taken over some of the empty space on the main avenue and already started doing their own renovations.

And in Las Vegas, even though he had just left he learned that the architects and designers had arrived and started taking photographs and notes of their own. Robert had been sending all of his notes to Jennifer while he had been there, so his list of ideas had been shared with the designers. To ensure disrupting business as little as possible they were going to start with some simple updates in the public spaces. And then portions of the hotel space would be updated and revitalized also trying to minimize the disruption and noise. The last thing Robert wanted to do was to get into this business and then drive away the guests.

The current estimates from the design and architect team was that it would take at least 18 months and possibly as long as 24 months before all of the work was done. That would give them 12 months of normal break-fix work before they would start updating and refreshing all of the space again. Robert had already determined that every 36 to 48 months they would be updating and refreshing the entire property. The biggest part of the project was going to be the pool area, in fact there were going to be two pools built out. One for adults only, so they could enjoy a little more quiet and not have to worry about noisy kids. After all, Robert was still hoping he could make this a family hotel as well as a great casino.

Glancing at the clock on the desk he saw that it was almost ten-thirty and since he had arranged to meet Shannon at noon, he knew he should get moving. As he stood up to get a shower his cell phone rang and he saw it was Joseph. He was wondering where he had gotten to, and Joseph explained that he had returned to the office early to follow up on some information about their "spying" employee. Apparently they had found some information on his computer, and with the help of the FBI they were tracking those leads down. But, Joseph had also arranged with a private firm to have the employee followed. Of course, Joseph didn't tell him that he had also searched his apartment and cloned his cell phone. There wasn't anything this person could do that Joseph wouldn't know about. Joseph had already talked to the FBI and arranged to give him just enough rope to hang himself, without doing any more damage to the company.

Robert reminded Joseph of his afternoon plans and Joseph assured him that the bodyguards were prepared for the day. Plus Joseph would meet him at the museum later. As he hung up Robert remembered when not too long ago when he felt that all of this was overkill. But he was the first to admit, even before Las Vegas, that he felt much safer having the SUVs and the bodyguards with him. Even on a date with a beautiful doctor, which if he didn't get moving he would be late for.

He took a hot shower and shaved, then after drying off and applying aftershave he went into the bedroom to get dressed. He slipped on jeans and a button down shirt, loafers and a blazer. He slipped his wallet into his pocket as he selected a casual watch for the day. As he stepped out of the bedroom he saw one of the bodyguards waiting for him. The man nodded to Robert and taking the lead led him out of the room where a pair of bodyguards were waiting. They quickly made their way to the waiting SUVs and made their way through the Saturday traffic to the museum.

Robert and his bodyguard made their way up the stairs and inside the museum. The main entrance was crowded with the usual visitors ranging in ages from teens to people in the 70s. It seemed as if everyone had come to the museum today and the main lobby was incredibly crowded. When Robert spotted Shannon across the room he broke into a huge grin and sighed in relief. A part of him he realized had been worried that she wouldn't show up. As he made his way towards her he was amazed again at how beautiful she was. With all of the artwork in the building he knew that she would top it all.

Shannon tuned and seeing Robert for the first time smiled broadly and just like that he stopped. His heart skipped a beat as he took one more step closer. He reached for her hand and held it softly, at the same time placing his other hand against her cheek. She slid her arms around his neck as he kissed her softly. He slid his arms around her and held for several moments, both of them completely unaware of the people moving around them. They finally broke out of their embrace, bought tickets and began to move through the museum.

The rest of the day was a blur to Robert and he was surprised when they were announcing that the museum was closing for the day. With the bodyguards following they walked to a local Italian restaurant for dinner and stayed for another couple of hours talking. Robert had never felt so at ease talking about his past and even his future as he did with Shannon. He had also never met someone who seemed so genuinely interested in his ideas - both for the Philadelphia and for the Las Vegas projects. She seemed especially enthralled to talk about his ideas for the hotel and even gave a few of her own insights as a traveler.

Despite it being a Saturday evening in New York City, the restaurant did not seem concerned with their sitting leisurely over dinner and coffee. And it wasn't until they were ready to leave that Robert realized most of the place was empty, except for Joseph who was sitting at a nearby table with a bodyguard. The look on his face told Robert all he needed, and now he also knew why the waiter had not brought the check. Sitting on the table in front of Joseph was the bill for dinner, along with his own dinner bill and a third for the table with the two other bodyguards. Robert assumed that Joseph was also paying for the empty tables around them, or more likely he was using the company card he carried.

"Robert, did he arrange for all of these empty tables?"

"I would assume so. Joseph still continues to amaze me with the things he is able to arrange. Especially considering that we decided to come here somewhat on a whim."

Shannon shook her head smiling, "he is quite a good guy to have by your side."

She started to walk out towards the front of the restaurant, but Robert took her hand. "You have no idea just how much he has meant to me in the past few weeks and months. Why don't we give them a few moments to settle up before we head outside? I am sure they have the SUVs waiting around the corner for us so there is no rush."

Shannon looked at him for a few moments, "they didn't empty the tables so that we could have privacy did they?"

Robert shook his head, "don't worry, these guys are good and I will never do anything to put you in danger. I would say trust me, but instead you should trust Joseph. I do."

The owner walked over to them to make sure that dinner and the arrangements were to their liking. Robert assured him that everything was excellent, including the arrangements. Then with a grin Robert turned to Shannon and said, "you know this would be a great place for an intimate fund raiser."

Shannon smiled, but he saw something in her face that said there was something else. And for the first time he remembered about the job offer in Philadelphia. He hoped that she had not made a decision, and if she had, he wondered if there was some way he could change her mind. Then again, he did like Philadelphia and there was no reason he couldn't move his office there. At this point in his career he didn't really have to be in New York City to be successful. But, he knew that the city was more than just a place where his business was. It was his home. Besides, who ever said she would want him to move. Just as that thought entered his mind she slipped an arm through his and rested against his shoulder.

As they rode in the back of the SUV Robert reached for her hand taking it in his. She turned, smiled, leaned in and kissed him softly. He did not want this evening to end, but if Shannon was thinking seriously about Philadelphia then it wasn't fair to push her. They had talked about it over dinner, but she hadn't seemed to have made a decision one way or the other. For that matter she had not even mentioned an offer, just how the interviews had gone.

When they pulled up at her building Robert opened the door and walked her to the door. Standing there awkwardly, like two teenagers they both seemed unsure of the other. Then Shannon asked if he wanted to come in for coffee and Robert agreed. As they turned and went inside Robert glanced back at the cars. He saw the lead SUV with Joseph pull away, but the other SUV stayed behind and shut off the engine to wait. He closed and locked the door behind him and when he turned found Shannon standing and watching him.

Robert moved closer to her and took her hands in his then softly kissed her on the mouth. She returned his kiss and wrapped her arms around his waist. Softly she whispered that she didn't really want coffee and smiling he tilted her chin up and kissed her again. Taking her in his arms he held her for several moments, their hearts beating almost in unison. Slowly they separated and Shannon led Robert to the family room where they sat on the couch. Briefly they held hands and again kissed, both tentative like a pair of teens sneaking some alone time in the basement.

The next morning Robert woke up early as usual and quietly slipped out of bed. He made his way to the bathroom, and when he stepped out found her laying with her eyes open watching him. He grinned as she pulled the covers back and patted the bed beside her. He quickly joined her then slid his arms around her kissing her passionately. Much later he woke up and found her side of the bed empty. Across the foot of the bed was an oversized terry cloth robe which he slipped on as the smell of fresh coffee rose through the air. He followed the scent to the kitchen and found her leaning over the island reading the paper.

Sliding his arms around her he said, "coffee smells good." She grinned and slid and empty mug over to him. Then pulling away she got cream from the fridge and filled his mug. He reached for the paper and quickly found the business section, scanning the headlines. As he quickly flipped the pages he suddenly became aware that she was watching him.

"You don't ever really turn it off, do you, Robert?"

Smiling he placed a hand over hers, "sorry, I guess its second nature for me. Coffee and the business section are how I always start the mornings. But, I um... did go back to bed... Which for me is very rare, not that I am complaining. In fact..."

Shannon blushed, and he thought she had never looked more beautiful. "How about we get some breakfast, then I will let you go to work?"

He pulled her into his arms again and kissed her again and again. "How about I buy you breakfast and then I have a little surprise for you."

She looked at him warily then smiled and nodded. They went back upstairs and got dressed. While he waited for her downstairs he called Joseph who said he would have a car pick them up in five minutes. Robert told him about the rest of his ideas for the afternoon and Joseph said he would make all of the arrangements. Robert hung up once again amazed that Joseph never asked questions, just made the arrangements.

They went to a local Todd English restaurant for breakfast and afterwards were taken to a helipad where there was a helicopter waiting for them. Shannon looked at him questioningly and he smiled and said, "trust me." The helicopter flew them out to the Hamptons on Long Island where a car was waiting. Throughout both the flight and the car ride they chatted and held hands. Robert had never felt more relaxed, and it was only as they reached the marina that Robert realized he had not looked at his phone once.

Robert explained that he had a friend with a boat and he was going to let them use it for the afternoon. They walked hand in hand along the docks passing all different types and sizes of boats. Finally they headed down a long dock and parked at the end was a huge yacht. Waiting at the base of the stairs was a finely dressed man in starched white pants and shirt, wearing the required white boat shoes. Shannon and he were both dressed in casual slacks and polo shirts and she asked if they were under dressed.

He laughed. "Its ok, my friends have clothes on board that we can borrow. I thought we could go for a ride and make our way over to Martha's Vineyard for dinner. If that's ok?"

Shannon grinned and held onto his arm, "well, I suppose it will have to do." Then she swatted his arm.

He was laughing as the man welcomed them aboard and guided them into the sitting area. He then pointed out the bedrooms, bar area, and sitting area outside. He offered drinks and got them fresh iced tea. The captain came into the room and apologized, but apparently they would not be able to go to the Vineyard - apparently the President was visiting. Instead he had made arrangements to go to Nantucket, if that was ok? Robert assured him it would be fine.

They went into one the guest rooms and found shorts laid out for them. They started to get changed, but ended up in each other's arms. Robert had never felt this way before and was determined to not let anything get in their way. Later, they made their way up to the upper deck where chairs and towels had been laid out. The crewman brought out iced tea, fresh fruit, and a cheese and bread platter. They both relaxed enjoying each other's company, the food and the amazing views as the yacht made its way to Nantucket.

They had to take a wide berth around Martha's Vineyard and Robert pointed out the submarine that was sailing in the area. He explained that any time the President visited either here or Kennebunkport there was a submarine nearby since there wasn't an airport close enough for Air Force One. Shannon was amazed by all of the other boats in the area, some Navy and some Coast Guard. She was also clearly taken by the lengths Robert had taken so the day would be perfect.

Once on Nantucket, they wandered the streets and it was only then that Robert seemed to notice the two bodyguards. He hadn't even realized they had gotten on board with them, and barely noticed they were there now. Dinner was excellent and Shannon joked about him not buying out the place for privacy. Everything moved at a leisurely pace and yet the time still seemed to fly by. Soon, they were back on board the yacht and heading back to New York.

Shannon fell asleep curled up on the sofa next to him as he finally looked through his emails, and read the news on his iPad. He softly woke her once they were docked and had the car drive them back into the city. Once again she dozed off next to him, and as much as he wanted her awake he was just as glad that she was that comfortable beside him. He walked her up to her townhouse and kissed her at the door.

"Robert, I had an absolutely amazing day today. And there is nothing I would rather do than invite you inside. But, I have to work in the morning and um... need my rest."

Holding her in his arms he smiled and kissed her forehead. "I am glad, I had a wonderful day as well. But mostly because you were with me. Sleep well and we will make plans to do this again. Assuming you want to, of course."

She ginned and kissed him again, "don't be silly. I will call you once I see my upcoming schedule and will definitely do this again." Then she turned and with barely a whisper was inside and closing the door.

Robert stood there for several moments before walking back to the car. It suddenly seemed very alone and quiet, and the two bodyguards in the front seat did nothing to fill the void. Back at the hotel Robert wandered around, picking up the remote and flipped channels for several minutes before turning it off. He moved to the desk and checked for new emails, but there were none. He even surfed the Internet for a while before finally heading into the bedroom and going to sleep. He couldn't fall asleep so he flipped through the channels again before settling on a baseball game and falling asleep with the TV on.

The next morning Robert woke up and made himself fresh coffee and then sat down at his computer. Half way through his emails he realized that he was going to have to go back to Las Vegas. Apparently there was some legal issues with the casino license and he would need to be there in person. While he sent an email to Jennifer to make the arrangements for the trip, and let his team know he was coming he realized something had changed in him. For the first time in his career he did not want to be in the middle of it, he wanted to stay right here in New York. He wanted to see her again, today, tomorrow and every day.

As if she had read his mind his cell phone rang and he saw it was Shannon. "Good morning, my dear. What a pleasant surprise. Did you know I was just thinking of you?"

Robert could sense the smile across the phone, "good morning, Robert. I am glad I caught you, I wasn't sure how early you went in to the office. I just wanted to say what a wonderful weekend I had. I hope we can do it again soon."

Robert couldn't help but smile, "Shannon, I had more fun than I have had in quite a while. I have to go to Las Vegas later today and then back to Philadelphia. I don't know if I will be back for the weekend, but if you are not working I would like to see you again also."

"I am not sure if I have the weekend free, but I would like that very much." There was a pause and Robert could hear announcements in the background. "I'm sorry Robert I have to run. Call me."

Just like that she was gone. Slowly Robert hung up the phone his smile not wavering for a moment. He was interrupted both by the door opening and Joseph coming in with a breakfast tray, and an email from Jennifer with his week's itinerary. As much as he appreciated her efficiency, he had to leave right away and find a way to focus on work. He brought Joseph up to date, only to find out she had copied him on the email so he had already made arrangements. The local bodyguards and SUVs would be waiting for them when they landed in Las Vegas and again when they got to Philadelphia.

Chapter 15

What was supposed to be just a few days in Las Vegas ended up being a week. There were so many meetings, dinners, tours of the facility, lunches, and even more meetings that Robert lost track of time. Before he knew it the weekend had arrived and then he "had" to go to Los Angeles to meet with several large investor groups. There were quite a few high profile investors that were already clients, and the Bellagio project had added a few more to his list. That meant even more meetings and a few private dinners with some of the celebrity investors.

By Sunday afternoon Robert found himself standing under the hot shower letting the water wash over him. He didn't know how long he had been standing there until he heard Joseph calling to make sure he was ok. He shook it off, finished the shower, shaved, and then quickly got dressed in the suit which had been laid out for him. Stepping into the sitting room Joseph handed him the information for who he was having dinner with. Robert had to smile when he looked at the list of names and saw several famous actors. They were not investors yet, he knew, but he was hoping to change that.

Much to his surprise when Robert arrived at the restaurant he saw that Martin Anderson was there as well. Robert walked over to him and shook his hand, he also told Martin that he did not feel it appropriate for him to be there. They stood to one side having this conversation, but anyone looking would see from Robert's posture that he was not at all happy with Martin's actions. Sensing that the rest of the guests were starting to pay more attention to them that Robert would have liked he broke away and everyone took their seats.

The two hour dinner took almost four hours and while he was used to meeting with future investors he found this dinner to be exceptionally tiring. Several of these people were already partner investors in several other projects, so it was more than convincing one person he had to convince all of them. Fortunately for Robert, the success of his company spoke volumes and that was the primary reason why he was even meeting with this group.

By the time he got back to his room he just barely got undressed before falling into bed and immediately dropping into a deep sleep. When he woke the next morning he realized it was not the alarm he was hearing but his phone ringing. He answered it slowly, but had missed the call. Apparently there were some serious issues brewing in Philadelphia and he had to get back there. He walked out to the sitting room and seeing Joseph, told him the news. He nodded and immediately called Jennifer getting her to make the necessary travel arrangements.

A couple of hours later they were boarding the plane and making their way to their first class seats. Settling in Robert got out his lap top and quickly went to work on reading updates from that team. All he could do was shake his head at some of the antics the politicians insisted on trying to pull off. He made notes, typed emails, and scheduled even more meetings. It was a wonder that anyone got anything done when they spent all of their time in meetings. Good thing he had some good people working for him, otherwise he would be broke.

As he and Joseph made their way through the Philadelphia

airport to the waiting SUVs he thought that the only good news was that being in the same time zone with Shannon meant he might get to talk to her. Plus, he would also get a chance to see Mikhail. The little guy still sent him emails and pictures, but it wasn't the same. Robert was pleased to see that Mark Thompson was waiting for him in the SUV and that a lot of the information he had requested had already been pulled together.

They spent the rest of the drive discussing next steps, but Robert was not planning on being very diplomatic. As they approached the hotel Robert had a change of heart and asked to be taken to the tent city. As they pulled up he saw Mikhail out playing soccer with a couple of the other kids, but as soon as he saw the SUV the boy turned and ran over. As soon as Robert got out the boy jumped into his waiting arms, and as usual Robert immediately felt a weight lifted off of him. They walked hand in hand into the office area where they met up with Pearl. Mikhail paid her no mind, and wouldn't stop talking to Robert telling him all about school and soccer and the teacher and the other kids. They all laughed when Mikhail finally ran out of steam and had to take a deep breath.

They spent the next hour sharing milk and cookies while Mikhail proudly showed Robert all of his drawings and how good he could read. Even Robert was somewhat amazed at the difference in the boy, and Pearl explained that clearly having a home was the difference. They went outside after a while and Mikhail gave Robert and Joseph a tour of the neighborhood. He had a running commentary of all of the big trucks that kept coming and going at all hours, and all of the people working.

Robert knew that they had been making good progress but was still surprised to see half a dozen houses fully built and another few partially built. Robert knew the interiors were still being worked on but this was good news. It meant that in the next month or so families could start moving into real houses. He also saw that several businesses were already open, including a corner store where Kim's had been located. He stood for several moments looking at the building before Joseph tapped his arm and they started moving again.

They made their way back to the SUVs and headed back to the hotel. Joseph had arranged for a quiet dinner and Robert fell asleep sitting on the couch watching Sunday night baseball. He rarely watched baseball and as tired as he was it was easy for him to doze off. He woke up the next morning feeling more refreshed than he had in weeks, and after a quick shower got dressed and over emails had his first cup of coffee. He kept working on the drive to his first set of meetings and by the time he arrived at city hall was prepared for anything. He met Thompson and a couple of staffers there and they strode through security as if he was coming in for a normal day of work.

His first meeting was with the city planning board commissioner and not surprisingly he had to wait. Robert was there fifteen minutes early and sat calmly while he waited. At exactly one minute before the meeting the secretary told Robert that the commissioner was delayed. It was another thirty minutes before he was told it would be another fifteen minutes. By the time the man arrived it was an hour and despite his apologies, Robert knew it had been a ploy.

His next scheduled meeting was with one of the state senators who had made it clear that he was not a fan of the project. Robert knew he couldn't reschedule it, so he sent Mark ahead of him. The commissioner continued to try and delay or slow down the meeting with Robert, who stayed patient. Even when the man took several "cannot miss phone calls" Robert remained patient. Even when the man needed to have the most basic things explained twice, Robert remained patient.

Finally he had reached his limit when the man reached for the ringing desk phone. Robert reached across the desk and held the phone down. "Sir, I appreciate that you are a busy man and that you run a large operation here. I can relate since I too run a large operation. That being said, I have given you the courtesy of being an hour late for a scheduled meeting. I have even given you the courtesy of interrupting this meeting several times. But if you interrupt this meeting again I promise that my next meeting will not be with the senator, but with the Philadelphia inquirer political and business reporters. Now, I don't want you to think I am threatening you in any way, Sir. I am simply saying that you should carefully consider giving me the same respect that I have given you. So, why don't we conclude this meeting so I can move on to the next political leader who will likewise spend a great deal of my time making himself feel more important?"

The commissioner took a deep breath and for a moment seemed to consider his options. Then with the smirk of an experienced politician said, "Mr. Cutter, I don't know how you do things up in New York. And this certainly isn't the big city, but we like to make sure things are done correctly. My job is to make sure that we are always looking out for all of our great city's citizens. You, Sir, are here in my office because you have friends in the government. If you don't think you are getting the courtesy of this office, then I suggest you reschedule time with the appropriate people in my department and they will review your plans with me. The way it should be done."

Robert stood up, and gathered up the documents that he had brought with him sliding them into his briefcase. "You are right. I have taken up too much of your valuable time. Please let me know who I should be meeting with and I will make sure that we do so immediately. I only ask one small favor, please make sure you consider the citizens of this fine city when you come to New York

City and ask me for a meeting. And that won't be a replacement of this meeting. No Sir that will be the meeting where you ask me to forgive you for wasting my time today. But, by that point it won't matter because the good citizens you claim to care about will know the truth. That you care of nothing more than your own importance. Have a good day, Sir."

Before the beet red commissioner could blink Robert turned and walked out of the office. He wished the secretary a good day as he strode past her desk and into the hallway. There were two staff people of his waiting in the outer room and they had trouble catching up with him. He waited for a moment at the elevator before moving to the stairs. As he started up he could hear the echo of the fast moving footsteps coming up the hallway. As he kept moving he smiled knowing the man would not catch up to him. At the top of the stairs he turned right and headed for the senator's local office.

He could hear the man panting at the top of the stairs, and almost felt bad for him. Robert did not have much patience for politicians, let alone career government people who acted like the commissioner. As Robert approached the senator's office door it opened with Thompson and the senator standing there. Robert approached them and shook hands with the senator.

"I apologize for the delay, Senator, but I was hung up down in one of the commission offices."

The senator smiled as he looked past Robert. He cocked an eyebrow and said, "it would appear that your meeting is not over yet. Perhaps you would like to use my office to finish that conversation?" Turning he smiled again at the commissioner and stretching out his hand said, "Mr. Commissioner, nice to you see up on this floor. I was just suggesting to Mr. Cutter that he could use my office to finish his meeting with you. Maybe if I joined the meeting I could help resolve any issues that two of you might have?"

Robert had to smile, for as much as he felt most politicians were just looking to the next election, the senator seemed to be a quick thinker. Or of course, he was just looking at Robert as a really big donor for his next election. Either way it worked and the commissioner told them there was no need and that Robert had supplied all needed documentation. That is what the commissioner had been coming to tell him. He would have all paperwork signed and sealed by the end of the week.

Robert thanked him and said he would have someone pick up the documents on Friday afternoon. Then he turned and walked with the senator back into his office. They spent the next hour talking about the project and the senator promised to take a tour the next day with Robert. After that they spent another thirty minutes talking about the project in Las Vegas. Apparently, the senator had been a guest of the Bellagio and was looking forward to the improvements Robert was making.

As they left the office Thompson was waiting for him as was a local reporter. The two stood answering the reporters' questions for another fifteen minutes. He had been at the original news conference, but admitted he had not been back since. The senator made the reporter promise to join them for the tour they were taking tomorrow, which he did. It seemed like this senator could get anyone on his side quickly and easily.

Robert spent the next couple of hours back at the hotel finalizing the plans based on the commissioner approving the rest of the project. On top of that he had to deal with an upcoming investors' meeting. Every quarter Robert met with his major investors to discuss the various new projects, as well as the existing business. Normally it was a couple of hours of business and an hour of socializing over a catered lunch. But he knew that this time would be a different meeting. They were already planning it as a working lunch and had added an extra hour to the meeting.

While he had a group of analysts that put together the basic presentation for him, he always finished it off adding his own commentary. His investors expected the best from a financial standpoint, and he had always delivered. But he knew that lately there were a lot of distractions, some bad and some good. Robert knew that he would have to be better than his best at this meeting. Not that he was worried about them leaving him, but these meetings were as much about the future as about anything else.

Robert spent the next several hours finalizing the presentation, answering the ever mounting new emails, and reviewing new design ideas for the Bellagio. It was an intense several hours, even for Robert who was used to long full days. There was something about the varied projects that was making it even more tiring for him. He closed his laptop, stood up and stretched then headed for the door feeling like he really needed some fresh air.

As he was about to open the door there was a knock and Robert stopped short. He stared at the door like he had never seen one before. As he reached for the handle the person knocked again, twice. Robert knew two important things - he was not expecting anyone, and his security was not supposed to let anyone close enough to the door to knock. For that matter, Joseph would not let anyone close enough to the door to knock either. As he was moving back away from the door his cell phone chirped. He looked down at the text from Joseph and grinned as he saw the words "open the door". Slowly he opened the door, seeing just enough of the person to draw an even bigger smile.

The red hair was as recognizable as the green eyes were shining, and the smile breath taking. "I was about to go for a walk, would you join me?" As he said the words he opened his arms wide and took a deep breath as Shannon stepped into his hug.

As he held her, he looked out into the hallway and saw Joseph smiling. They stood in the embrace and Robert could feel the stress slipping out of his body as if a magic wand had passed across him.

Breaking the hug they left the room hand in hand, and if asked Robert would have admitted that for the first time he was truly oblivious to the following trio of security guards. They passed through the lobby into the indoor mall with the Williams and Sonoma, stopping at the Starbucks for a drink. Leaving the building they walked down Walnut Street stopping from time to time to look in the various windows. They walked down to Rittenhouse Square and turning walked up to Parq where they had an early dinner.

After dinner they left the restaurant and as they stepped outside saw Joseph standing beside the waiting SUV. "I thought you might like a ride back to the hotel folks, and cabs are so hard to find." They all laughed because as if on cue a cab pulled up to the curb. It felt like a long time since Robert had laughed and even a longer time since he had felt relaxed. They rode back to the hotel in silence, holding hands again. Shannon rested her head against Robert's shoulder and he kissed her forehead softly.

They spent the next several hours in each other's arms and then Robert fell sound asleep. He slept so soundly that in the morning he didn't hear Shannon get in the shower or get dressed. He woke up and immediately smiled as he saw Shannon standing beside the bed, but just as quickly it slipped as he realized she was already dressed.

"You have to leave so early?"

"Sorry, Robert, but I have a couple of meetings early this morning. That job is still in the offering, and I am trying to work out what the details would be. I have my team to consider and what resources I will need. There is more in this case than just my salary to consider." As she spoke she placed a soft hand against his cheek, caressing it lightly.

He smiled and placed his hand against hers, "it sounds like one of my projects. If there is anything you need help with, let me know and I will give you whatever it is. But, I have to admit, I would rather you stay in New York." He leaned forward and kissed her softly "but I do understand you have to go where the work is." No matter how hard he tried to smile though, the look of sadness creeped into his eyes.

Shannon put on her best smile and returned his kiss. "Robert, New York is not that far and this is not a done deal by any stretch of the imagination. And as long as you will let me I will spend as much time as I can with you."

Robert took her hand in his, "you will always be welcome, because if you haven't noticed I enjoy every moment I have with you."

They looked at each other neither knowing what else to say. And before they could there was a soft knock at the door. "Sorry, Sir... But, we only have about an hour before we are meeting the senator at the site."

Robert nodded and glancing at the clock was surprised to see that it was already almost 8.30. He looked at Shannon who was smiling again. He kissed her as he pulled her into a hug and held her for an extra moment. "Well you heard the boss. Call me later and we can have dinner again!"

She smiled brightly, "that will be great! But then I have to go back to New York tonight."

His smile faltered for a moment, but then he said he would make the arrangements. Then getting out of bed, he walked her to the door. As he opened it, Thompson was about to knock and he slipped past them. They kissed and said goodbyes, then as he closed the door Robert was back to being all business. He headed for the bedroom with Thompson trailing him as he gave him some instructions for the morning. After a quick shower and shave Robert was dressed and having his first cup of coffee as they left the room.

Robert was on the phone with Jennifer during the drive over to the site, following up on some emails he had sent to her yesterday. As soon as he hung up he went to work going through his emails on his iPad. As they drove through the neighborhood leading up to the site Robert was again amazed at the transformation. Not only from the time of the fire itself, but even from before that. New businesses were being built and decorated, signs going up all over announcing when they would be open. And almost more importantly there were signs going up offering employment.

As they made the last turn Robert was greeted by an amazing site - a coming soon sign had been put up for Wal-Mart and they had already found a location for a temporary hiring office. He found himself smiling broadly because he knew that despite all of the detractors and critics you certainly couldn't argue with signs like that. As he pulled up to the site Robert saw not only the reporter from yesterday speaking with a group of people but there was the local ABC station setting up a camera.

As the SUV pulled up to the curb the reporter approached to ask Robert a few questions. But, he was surprised to be stopped short by a gentle hand on his arm. He turned to see who had stopped him and was surprised to see one of the biggest men ever standing there. Knowing it was a body guard he was a little surprised they would stop a reporter. But then the man nodded towards the tents and the reporter watched as a little boy ran full speed at them. The boy vaulted into the air without a word, and landed straight against Robert. The reporter was shocked by this attack, until he saw that Robert was actually holding the boy and the two were laughing away.

"Sorry about that Mr... Sorry, I don't think I caught your name yesterday?"

"Paul, Mr. Cutter. From the Inquirer."

"Good morning, Paul and thanks for coming out. Your crew is welcome to film whatever they need, I simply ask that you give these folks their privacy. Remember this is still their home."

Before either of them could say anything else, the boy spoke up, "my name is Mikhail. Are you a friend of Robert's?"

Paul smiled at the boy, "not yet, but I think that would be nice. Is Robert a good friend of yours?"

The boy nodded his head enthusiastically, "is he ever! He built us these cool tents, and is building new houses for us. And when he first got here he made us a big dinner, and it even had ice cream and pie. And he got me books, and crayons, and even took me to a baseball game. Do you like baseball? Oh... But he does make me go to school." When he paused to take a breath they both started to laugh.

"Well, Mr. Cutter certainly sounds like a fun friend to have. Tell you the truth, I am more of a football fan myself."

"I have never been to a football game. Robert, can we go to one? Can we?"

Robert smiled as he always did, "well, they don't play during the summer. But sure... When the season starts we can go to a game."

And as only a seven year old boy could do he jumped up and down in his arms, "yippee!"

Robert set Mikhail down as they walked inside, Paul asking Robert questions about the project and how it was going. Inside they sat at one of the tables drinking coffee and eating muffins that one of the women had made. The women took turns now cooking meals and snacks, not just for the residents but also for the construction workers. Who were only too happy to take a lunch break and get a good meal instead of something packed or fast food.

"Paul, this is their way of giving back to the workers. Some of these folks are learning a trade while building their own homes, and for those who can't they find other ways to help out."

Robert stood up as the pastor entered introducing him to Paul. The three men sat together and while Paul asked a lot of background questions the film crew either filmed the men or wandered around taking file footage for the story. They talked about the future plans and how they seemed to be coming together better and faster than anyone expected. Eventually Paul got to the questions he was most curious about, things they had asked Robert about before.

"Mr. Cutter if you don't mind my asking. Why here, why now? I know you have said that this is just an investment for your company, but our financial people tell me it will take years to break even. And you may never make a profit."

"That is a question I am sure you know that everyone has asked and you are right - I have answered before. The simple answer is - why not? It's true that it may take years before we break even. But this is a simple investment, and it is real estate which as I am sure you know is always tricky. But the financial people are also assuming the break even based on the old value of the property. Look around. There are new houses going up everywhere, a park is already in place and will be expanded, new businesses including a Wal-Mart are moving in, and even the apartment complex is getting a face lift. When you consider the increased value of all that all of a sudden break even does not seem such a stretch, and profitability cannot be far behind."

Paul smiled, "that all sounds reasonable, and I am sure on paper it makes sense. And I have to admit, that looking around I can see how that would be true. But, if you don't mind my saying so, seeing that little boy makes me think there might be more than just profits involved."

Robert smiled and after a moment's hesitation said, "I won't deny it. At first I saw a huge opportunity even without a real estate background. In business, any business, if you can buy a distressed underperforming business and invest enough to make it better and insert the appropriate improvements then you can make a profit. If the basis of the business itself is sound and you have the right people doing the day to day work and anything is possible.

Here it really is not much different. This was definitely a distressed piece of real estate - even before the fire - but the basic underlying business was sound and strong. The people, Paul, they are the basis for this business and I can tell you they are a strong and proud people. None of these people *want* to live in squalor and despair. They have just never been given a chance to do more, more with their lives, with *their* business.

Do you see that woman? Her name is Pearl and she was working three jobs when I first met her. And that was to keep a crumbling house around her and her son. Just so they could be dry and have a somewhat safe place to sleep and eat. But the price of that security was that Mikhail was alone most of the time and without a mother. I invested in her business and now she coordinates this entire operation here. Why? Not because of anything more than I knew that someone who could work three jobs, could easily manage one big job. All she needed was the tools. That is what will make this investment a success - investing in these strong and proud people. Not building new houses or businesses, but the people."

Before Paul could respond they heard a strong voice behind them, "now that is a speech! Robert, if I had you beside me in the senate there isn't anything we couldn't do!"

They turned and standing saw the senator. Robert laughed

"being quite candid Sir, I don't think I would make it as a politician. I don't think I have the patience or the temperament for it."

"Considering how you handled the commissioner yesterday, I think you would be a breath of fresh air."

Robert nodded and then led the three of them around the tents and throughout the neighborhood. A few of the houses were already being lived in and several others were almost finished. They walked and talked for quite a while and then sat and talked some more. Mostly it was Robert and the senator discussing what the challenges were and how he could help. Robert liked him immensely because he seemed honest and genuinely willing to help. He was sure that it was to get the voters, but Robert hoped that was not the sole reason.

He spent the rest of the afternoon working through emails, reviewing reports and analyses, and still putting the final touches to the board presentation. That was tomorrow so he was heading back to New York later in the evening. He and Shannon were planning an early dinner then she was going to ride with him back to New York. They had dinner at a wonderful little place that was more of a neighborhood gem than one of the more well-known restaurants. Then a nice quiet drive back with just the two of them in the SUV and just the driver. He had gotten Joseph to agree as that was as much privacy as could be afforded with their security even driving along the turnpike.

Slipping his arm around Shannon's shoulders and pulling her against him he couldn't wait for this whole thing to be over. With a chuckle he kissed her forehead thinking that the downside was they couldn't do this. He heard her deep sigh as she pulled her legs up into the car seat and resting his head against hers they both dozed off. It was an uneventful ride back into New York and too quickly they had arrived at her apartment.

Back in the city now, as Robert kissed her goodbye he watched security switch cars. So much for being alone. Back in the SUV he got a call from FBI agent Simmons asking if they could meet at his office. Joseph has gotten a similar call and let Robert know that they were ready to wrap up the investigation and make their arrests. Robert told Joseph that he wanted in on it, and didn't think the "mastermind" would be dangerous at all.

In the lobby of the office they found agent Simmons, two other agents, plus several New York police detectives. They followed Robert into his office where agent Simmons laid out all of the information they had found regarding the group. Throughout the discussion Robert sat back and just listened. He couldn't believe that behind all of this was nothing more than smuggling drugs and money. At the end they discussed next steps and while the FBI was initially against Robert's being involved they seemed to understand and finally agreed.

When everyone had left Robert sat quietly in his office not wanting to be disturbed. Suddenly the board meetings, hotel restorations, and even the Philadelphia project seemed less important. All of this had been for money plain and simple. Had the man come to Robert he could have helped him, instead it had come to violence - intended or not, people had died. The only benefit to this entire thing was that he had met Shannon, and now she was planning on moving away. Of course Philadelphia wasn't that far, they could figure something out.

He spent the next several hours with his thoughts and ideas about his future. If the past few months had shown him anything it was that maybe money wasn't everything. Having grown up with nothing and no one to teach him different all he ever cared about was making enough money to eat. But, obviously that had changed to focus on money being everything. He would never go hungry again, but now he realized he had been hungry all along and that money couldn't change that. Only he could.

He left his office with the security team in place, had a quiet dinner and then went to bed early. He watched baseball for a while knowing that would put him to sleep - which it did. He slept fitfully tossing and turning. His dreams mixed between a young homeless boy scrounging through the trash for a nugget of something to eat and a young man working as hard as he could to learn everything he would need.

***

The young man stood outside the building trying to fix his tie in the reflection of the gleaming metal and glass facade of the building. He had walked past this building every day for the last two weeks to see how the people working here dressed and acted. He even went to a local deli to hear how they spoke, hoping if he got the chance he could sound like them. He tried to fix his hair wishing he had an extra five dollars to get his hair cut, but this would have to do.

His suit barely fit him but it had cost him everything to buy it, and that had also meant working for the tailor without pay just to get it. His scuffed shoes didn't fit, one was too tight and the other too loose. Taking a deep breath he stepped inside and mustering all the confidence of his street life he strode up to the desk and asked to speak to the CEO - a term he picked up in the deli and then researched in the library. Security looked unsure of letting him up but he said he had an appointment he was late for.

He took the elevator to the top with a group of senior executives, or he assumed they were based on their shiny shoes, and perfectly tailored suits. As they went higher in the building he started to lose some of his confidence when an elderly man standing beside him leaned over and said, "don't worry, son". When the young man looked at him, he just winked and smiled. The doors opened and they all stepped off, except for the young man who felt like there were bricks in his shoes.

"Don't quit now, son. We haven't even started." Then the old man crooked a finger at him and he had no choice but to follow. The man led him around corners and down long dark paneled hallways. Finally they approached a set of large wooden doors and sitting in front of them at a pair of gleaming mahogany desks were two of the most beautiful and elegant women the young man had ever seen. They greeted the man and he realized that the old man was the CEO he had wanted to meet.

The old man turned to one of the women and seeing the young man hesitate smiled and said "Sheila when this young man is ready, bring him and my coffee in."

"Yes, Sir." As he passed her she said, "I would go in before business takes over and he forgets you are here."

He took a deep breath and walked into the office. He strode purposefully towards the desk where the old man stood but slowed and eventually stopped midway. He had never seen anything like this, except maybe in the movies that he had snuck into. Everything was gleaming wood, and there was two of everything. Two oversized desks, high backed leather chairs, two oversized TV screens, and a wall of glass that made up three of the rooms walls. In the one corner was a round table surrounded by high backed leather chairs and against every available space were awards, magazine covers, and photos of two men shaking hands with a lot of very important looking people.

The old man walked over to him and took his hand in his, shaking it fiercely. "My name is Martin Anderson. But I think you know that. And since we have an appointment I must have missed it in my schedule today, what can I do for you Mr..."

Quietly he started to answer "Robert... um... Cutter... sir."

The man shook his hand even harder "speak up son. It's your name say it like you mean it."

Robert looked like he was going to run or melt under the man's gaze "Robert Cutter, Sir. And I am here to learn about the business from the best."

"First rule of business... don't flatter the other person to get what you want. Unless of course you really mean it." Then there was that disarming smile that made Robert feel totally at ease. They were interrupted by the woman with coffee and bagels. Robert was starving but didn't want to eat since he had heard that was bad manners at an interview.

"Ok, son. Second rule of business. Don't just know who you are meeting and why, but know everything there is to know about him and his business. And don't just know why you are meeting but believe in it fully. It's never a question of having the meeting or being successful, the question will always be - why not.

You look like a smart kid, so here is what I am going to do - give you a chance. I have a feeling you have been working up to walking into this building let alone into this office. And if I am right you didn't really have a plan when you got in here. So next rule - always be prepared, don't let anyone surprise you. I will give you a month and if in a month I don't see what I think there is in you then we are done. Fair enough?"

Robert didn't blink and then with the wheels turning in his head he said, "no sir, that's not fair at all. It will take a month for you to get used to me. Give me three months and after that you can kick me to the curb if you want to."

The man laughed loudly and clapped Robert on the shoulder, "son that was exactly what you should have said." Then he walked around to his desk and pushed the button for one of the women. As she walked over to the desk he continued, "today we are going take the day off. Because rule number four is to always dress the part. No matter what or where the meeting is to know who you are meeting and dress accordingly." Then he turned to the woman and said "tell my driver we have some shopping to do. We will be back at 1.30. Call an executive meeting for 2.30 so my new protégé can meet the team."

With that the man took his arm and led him out of the office down the elevator and into a waiting Mercedes Benz. They spent the next several hours shopping after a proper breakfast - the first Robert had had in ages. Throughout the whole morning Martin gave Robert the background on his executive team. And he made sure that Robert remembered their names, and what their jobs were. It was a lot to take in for him, but he found that if he focused he could remember it all clearly. They also talked about business and some of Martin's rules, there weren't a lot of them but they were important.

The next time Robert strode through the front doors of the building he felt stronger and stood straighter than he ever had before. His ambition alone was not going to be enough. He knew that now and he was determined to learn everything he could from Martin in the next three months. Just that quickly he wanted this man to be proud of him, he had taken a risk on Robert and he wanted to pay him back.

Robert always wondered about the second desk, but didn't want to be rude and ask. They found that a laptop and a portfolio and pens had been dropped off for him. Robert learned that he had been assigned a small office down the hall, but Martin already told him he would spend most of his days with him. When the executives assembled for the meeting they were surprised to see Robert there, but Robert shined and knew all of them. He made the old man proud by not only remembering their names, but also their exact jobs and responsibilities in the company.

That day that Robert went back to his rented room and sat on the edge of the bed looking around as if seeing it for the first time. In the small closet in his room hung the new suits Martin had bought for him, alongside the ten dress shirts. In the bottom of the closet were several pairs of new shoes and in his dresser he now had plenty of socks and underwear, all of which not only fit him, but also matched. This morning when he had left to go to see the old man, he had hoped not to get thrown out. Now he had all of this and for the first time - someone who actually believed in him. And as he sat there he was totally focused on proving him right.

Starting the next morning and for the next three months Robert worked from dawn until well past midnight. He was too intent on learning as much as possible to worry about anything else. And unlike any of the other people he met he didn't have a wife or a family. Truth be told he had no idea if he ever had a family, but it didn't matter to him. What mattered to him was the old man and making him proud.

The three months passed quickly, more quickly than Robert would have liked since he felt like he needed to learn so much more. All he had was the hope that he had done well for Martin and that he would keep him around. As usual he walked into his small office just as the sun was beginning to rise. When he opened the door he was surprised to see a suit bag hanging from the back of the door. Attached was a note that simply read "our three months are over and this is your last lesson."

Robert carefully opened the suit bag wondering what exquisite suit Martin had bought. Instead he saw his own suit from that first day hanging carefully on a hanger. With it were the shirt, tie, shoes, and even the underwear. Robert stared at it for several moments before he understood Martin's lesson to him. He realized that Martin must have dropped it off this morning, so he walked down to his office. He found the door slightly ajar and stepped inside.

He found Martin sitting not at his desk, but at the other desk. At first he thought Martin was resting until he noticed something wrong with the angle. He ran over and tried to lift him into a sitting position and that is when he saw the lifeless eyes staring back at him. Robert didn't know what to do and after a moment he grabbed the phone and dialed 911. Even while he told the police what happened he could feel the warm tears slide down his cheeks.

The police came. The receptionists came. The executives came. Robert never saw any of it. All he saw were the lifeless eyes of the second person in his life to trust him. People stopped by his office but all he could do was sit there and stare at the old suit. No one asked about it, and even if they did he wouldn't have known how to answer them. The police confirmed that Martin had died of a massive heart attack and it was likely that he never knew what hit him.

Robert finally went back to his small room not knowing what to do the next day. At 6am he got a call from Sheila, Martin's old secretary. The executive team was holding a meeting and they wanted Robert to be there. He was sure they were going to toss him out, since he was Martin's experiment not theirs. When he entered the main conference room they were all their waiting for him and each one walked over and shook his hand. After a moment of respectful silence the senior lawyer started the meeting. They all took a moment to tell their favorite memory about Martin, but Robert heard none of it. When it came to his turn he just nodded, so they moved on. When everyone had said their piece, Robert was surprised to hear that a letter had been left for him. He started to read it out loud, but then had to stop and handed it back to the lawyer.

> "Dear Robert,
>
> The past three months have reminded me of why I got into this business. And despite what some people think I am hoping you know

better. It was not for the money at all. You never asked me, but I know you were curious.

The second desk - it belonged to my younger brother Adam who worked by my side for more than thirty years. Then one morning he was gone. The good Lord had taken him from me too soon and I never had the chance to tell him how much I loved him and loved working with him. I see a lot of him in you. I see the same hunger to learn, to grow, to build something special.

Never lose that Son, never forget who you really are. If you are reading this letter then I will assume I have gone. Don't be sad, Son. My wife, God rest her soul passed away twenty years ago this month. She has waited a long time for me, and I am finally ready to join her.

I know you think I call you Son because I am an old man. But, I want you to know that it is more than that. I have two children that you may meet in the coming weeks. My daughter lives in California with her third husband and three children. I see them in the Christmas cards they send me. I have always been too busy to go and visit, and I suppose they too have been too busy. I always thought there would be a tomorrow. I also have a son and he bears my name - Martin Jr. has a job, a title, and a salary at the company. But since you have never met him I am sure you can guess what that means. I always wished that my son was... well, more like you. So when you came along it was perfectly normal for me to call you Son.

I want you to know that both my brother and I will be watching over you and if there is a way for me to let you know that, I guess only you will know. Don't be sad for me either, I will miss you more than you may know. I am proud of the man you have become in a short three months, but I am even more proud of the man I know you will become in the coming years. Thank you for the past three months, Son, they have meant a lifetime to me."

The room was silent for several moments. The senior lawyer carefully folded the letter and placed it back in the envelope and put it down in front of Robert. One by one the executives all left the room passing Robert and placing a hand on their shoulder as they went out. They closed the office that day, and Martin's passing was felt by all. The stock exchange lowered flags all over to half-mast and there was a moment of silence in his honor.

The rest of the week went by in a blur and Robert knew that he was just moving through the paces. Friday came and went and at the end of the day he was ready to go home. When he was leaving the building the security guard at the elevator stopped him and said, "Mr. Anderson was a good man. I will miss him."

Robert smiled for the first time all week and then said, "yes, he was the best!" He stood there for several moments, walked out into the street then turned back towards the building. The glass and steel shining as it did on that first day and when Robert saw his reflection he knew he had been changed. Forever.

Chapter 16

Robert woke early and after a hot shower and a shave he got dressed and left the hotel. Robert knew that when they got to the office the staff would already be hard at work. But, this morning he wasn't going to the office - at least not directly. Instead they walked around the corner and up a short block to a small coffee shop. Joseph had already installed two bodyguards who were waiting outside and stopping people from going in. Most people would have just assumed it was for security, although there was no one inside the shop yet.

Had any of the shop's regulars looked in they would have known something was different. Of the two baristas behind the counter, one was the owner as usual. The other barista was not his business partner, rather it was agent Simmons trying to figure out how all of the machines worked. Had they been inside the store they also would have heard him say, "this is why beat cops drink straight coffee black!"

During the night they had installed several high resolution cameras and many more mini microphones so that not one word of the discussion would be missed. They had all of the evidence they would honestly need, but Robert insisted on getting a confession from him as well. There were two other agents in the coffee shop's back room and several undercover police officers were arranged up and down the street.

Robert walked down the street, Joseph beside him and a bodyguard both in front and behind him. As they approached the coffee shop a black Cadillac limousine pulled up and the man they were meeting with stepped out of the back seat. He barely waited for the car to stop before he had stepped out and squeezed between two trucks parked at the curb. Even Robert was impressed with the outfit he was wearing, and given the man's financial situation was surprised he could still afford them. But, Robert supposed he was wearing it for the board meeting later in the day.

He waited for Robert at the door, which he couldn't have gone through since the bodyguards were not moving. As Robert approached he turned to face him and stuck out a hand to shake. Robert shook his hand and thanked him for meeting him early. Then they stepped inside the shop and ordered coffee and a couple of chocolate croissants. They sat at one of the small tables, well actually the only table since the only other seats were counters.

Once the coffee and croissants were brought over Robert nodded and the two baristas left the front of the store.

"Boy, when you want a private meeting you really get it private."

"Martin, I felt that perhaps our discussion should be as private as possible. And since this store is small enough I can easily control it. To be honest, I like it so much I might just buy it."

The man laughed, "well, let me know if you do because I will be your first investor!"

Robert hesitated, a troubled look crossing his eyes before he spoke again. "Martin, I think we need to talk. You and I both know that you can barely afford a cup of coffee in this store." He held up his hand when Martin started to protest. "I don't quite understand how you don't have any money left, after all you get a check just like all of my other clients every month. In fact, because of your father, your shares are larger than everyone else's. If you were having money problems why didn't you come to see me? I need to understand this, and please don't tell me I wouldn't understand."

"Robert, I don't know where this is coming from. Look at me. Do I look like I am hurting for cash? I think not, and even if I were, you definitely wouldn't understand. And thanks to *my father* you would be the last person I would come to. That old man gave *you* everything on a silver platter. *Everything!* It should have been ME! Instead that senile old man gave it all to you, he probably thought you were his other son."

Robert shook his head. "Martin, there was nothing wrong with your father. Except perhaps that he always saw the best in you, no matter what. Do you know the funniest part of that? It's that he did want you to take his job at the firm. But apparently when the board called you the response was 'not interested'. Really Martin? Your father and uncle spent their lives building a hugely profitable business and when it came time for you take the mantle your response was 'not interested'!

Let me tell you something else, Martin, for the past fifteen years I have kept you on. Not because I promised him, but because I felt that it was the right thing to do. And how do you repay me? By using inside information against me, and then causing all kinds of disruption and violence. You put innocent people at risk! Why? Because you were too stupid to realize that all of your life *other* people have taken care of you!"

Martin hesitated and realized he had lost any chance at arguing. "Robert you really don't have a clue do you? That old man gave me a title, but never a real job. Never an opportunity to make a name for myself. Instead he gave that to you. For three months all I ever heard about was YOU! It was sickening! The only reason I was not interested was because you were there.

But the truth is that I never planned for any of this. A few years ago I got into some trouble gambling and no matter how much I tried it just kept getting worse. Finally I got approached by an associate of the people I owe money too. They made me an offer - all I had to do was give them access to information and the slate would be cleaned. Unfortunately, while it cleaned the slate there was always another game to bet on."

Robert shook his head. "Martin, I am going to introduce you to FBI agent Simmons who is going to read you your rights, then arrest your dumb ass, then you are going to tell him everything you know. And if at any point you decide not to cooperate I will have your ass in jail so fast you won't have a chance to rethink anything. Is that clear?"

Robert then stood up and without a word turned and walked out of the store. The two bodyguards outside stayed there. As he stepped to the curb Joseph stepped up beside him and before either could take a step the SUV pulled up. They both climbed inside and as the SUV pulled away Robert sat and looked out the window. He couldn't believe some of the things that Martin had said. He wondered if it was true that he had been that insensitive to Martin's needs. Or if the old man really never gave his son the chance he wanted.

Upstairs in his office, Robert sat on the couch drinking a cup of coffee. He knew he only had another hour or so before the board members started to arrive. He looked around the room, looked at what he now had and thought about his accomplishments. The accomplishments showed in the *stuff* he had acquired over the years. He remembered Martin's office with all of the awards and the photos of famous people on the walls. Robert had none of that, no framed covers of Time or Newsweek, no framed photos of him with the Mayor, Governor, or Senators. Just stuff.

He had never wanted the fame that went with the success, but to be honest he had wanted the success which meant the money.

He had grown up with nothing and once he was old enough to understand he became determined to never go hungry again. If that was the definition of success then he had certainly succeeded. But today he knew that the very idea of success had changed, and having nice things and plenty of money just wasn't enough.

He got up and went over to his desk spending the next hour reviewing emails and daily reports and then spending a last few moments with the morning's board presentation. This time more than any other, everything had to be perfect. He had even gotten some last minute updates that he would need should questions come up. He knew that the board would expect him to be at the top of his game and that was where he had to be.

The board members started to arrive and were being ushered into the conference room. Jennifer had brought in a caterer in who had set up a breakfast of fresh fruit, bagels, muffins, coffee, and tea. The board mingled and chatted quietly since several of them only saw each other at these meetings. Robert knew that his executive team would already be in there as well mingling with the members. Some would stay for the meeting as they held positions on the board, primarily Frank and Lowell, but a couple of others stayed in the background.

Robert entered the room through his private door and for a moment there was a lull in the different conversations and then it picked back up. As he made his way over to the coffee service he shook hands with each of the board members. He spent several minutes with each member, making idle chit chat about their families and vacations taken. Robert had always seen this as a part of his job but now he saw it as an opportunity to learn more about the members. He didn't want another "Martin" situation.

After a bit more socializing they closed the doors and the members took their seats. They had some official formal issues to deal with and Robert always let Lowell handle these things. This took about thirty minutes and during this time Robert collected his thoughts. He looked around the table at the eight men and the three women seeing pillars of industry, fellow executives, lawyers, and accountants. Or at least they had been, several of them were now professional board members. But Robert trusted their experiences, insight, and varied knowledge. They all brought something to this table, which was why Robert had originally selected them as members.

Someone asked about Martin and Robert just shook his head. They could ask questions, but they had all seen that look and it meant he would have no answers. When Lowell was finished they spent the next thirty minutes reviewing the past quarter's financial results of the firm. Robert had to admit that they had done incredibly well over the past few months and the smiles around the table were further proof of that. But, Robert also knew that while the past results were important to this group, the future held just as much importance. Everyone in this business knew that you were only as good as your last financial report.

They took a short break to refresh the coffee and for bathroom breaks. Robert took a few minutes to go into his office and private bathroom. As he stepped out he found Joseph waiting for him. He walked over to him put a hand on his shoulder and said, "Robert, we have known each other a long time. I believe in you."

Robert nodded his thanks and wondered about Joseph. It seemed like Joseph always knew what he was thinking. He headed back into the conference room and was pleased to see the presentation was ready to go. The other members returned to the room, the lights were dimmed and Robert began his presentation. He spent the next thirty minutes going through the first half of it. This part focused on the existing projects and how he saw them going forward. It was the second half that he knew was going to be a challenge.

Robert started off by going through where they were with the Bellagio and what the plans were. They went through some of the renderings for the renovations and the board asked a lot of questions. Some seemed to be more interested in colors and design choices then what it would mean financially. But Robert knew it was not out of disinterest, but more because they trusted him on the financial side. Plus, he knew they would want to know everything possible about the project.

One of the members was managing partner of a highly profitable interior design firm, and they had been given the project. Because of this he was able to answer some of the more specific questions and the overall design plans. Another of the board members was also on the board of the Hilton Hotels, but he had to step out during this discussion. They had to be very careful about what information was shared to avoid any potential question of impropriety.

They took another short break after that part of the discussion which was fine since Robert knew the members wanted to spend a lot more time discussing the Philadelphia project. As Robert was sitting quietly with a fresh cup of coffee his phone buzzed and he glanced down seeing it was a text. Normally he would not be bothered with his phone but smiled when he saw it was from Shannon. It read, "hi darling, I know you have your board meeting today and wanted you to know I was thinking of you."

He was about to respond when everyone came back into the conference room and took their seats at the table and they picked up the presentation. Although Robert had used primarily all of his own money, he had leveraged quite a bit of his assets which meant that if it went bad the banks could move in and take control of the company. He was betting a lot more than just money on this project and everyone knew it.

He took his time going through the project background and

the financials, spending the next hour going through it at a more detailed level than on any other project. He spoke with the normal confidence and assurance that he always did, and laid things out in the most unemotional way possible. He understood that this was more about the financials than it was about emotions. So that is what he gave them - the financials.

When he was finished with the formal presentation everyone sat quietly while he took a drink of water. The questions started off with a lot of the same questions that had been asked by reporters since the project had started. One of the members even mentioned his comments to the reporter from the day before, and Robert confirmed again what he had said. Everyone was very congenial during this question and answer time and Robert noticed that only one member had not asked any questions or made any comments throughout the discussion.

Finally he turned to the man and said, "James, something on your mind?"

The man in question was a famous lawyer whose firm represented companies all over the world. He was well known throughout the business world as a legal genius with a sharp mind. Someone generally able to see beyond what the normal business person saw. More than once Robert had spoken with him privately prior to a deal just to get his opinion. Having him on the board had given the company a huge amount of credibility and Robert knew it was one of the reasons for his success in gaining new investors.

"First, Robert, tell us why Martin is not here today. He has never missed a meeting, so I honestly doubt something came up."

Robert hesitated then said, "Martin found himself in some trouble, and unfortunately did not come to me but decided to try and resolve things himself. It didn't work out and his problems have been compounded exponentially. In fact, I was going to ask this at the end of the meeting, but we should start to consider a replacement as I do not think that Martin will be returning."

James smiled, "very delicately and diplomatically put, Robert. You have done an excellent job in selling us on the project and I firmly believe that it has the potential to be an incredible boost for the company. Both financial and politically, which in this environment is not a bad thing." He paused briefly as if weighing his next words, but anyone who knew him knew that he had planned for this question carefully. "What is your exit strategy for this project, because we all know that the exit strategy is just as important as the entry strategy?"

Robert sat back in his chair and smiled, it was the one question no one had asked him since the beginning. "James, you really are one step ahead of everyone else. My exit strategy is a simple one - build the neighborhood to its potential and then sell the mortgages, loans, and remaining properties at a nice profit to the mortgage banks. Or roll it up into a mortgage backed package and sell it on the open market. Either way, my exit strategy is the same... make sure that these people are settled and secure before doing anything that might ruin their chances.

I am going to tell you the same thing I have said over and over again. These are some of the strongest and proudest people I have ever met. They weren't born with wealth and most of them will never even have a chance to earn a small portion of the wealth that we all have. But they have something that a lot of people do not have - heart and desire. There are a lot of people who go to work every day with the same purpose - to get a check. These people go to multiple jobs every day with a different purpose. They go to live, to stay alive, and to have the mere basics in life.

Let me ask you a question, James. If I spent ten or a hundred times as much money to buy a struggling football team would you expect the team to win the Super Bowl the following year? No, Sir you would not, you would expect me to spend even more money and build up the team to at least give them a chance to win the Super Bowl. Not the first year and maybe not even the second year, but you would be thrilled if they showed promise and had at least a winning season. Right?"

"Robert that would be a good analogy except that a football team has the ability to make money even when they are losing. And often with a new owner the team will automatically gain in value. But you and I both know that this is a very different situation. So, please tell me that you bet your own fortune and the potential for this company on more than a football analogy?"

Robert shook his head. "James, the value of the neighborhood is already increasing every day. Where before there were closed stores and no one would even bother consider opening a new one, there is now a long line of companies looking to open new businesses. There are franchise organizations offering special financing to prospective owners. There is a Wal-Mart already in the process of being built and the hiring has already started.

I have even had an offer from a real estate management company to buy out the apartment complex with the understanding that the renovations would still be done. They explicitly said they understand how integral that is to the success of the neighborhood. They aren't offering enough money, so I told them to go back and rethink their offer, I fully expect a second offer within the next week, and that will be an offer this board will be asked to weigh in on."

James nodded his head then said, "so, what is *your* exit strategy?"

Robert smiled again and spoke honestly "I don't have one yet. Except to say that I have a fantastic group of executives working with me every day. And an even more fantastic group of people who work for the company making us all successful. I couldn't have done half of what we have accomplished without all of these people. But, you don't really have to worry. I am not going anywhere and if I do, I will simply open a second office to work out of."

The room was quiet since no one had expected a lot of what had been said. After several moments James stood up and extended his hand. "Robert, I won't speak for anyone else at the table. But, I am damn glad to hear it. When no one else saw the sliver of hope or potential, you did. Martin Senior would have been proud of you, and I personally am damn proud to call you an associate and a peer."

As they shook hands the rest of the members stood up and all moved forward to shake his hand as well. Someone moved to the door opening it and the caterer brought in lunch. As it was set up various members came over and chatted with Robert. The meeting was over and they could move on to the social part. He saw Joseph standing in the doorway and he made his way over. He handed him a slip of paper and on it was written a note from Agent Simmons.

> *Mr. Cutter,*
>
> *We have what we need from Mr. Anderson and will be moving on the rest of the people involved. Thank you for your help today. I will ask you to keep this confidential until all arrests have been made. We will need a final statement from you, Sir, but I believe you can finally rest a little bit easier.*

Robert breathed a huge sigh of relief and placed his hand on Joseph's shoulder. Then he folded the note carefully and put it in his jacket pocket. Turning back to the room he felt as if a huge weight had been lifted from his shoulders and that he could breathe again. He hoped the rest of the arrests would go quickly so he could get back to a more normal life. He shook his head trying to remember what exactly that was, since it had been so long since he had driven himself anywhere let alone gone without security.

Lunch was a much more relaxed experience than the rest of the meeting had been and it was a full hour before all of the board members had left. Robert went into his office and walked over to bar where he poured himself a tall scotch, then sat down on the couch and closed his eyes for a few moments. Before he had a chance to take a drink his cell phone buzzed and looking at it he smiled. The text from Shannon said that she would be finished with her shift early if he wanted to catch some dinner.

For the first time in many months he closed his eyes and leaning his head back felt himself truly and completely relax. Business was one thing, and it was certainly loaded with stress, but nothing that he had not grown accustomed to over the years. Everything else had been something totally new and now that it was almost over he could focus on the good things. And holding his phone in his hand he knew this was one of better things life was offering him. And then just as quickly, as he felt happier than ever before, it all slipped away.

The first gun shot was loud, louder than anything he had ever heard before. Robert jumped up off the couch and started for the door. No sooner had he taken two steps did the door burst open. Two of the bodyguards entered and taking his arms led him over to his desk. They sat him down and then rolled the chair to the corner, the desk between the door and Robert. One of the men knelt in front of Robert placing himself between Robert and the door.

The second guard knelt in front of the desk, both men had their weapons drawn and pointed at the door. Robert didn't have to think or ask, he already knew they would not go down without a fight. As Robert made himself small in the chair he heard more gunshots, two distinctly different weapons were being used. As if reading his mind the man in front moved slightly to one side and held up two fingers.

The gunshots got closer and Robert realized one was more of a blast sound than a shot. Suddenly he heard shouting that he recognized coming from the far end of the hall. Then more shouting coming from the conference room hallway. The blasts and shots came more frequent and now there was a lot more shooting. It seemed to come from all around the area outside of his office and Robert hoped that people, his people, had found places to stay out of the way.

There was more shouting and more gunfire, then a blast hit his office doors. They shook inward on their hinges, but held. The second blast hit the doors and this time one of them fell inward hanging awkwardly off its broken hinges. As the gunman burst through the door Robert could hear gunshots on the other side of the door, and he realized there had to be more than two gunmen. But, before he could pull the trigger on the shotgun both guards opened fire and the man went down in a heap.

Out in the hallway there were still more gunshots, then it all went quiet. Almost too quiet. Neither guard moved nor flinched, not a muscle twitched. Then they heard a voice call out "clear" and one of the guards responded "clear". The response was a distinct "FBI stand down." Robert started to rise up, but the guard put a hand against his chest and held him in the chair in the corner. He didn't turn and look, but kept his eyes and his gun firmly pointed at the doorway.

The badge came first followed by agent Simmons' face. "Stand down gentlemen, FBI." He repeated again and then slowly entered showing his empty hands. Both guards immediately lowered their weapons and stood up. Robert followed their lead and only then did he stand up as well. "Mr. Cutter, I apologize we didn't get here any sooner. Fortunately, the shooters were not very good and your security was better."

Robert immediately left his office and found Joseph and Jennifer standing off to the side. Jennifer hiding behind Joseph, who was standing in a doorway. First Robert saw the gun in his hand then he noticed the blood dripping off his hand. "It's nothing Robert, just a little flesh wound. We got lucky here."

Slowly, people started to come out of offices as the EMTs came down the hall. They stopped at each doorway to make sure there were no injuries, and amazingly Joseph was indeed the only person injured. The EMTs were followed by police and several more FBI agents including their hostage rescue unit. Police went to each office and interviewed each person one at a time. The coroner and CSI teams arrived to do their jobs and take the bodies away.

Robert, Agent Simmons, a patched up Joseph, and the two body guards sat in the conference room. Agent Simmons explained that when they arrested the first group someone got word out to this group of thugs. These were the people who had actually been responsible for everything that had happened over the past six months because of the intelligence from Anderson. They had been given instructions to finally end it all, which meant killing Robert.

The bad news was that the ring leader had actually managed to get away. It had been because of the security that Joseph had installed that the gunmen were slowed down enough to allow the FBI time to arrive. Amazingly, despite the overwhelming force they faced they kept going with one purpose. The good news was that one of the men had a cell phone pre-programmed with the ring leader's number. They had already sent a text that the job was done. The FBI had also published a report saying there were many dead including Robert. It was only a matter of time before the receiving phone was traced and they would have him.

There was suddenly a commotion out in the hall and Shannon

burst into the room. She was flushed and breathless and there were tears in her eyes. Jennifer was right behind her and had obviously brought her back. Robert jumped up and took her into his arms holding her tight. He held her as she cried into his shoulder and kissed her forehead whispering to her. Finally she had calmed down enough and Robert moved to pull over a chair, when they all got an even bigger surprise.

"Sam... What are you doing here?"

"Shannon?" The two stared at each other and then hugged briefly. "I have been working on Mr. Cutter's case for months. I had no idea you knew each other!"

Shannon and Robert looked at each and Robert took her hand. "I take it you two know each other Shannon?"

She laughed "Sam is my brother Robert!"

Robert stared at the two of them then started to laugh. Simmons finished telling Robert what they had learned that day and despite everything they knew there were still some holes. The entire time Shannon sat by Robert's side holding onto his hand like she would never let go. At one point she interrupted to say "I heard about the shooting here and had to come right over."

Simmons shook his head and laughed, "so much for being the level headed one in the family!"

By the time they finished it was dusk outside and with the bodyguards still in place they all climbed into the SUV and went for dinner. They went back to that small Italian restaurant Robert and Shannon had gone to, but this time they only had their table. Simmons and Shannon caught up on family stuff throughout dinner and well into a second cup of coffee.

When they were getting ready to leave Agent Simmons got a call. He quickly took it outside and Robert could see him talking through the windows. When they came outside he explained that the phone had been off this whole time, but it had just been activated. The phone was in Las Vegas and a team of agents had just been sent to watch him. Simmons was getting on a plane and flying out immediately to personally make the arrest. He was not going to let the man get away again.

As he turned to get in a waiting sedan Shannon gave him a kiss on the cheek "I won't say it, Sam." He nodded and then was gone. She and Robert got into the SUV and headed over to her apartment. This time a bodyguard checked the place first before they could go inside. He stayed in place in the living room, another was stationed at the back of the brownstone and two more were sitting in the SUV. Robert and Shannon went upstairs to bed and eventually fell asleep.

Robert woke the next morning to the smell of amazing coffee. He rolled over and felt the empty spot in the bed, got up and went downstairs. He found Shannon talking to the bodyguard, both of them holding coffee cups. She poured a cup and handed it to Robert, who looked surprised to realize it was his own blend. He was about to ask when Joseph stepped in from the back patio, smiling and holding his own cup.

"Joseph, I would like to get back to the office as quickly as possible. I know I told everyone to work from home for the next couple of days, but I want to get the office back up and running."

He kissed Shannon on the cheek as he took the cup from her. "I could get used to this."

She laughed and said, "don't get too used to it, Mr. Cutter. Remember I work also."

"Indeed. Joseph give me fifteen minutes and then I will be ready to go."

With a girlish giggle she slipped her arm into Robert's and the said, "maybe thirty minutes".

Robert laughed as they went upstairs together, but true to his word he was dressed and back downstairs in just under thirty minutes. They loaded into the SUVs and rode over to the office, Robert wondering if this would be the last day for the security. They rode the elevator in silence and when the doors opened to his office lobby he got another surprise.

There were painters and workmen already in place patching holes and repairing damaged desks, windows, and walls. All of the staff was already in the office, and if not working at their desks then they were straightening up. Jennifer was walking around with a clipboard in hand and was making a list of replacement items. She smiled when she saw Robert and followed him back to his office. Somehow his doors had already been removed and the main reception area was being worked on by several people. This was where the bulk of the shooting had taken place and it was clearly where they had started.

Robert looked at Joseph who just shrugged, so he turned to Jennifer. She smiled and said, "well, someone had to do it."

He grinned and went into his office and walked behind his desk. The news was carrying the story as a top story, but had no real explanation. Jennifer followed a minute later with a fresh cup of coffee and as he got to work he saw the two bodyguards standing in front of his door.

He spent the next several hours going through his emails which seemed to pile up even as he read them. There were still reports to review, plans to go over with designers, and media people to speak to. Several of the people he worked with on projects outside of the company were trying to reach him to make sure everything was ok. Just like everyone else who had come back to work today, the job went on. He had a business to run and there were a lot of people relying on him to make sure it ran well.

He tried to focus on work but was still waiting to hear from Agent Simmons. He still couldn't quite think of him as Shannon's brother and hoped the rest of her family was just as nice. He would have to make it a point to meet them all. Perhaps when this mess was over he could invite them to his shore house for a party. Heavens knew he needed a reason to smile, and a party would always be fun. Maybe make it a picnic in the park and invite the entire company.

Towards the end of the day Robert called the entire staff into a meeting. He spoke openly about everything they had learned and what had happened and been happening. He held nothing back and explained about Martin and some of his problems. The purpose was not to broadcast the dirty laundry, but to explain and hope that would help make people feel a little safer. The other reason for the meeting was that Robert wanted a chance to see the faces of his employees and know that there was no one else involved.

The FBI had several agents placed around the room keeping an eye on the staff. He kept talking, watching the agents until he saw one nod. Then he found a way to end the meeting. They spent time on questions and there were a lot of them. Robert did his best to answer them, but some were still considered confidential because the case was still active. The meeting ended and Robert stood shaking hands with each person, assuring them they would do their best to make sure this didn't happen again.

It was another couple of hours of working before Robert's office phone rang. As it did Joseph walked in and nodded. Robert hit the speaker button as Joseph reached the desk.

"Mr. Cutter, this is Agent Simmons. I wanted to let you know that we have arrested him. Once we told him what had happened in the office and about all of the arrests made there he seemed to recognize it was over. And it is."

"That is excellent news, Agent Simmons. I appreciate you making the call."

"No problem, Sir, and my agents told me that based on what

they saw at your office they think that there are no other moles. But, it is possible that Anderson had someone helping him so I would suggest keeping an eye on things a bit longer. Nothing dangerous, just information I am sure."

"This is Joseph, Agent Simmons. Thank you, we have already some things in place and are starting to look through the history to find the inside man. Did you find out what the end game was?"

"Actually we did. I can't quite get into the details yet, but he was using the company's airplanes for smuggling "things". We think it was drugs, weapons, and even people but we are not sure to what extent or who his customers were. Yet. But we don't think he was actually working for anyone specific. Just offering services to whoever can pay for it."

"Thank you, Agent Simmons. We have been going through the financials and FAA documentation and didn't find a thing. But, we have people going through the service information. If there is anything that is where it will be and when we find it I will get it over to you."

"Thank you, Mr. Cutter. On behalf of the FBI I appreciate all of your support and patience."

"It was my pleasure, Sir. If there is anything more you need from me or anyone here at the company please let me know. And personally, Agent Simmons, the next time you are in town let me know... We can have dinner, I would like to get to know you better."

"Will do Mr. Cutter. Take care, sir." And just like that the line went dead.

Robert sat quietly for a few moments then looked at Joseph and smiled. He then stood up and at first shook hands with Joseph, but before Joseph could react he pulled him into a hug and whispered "thanks". Then just as quickly he let him go and headed over to the bar. He poured himself a drink and a second one for Joseph. They toasted the end of this problem and Robert hoped that it truly was over.

Chapter 17

Over the next couple of weeks things gradually returned to normal. Work was just as busy as usual, but Robert felt that he could give it his full focus now. He knew that people wondered what would happen now that it was over, and if he would go back to the way he had been before? But Robert knew that he could never really go back to the way he was. Somewhere along the way he had lost himself, gotten so focused on making the next million that he forgot where he had come from.

He had no plans to change anything and just wanted to focus on getting back to normal. Just to be safe he and Joseph had decided to keep the security for a couple of weeks. He and Shannon had found more time to go out for dinners and spend time together. But no matter how hard they tried they were both back to working hard and their nights together grew shorter and fewer. Robert had not changed how he felt for her, and he hoped she still felt the same.

They had plans to spend the weekend together because on Monday he was heading to Philadelphia for a week, and then Las Vegas for a week. Robert planned a romantic dinner at Asiate at the top of the Mandarin Oriental on Columbus Circle and then perhaps a leisurely walk back to the hotel. Shannon had already arranged her schedule so she was going to stay with him. He had also scheduled a morning visit to the spa, and then an afternoon tea. The Plaza was well known for the formal tea and he knew that she was looking forward to it. Possibly even more than the spa itself.

And so now Robert found himself for the first time in life sitting in his office at 3pm in the afternoon daydreaming. He was sitting at his desk, but he was facing the wall of windows and looking at the city beneath him. He realized that he was not going to get any more work done, so he finally stood up and rang for Jennifer. She was shocked when he said he was leaving for the weekend. But all the same she packed his briefcase for him as she always did, knowing that with his iPad in hand he was never that far from work.

As he was packing up, Lowell stuck his head in the doorway "Robert, may I have a moment?" Robert knew that it would be easier to deal with now, so he nodded. Jennifer left the office, quietly closing the door behind her. Robert and Lowell sat down on the couch and Lowell began.

"Robert, we have been together for a long time now. And it has been the most rewarding years in my career - both professionally and financially. But... I think I am ready for more. I know there was a lot going on, and honestly I have waited until all of this blew over."

Robert looked at him and then nodded. "I know that the past few months have been a challenge and that we haven't always seen eye to eye at times. I can't tell you how much it has meant to me knowing that you have been beside me over the years. Knowing I can count on you for your honesty and analysis has given me the ability to stretch myself and the company further. I have been thinking about changing things also and you are going to be a huge part of that."

"Thank you for that, Robert. I won't lie to you, the past few months have been very difficult for me because I haven't felt like you and I have been on the same page at times. As I am sure you know I get approached all of the time with opportunities, but none of them have even come close to anything I would consider. That being said, there is one position that I would like you to consider. As part of the Vegas project we have always said that we would need new leadership. I think that I can fill that role nicely. Before you say it, I know that I don't have hotel or casino operational experience. But, as you have shown me - with the right people you can accomplish anything."

Robert laughed, "great, so then you are going to use my own words to prove it would be ok for you to leave? That's not really fair. Seriously, I think you would be incredibly good in that role and probably the only reason I haven't considered it was because it means I have to lose you. But, then again - we do own the hotel. Obviously, the board will be doing the executive search but I will back you if this is what you really want. But, I am being a little selfish because then I know you won't really be leaving me and that there is an executive in place I can truly trust."

"Robert, thank you for understanding. And I appreciate your trust in me. And so you know, even if I were thinking of truly leaving I already have a few people that could step up and take my role here." He stood up and Robert did as well, then the two men shook hands. After he left the office, Jennifer came back in to finish putting his things together. She was surprised to find Robert at the bar pouring himself a scotch.

"Everything ok, sir?"

"Couldn't be better Jennifer. Well, except perhaps if you were to call me Robert!"

"Yes, sir. Your laptop and files are packed up so you are ready to go. I also let Joseph know and he said he has the car ready for you."

Robert thanked her and then wondered how long he would need

to have "a car" waiting for him. Although, as much as he enjoyed driving he had to admit there was something very nice about not having to deal with traffic. Maybe he could keep one of the SUVs and bodyguards for a driver. As he turned to leave, briefcase in hand he was stopped by a news broadcast. They were showing a live broadcast of the FBI marching the ring leader that had been after him all of these months into court. Apparently he was going to be booked immediately and spend at least the weekend in jail.

Robert found himself looking at the screen intently since this was the first time he had seen the man. He looked terrible - his face drawn and tired, hadn't shaved in several days, his eyes were blood shot and darting all around. He looked like he had been hiding from more than just the FBI. The man was surrounded by FBI agents and wore a bullet proof vest. Robert wondered what the concern was when a gun shot rang out, and as if in slow motion Robert watched as a bullet ripped through the man.

As Robert stared the man crumpled to the ground already looking dead before collapsing. But what also caught his eye was the FBI agent in front of him who also went down. Then all hell broke loose with reporters and other people running everywhere. The FBI agents were all crouching around guns drawn and pointed upward and looking around. No one knew what was going on, but it couldn't have been good.

Without Robert realizing it, Joseph had walked in and stood beside him. He placed his hand on Robert's shoulder and said, "now it is over." For a brief moment Robert looked over at him and wondered if he had something to do with it. But he was sure that was not possible. As if the entire universe knew what Robert was thinking, his private line rang. Still staring at the TV he walked over to his desk and picked up the phone without looking at the caller ID.

"Robert, I am sorry we did not learn of this sooner. You will no longer be troubled by this."

And just that quickly the phone went dead. But Robert would always recognize the quiet, subdued voice of the elder Anthony Salvatori. Still holding the phone in his hand he looked at Joseph who simply nodded to him. Maybe he did know more about this than Robert thought possible. As Robert looked back at the TV he was shocked to see that the FBI agent that had gone down was now sitting up. Even on TV he could see that the man was white as a ghost and a little shaken.

He could also see that it was Agent Simmons. Still holding the phone he quickly called Shannon. He didn't want just anyone to tell her. He had to smile even though she wasn't answering because he watched on TV as Simmons reached for his own cell phone and answered. The cameras kept the dead body out of the shot, but stayed focused on all of the FBI agents. The EMTs arrived, checked on the dead man and then moved to Agent Simmons.

The cameras finally switched back to the newsroom as they were helping Simmons onto a stretcher. His phone rang and he answered it again without looking. He listened briefly then said that he understood, and hung up this time putting the phone back down on its cradle. He looked at Joseph again who simply nodded and walked out, presumably to get Jennifer to cancel his weekend plans.

Robert was torn between being disappointed and also happy that agent Simmons was going to be ok. He buzzed Jennifer and told her he didn't want to be disturbed and he would let Joseph know when he was ready to go home. He had been alone for all of his life, but now he really what it felt like to be lonely. As he sat and stared out the window he didn't like it and knew that something would have to change.

He sat there a bit longer as he contemplated where life had taken him recently. He had to smile thinking about where he had been a year ago - focused on making his next million, dating the next beautiful woman, and buying the next big toy. Now he sat in his office feeling lonely as his weekend plans with a truly wonderful woman collapsed around him. But, he couldn't blame her or himself or anyone. It was simple fate stepping up and giving him something to think about.

But, if he were to be truly honest with himself what was there to think about? So they had been dating for the past couple of months, and she was certainly a wonderful person. Did that mean he had to change his whole life? For a woman? If there was one thing Robert could say without any hesitation, no woman had ever been the deciding factor in anything in his life before. So why should she be any different. Why indeed?

Chapter 18

Robert spent not the next two weeks traveling, but the next month. As much as he wanted to be in New York finding excuses to see Shannon it seemed like there was always something. The week in Las Vegas was extended because of architecture and design challenges. For a guy who had spent his whole career surrounded by finance professionals, lawyers, and now politicians the designers and architects were just as challenging if not more, to deal with.

And then some of the investors had decided on an impromptu visit for the weekend so they could have a full tour and update on the construction and changes already taking place. Robert had decided to give Lowell a taste of the business and flown him out for the weekend so he could meet with the investors as well. While he sorely wanted to be back in New York with Shannon he also admitted some of the discussions and decisions were thought provoking. And he was always looking for a new challenge.

The following two weeks he spent in Philadelphia meeting with politicians and business leaders. With all of the changes in the area people were concerned that the neighborhood would again attract the wrong kind of people. Interestingly, despite the tents being completely unlocked no one had attempted to rob anyone. It could have been because there were always people around, or it could have been because there was still nothing really to steal. Or it could have been because people knew that the local organized crime families were supplying a good portion of the local labor.

Regardless of the reasons, it was a reasonable concern. And even though the city police were back to patrolling the streets regularly, they were concerned it would take more than that. Robert didn't have the answers either, and it certainly wasn't his responsibility as part of the business operation. But he did feel some responsibility to help these people have a normal, safe life.

Aside from that it seemed that some of the new small businesses were having some issues and that Robert could help. He had made people from his staff available for ongoing seminars regarding financials, general management, and even supplier management. This was a good opportunity for Robert to meet with them and give them some of his own personal advice. And at the end of the second week he found himself refreshed and feeling better about his role in this project and in general. It also gave him some ideas of some of things he could change in his own future.

And then he got the best surprise of all when on Thursday evening as he was heading to the hotel restaurant having just come in from his office at the tents. He saw Shannon standing at the receptionist desk. She must have sensed him because no sooner did he walk through the doors than she turned and saw him. He stopped short when he saw her and then laughed as she skipped across the small lobby and threw her arms around his neck. They kissed tenderly as they held each other and then slowly they broke the embrace.

Robert glanced over at Joseph as they broke the embrace and saw him grinning. They waited for the elevator holding hands until the doors opened. Then as they were about to step aboard Robert slapped Joseph on the shoulder and they all laughed. Joseph let them aboard then turned with a nod went back for her bag. He let the doors close and they rode up to the restaurant where they had a fabulous dinner. Apparently, once again Joseph had thought of everything. They spent the evening catching up which was both wonderful and sad. While Robert had been busy with his projects, Shannon's job offer in Philadelphia had finally come together. She had to give her current employer until the end of the summer, but effective September first she was going to be working and moving to Philadelphia.

After dinner they went back to the room and spent the rest of the night making love and holding each other before falling into a deep sleep. Robert woke once during the night and found Shannon lying against him, he grinned to himself and simply pulled her closer. Her body felt good against his, and even the light snort that she made when moved was attractive.

The next morning they ordered breakfast in the room and while they were eating Shannon got a call from her sister. Since Shannon was in Philadelphia her sister wanted to come into town and see her. She even suggested getting together at their mother's for dinner like they used to. Robert told her to go ahead, and Shannon brightened suggesting that Robert join them. Naturally he agreed, he couldn't wait to meet the rest of her family.

They agreed to meet at the family home later in the afternoon, so Robert and Shannon decided to take a walk. They left the hotel and wandered down Walnut Street stopping in store after store, making small purchases here and there. When they reached Rittenhouse Square they walked down to one of the cafés and found a seat outside. They ordered coffee and a light snack and just sat and relaxed, holding hands and chatting.

As they walked back to the hotel, Robert realized for the first time all day that the constant bodyguard's shadows were not there anymore. And he was not alarmed or worried in the least, in fact he felt quite at ease. As they strolled down the street hand in hand, Robert felt more than just at ease. He felt content and incredibly happy. And even Shannon's news about moving to live here permanently couldn't dampen his mood. He had made millions of dollars on investments and rebuilding struggling companies, he could figure this out as well.

They showered and then rode over to her mother's house in south Philadelphia. They stopped along the way at a popular Italian bakery for cookies and fresh bread. Then walked the last couple of blocks to the house. When they got there, Shannon's sister, Olivia was already there along with her four year old son Jack. Robert was thrilled to meet them both, except that Shannon's mother was not home. So they sat in the small back yard and talked.

Jack was sitting quietly and seemed to be dozing off and Robert asked him why he was so tired?

"I didn't sleep well, I think the monster in my closet was snoring!"

Robert smiled and then said, "you know, a friend once told me that the monsters only come to little people because they are afraid of adults. And really they just want to make friends. Next time you hear him just say hello and tell him you will play with him tomorrow."

Jack looked at Robert wide eyed and then smiled. "That is what my mom always tells me!" At that moment, Robert realized that both Shannon and Olivia were staring at him intently.

"Robert... where did you hear that? That is what my father always told us when he tucked us in at night?"

But before he could answer Shannon's mother came out of the back door. Immediately Robert jumped up and introduced himself and the topic was quickly changed. He didn't know how to explain his policeman friend and wasn't quite prepared to at the moment anyway. They started to go into the house, but Jack had fallen asleep so Robert turned back and carried him into the house. He laid Jack down on the couch and covered him with a blanket.

When he turned around he saw Shannon looking at him with a lot of questions in her eyes. She must have recognized he wasn't prepared to answer them so instead she walked over and kissed his cheek. They started to turn towards the kitchen when one of the many pictures from the bookshelves caught his eye. He stepped over and lifted it up bringing it closer for a better look. As he did Mrs. Simmons walked into the room and saw him holding the old photograph.

"Robert, of all of the photographs you picked up that one?"

He turned to her, gripping the frame and staring at it, "is there something special about this one?"

She walked over and ran her fingers across the glass and rested them softly on his arm. "Sam Senior never told me much about it honestly. All he would ever tell me is that it was his one failure, his one regret in life. The day he died he promised to finally tell me after his nap. He never got the chance."

A small tear formed in the corner of his eye and as it slid down his cheek he turned to her. "Mrs. Simmons your husband was a good man stuck in a difficult time. He didn't fail, he saved a life."

Shannon just stood there staring at him and Mrs. Simmons turned to face him. She brushed away the tears on his cheek and then kissed him softly. "That's sweet of you to say dear, and I would certainly like to think so. I wonder what ever happened to that little boy."

Robert glanced at Shannon and could see that she was starting to understand. Then he took Mrs. Simmons' hand and led her over to the love seat and sat her down then sitting down beside her.

"I will tell you something I have never told anyone. When I was about six years old I was living on the streets, in an abandoned warehouse. A policeman found me and gave me some food and fresh clothes. During an incredibly bad storm the warehouse collapsed and I barely managed to escape with my life thanks to that same policeman. I spent the rest of that day in the emergency room and he opened his house to me letting me live there. It took the department of child welfare six months to decide that I needed a home with a *real* family.

I was too young to understand and always thought he didn't want me. Over the next six years I bounced from family to family until one of them packed up and moved to New York taking me with them. And about 6 months after we moved there I came home from school one day to an empty apartment. Apparently they had decided that they had enough of being parents and left. I guess they forgot that I was only thirteen years old. They had paid through the end of the month, and their deposit got me one more month but after that I was back on the street.

The next few years I was moved from shelter to shelter, and got some help from a couple of churches in the city. I won't lie, there were even times when I thought about quitting but then I thought of Officer Sam. He used to tell me that God sent him down that street for a reason, and while it might not be obvious surely He had a good reason. So I kept going. He also told me, even at six, how important school was, so I kept going to school.

I never forgot him, or the things he told me. In six months your husband meant more to me than any *real* family I lived with for the next ten years. When I was older I tried to find him, but this was way before the internet. And as a regular street cop he never hit the news, so there wasn't much. Plus, I never knew him as anything more than Officer Sam. But, I never stopped wondering who he was or where he was."

No one said a word. Mrs. Simmons broke the silence first. "Robert, Sam never forgot you! Every Christmas he laid a gift under the tree and we never who knew who it was for. All he ever said was that it was for an old friend." Slowly she stood up and moved over to a cabinet, getting a wrapped gift out. She came back and sat down next to Robert handing it to him. "It never felt right to me that I should open this, and every year I have continued the tradition for Sam."

It was a small package, about the size of a cigar box. It was wrapped very carefully, but the extra slips of tape and the faded wrapping paper were witness to how old the package was. Robert didn't have to unwrap it, instinctively he knew what it was. A tear slowly trickled down his cheek as he ran his fingers softly across the top of the package. And then in very faint ink in one corner was written "to the kid from Santa".

Carefully he pulled the tape away from the paper revealing a worn, cracked wooden box. Robert carefully folded the wrapping paper on his knees and then even more carefully held the box in his hand. In his mind's eye he could see a small hand gripping the box as the rain crashed around him. The last time he had seen this was the night of the storm when the warehouse had collapsed around him. When he opened the box he saw a carefully folded note.

In careful block lettering it said, "Kid, I found this in my squad car and wanted to surprise you with it at Christmas. You were gone by then and I always hoped I would find a way to give this back to you. Sam"

"That was Dad's handwriting. But why did he call you kid?"

Robert turned and looked at Shannon "I never knew my real name, and people always called me 'kid'. So it stuck. He told me once that his favorite author was Robert Ludlum, so whenever I needed a name I used Robert."

He looked again inside the box and carefully pulled out a chain. On the end was a small medallion of Saint Pancras, the Patron Saint of Children. Robert's fingers slid through the metal chain and holding the medallion in his fingers gently rubbed it with his thumb. Holding the medallion in one hand he looked again in the box and pulled out a faded photograph. He held his breath as he unfolded it, and they all leaned in to see it. It was faded, but you could see a small boy. Or at least they all assumed it was because he was bundled up so tightly you could hardly see his face.

Robert leaned down and looked into a corner of the box and then lifted out a thin wedding ring. It was a plain gold ring and small, even for a woman's finger. There were no markings, no engravings, nothing to identify it. "I found this in one of my pockets one day and always assumed it belonged to my mother. Or maybe I just wanted to believe it."

Carefully he put everything back in the box, including the note from Sam. He gently closed the lid then stood up and carried it outside to the backyard. He sat down in one of the lawn chairs, the box resting in his lap as he stared off into the distance. The memories a jumble in his mind as they as they all came flooding back. He felt the tears begin to flow and sat and cried. He cried for the lost years, and for the pain that Sam must have felt every year when he put the box out. How he wished he could have found him one last time to say thank you. He had always assumed that the cop had never really cared for him, just like every other "parent" in his life. But now he knew just how wrong he had been, and for that he cried as well.

In the end it was Mrs. Simmons who came outside and placed a gentle hand on his shoulder. "Robert, don't be sad for Sam. I know that he is watching over our family and guiding us in his own way. And now I know that he is finally smiling knowing that you have found him."

Robert stood up and hugged her tightly. They stood in the embrace for several minutes, both of them lost in their own memories and thoughts. When they finally broke apart and started for the back steps they were surprised by a male voice, "hey... What's all the hubbub? Mom, why is Shannon crying? She told me everyone was coming in and I just couldn't pass up a chance to have some of your famous pasta gravy and meatballs!"

She walked over and hugged Sam Junior tightly. Then they all went inside and were given different chores by Mama Simmons in helping with dinner. They set the dining room table and had one of the best dinners Robert could remember. It didn't hurt that everything was fresh and homemade, or that Shannon was beside him either. But he listened to stories of Sam Senior from the three of them and by the end of dinner he felt like he was truly a part of the family.

That night he and Shannon talked for hours about the future. About her move to Philadelphia and how he had been feeling lately. They talked about what they both wanted and how they would get there and make it work between them. They both knew it wasn't going to be easy and that there were certainly a lot of challenges ahead. They also talked about the past with Robert telling Shannon more details of his growing up. It was his past and it was what made him who he was today.

Epilogue

The woman stepped off of the elevator, a small four year old boy holding her hand. She smiled at the receptionist as she strode through the main doors. She was walking a little slower these days, but being seven months pregnant seemed to make everything a little slower. Except for going to the bathroom which seemed like a constant event.

At the end of the hallway she saw the large mahogany doors closed, and the secretary sitting behind the desk start to stand up. "Is he free? Sam and I were hoping he might have time for lunch."

Jennifer smiled and coming around the desk gave her a big hug, "we can shift a couple of things around today to make the time. You know he never says no to this little cutie... or you! He is just finishing up a video conference with Lowell, so I will let him know you are here."

Shannon thanked her and then they went into Robert's office. It was similar to the office he had in New York City but with just a little bit of a different view. Instead of his bar here being stocked with alcohol she knew it would have water and juices, so she got a small apple juice for Sam and water for herself. Sam sat beside her quietly playing with a couple of his action figures he had brought in from the car.

Robert strode in and gave Shannon a quick kiss before grabbing Sam and lifting him into his arms. "Hey buddy! This is a nice surprise! Are you being a good boy for mommy?"

"Yes, Daddy! And I even helped Mommy with the laundry this morning!"

Robert tousled his hair, "that's my little man. And how is Mommy feeling today?"

Shannon smiled brightly seeing the two of them as she always did. "Mommy is feeling just dandy today. I don't know if it's a boy or a girl Robert, but she will definitely be a soccer star. How is Lowell?"

He laughed, "he is good. The quarterly results for the hotel are above expectations and the casino is doing even better than anyone expected. Some of the changes he has implemented have really made a huge difference. He wanted to come back for Christmas, but there is a lot going on this year. I think he misses the cold and the snow."

"Well, we can always ship him some of the stuff. It may only be November but I have already had my fill of it. Unfortunately I don't think I can travel anymore, but you are welcome to go if you want. I saw Pearl had a group of people in her office, is everything ok?"

"Pearl always has a group of people in her office. Now that everything is done, including the apartment building we are putting the final touches on the park. If you had asked me five years ago I would not have expected it to take this long. But, apparently building houses is a lot easier than refurbishing an entire apartment building."

"That's great news. I know she has worked very hard on this, so I am glad to see it finally coming to an end. Maybe you can give her something that will be less stressful?"

He laughed again "Mikhail is stressing her out enough I think. For a kid his age I think he already has girls fighting over him. Which reminds me, he has a big basketball game this week for the city wide playoffs. Pearl said that if they can win this game and the next one then they will play the regionals and maybe even go to state."

Shannon shook her head and then he helped her up. Hand in hand they left the office and as they passed Jennifer's desk she reminded him about his class. "I'm sorry Robert, I forgot you taught today. Are you sure you have the time?"

"Absolutely honey. We can drive over to Cosi for lunch and then I can have the driver drop me at the high school before taking you home. Speaking of which, there is this one kid in the class who is absolutely amazing. I have already talked to him about coming to work for us over the summer, and I am going to meet with his parents next week."

Shannon was very proud of Robert and how he had taken on this class. It had been an idea of his when they first opened an office in Philadelphia as it gave him an opportunity to give the junior and senior high school kids a real taste of what Wall Street could be like. Each class was half of the year and the students had to put together a resume and interview for a spot in the class. And every year so far they had more kids than spots. Plus, usually there were one or two kids that had the opportunity to work either here in his office or at the office in New York City.

***

Six months later there was a large group of reporters, politicians, supporters, neighborhood business owners, and people standing in the new park. It had been finished in April, but they were finally ready to inaugurate it and he had one final surprise for Shannon and her family. As with everything else in this project Pearl had dedicated her time and effort to make sure it came off perfectly. It hadn't looked like there would be nearly enough space for everything, but there was. And there was even space for a small picnic area with trees to attract more families.

On one side there were basketball courts with low fencing so the ball wouldn't have to be chased too far. On the other side was a huge play are for the smaller kids, with swings, a jungle gym, several climbing areas and sliding boards. The entire base of the area was made from recycled tires and it was very soft and comfortable for falling down. Stretched across the middle was the picnic area with several built in barbecue pits so the apartment families could have a place to cook as well. And going around the entire park was a path for walking or jogging.

Across one of the central paths was a big red ribbon which had been hung for the occasion and alongside of it was the podium. Once again Robert would be speaking on this same spot that he had almost six years earlier. Looking around he saw some familiar faces - a couple of reporters, the senator had returned from Washington and the former Councilman, now Mayor of Philadelphia came out.

"Ladies and gentleman, if we can get started. Six years ago a devastating fire tore through this neighborhood destroying everything it touched. Businesses were ruined, homes were destroyed, and people's lives were upended. People who had very little now had nothing. If you look all around you today you will see what a difference time and healing can make.

Six years ago there was a long line of smoldering mess that is now a neighborhood of beautiful homes. All built by the people who now live in them. Down that street is a row of shops and businesses that once ran from this neighborhood and now I am pleased to say - are hugely successful. And behind me you can see what was once a dilapidated, uncared for apartment building. It was once barely inhabitable except by people with little hope and even less opportunity.

Today is a very different day here, because today is the day that we can say 'life has returned'. A long time ago a friend of mine told me that no one should ever be forgotten or overlooked. This friend dedicated his life to helping people and serving them in the way he knew best. And after much research I have found that he did just that. He treated everyone with great respect and dignity, even though he sometimes saw them at their worst.

I didn't know him for very long, just a short six months. I was about six years old at the time and yet, he changed my life forever. He wasn't a politician or a doctor or a lawyer. He was a cop, and a beat cop at that. He rode the streets that most people would have avoided. And it never got him down. Even after he retired he continued to help the community that he had loved and served. He wasn't a great man, except to me. He wasn't my father, but I would have been proud to have called him that."

Robert paused briefly and glanced at Gram Simmons. Seeing the tear slide down her cheek made his own voice crack as he continued. "Ladies and gentlemen, it gives me great pleasure to introduce you to an amazing woman. Mrs. Simmons was the wife of this man, and together they raised an amazing family. One I am also pleased to now call my own."

As Mrs. Simmons stood up and waved quietly he walked over and kissed her cheek. Then he took her hand and led her over to a sign post. "Gram, it is my honor to have this park officially named the 'Officer Sam Simmons Memorial park'." With a bit of a flourish he pulled the cover from the sign post which read that. It also listed his birthdate and the dates he worked for the police force. They stood quietly for a moment before the reporters moved in for photographs.

He then moved over to the ribbon and with the help of the mayor and Pearl they cut it. Everyone cheered and clapped as Robert moved away from the crowd letting the politicians have the spotlight. One of the photographers insisted on taking several pictures of Mrs. Simmons with the plaque, and then Robert and his family. He was pleased to see that Sam had driven up from Washington where he was now working as one of the FBI's assistant directors.

They had arranged for a local restaurant to barbecue for the rest of the afternoon and Robert even found a few of his students had come for the festivities. Lowell and Frank were there too because they knew how important this was to Robert. But what pleased and surprised him most was seeing Joseph and Jennifer standing together. He glanced at Shannon who smiled at winked and he held her hand in his. As he leaned down to kiss her hand he saw the thin plain gold band on her hand and smiled.

THE END

About The Author

I live in Southern New Jersey with my amazing wife and best friend. We live just outside of Philadelphia and about an hour from an awesome selection of beaches. It was on a beach that I wrote my first short story and love to spend as much time as possible there. There is something so invigorating about the sun and the blue skies.

While this is my first novel, I am already working on my second of many to come. While not working on writing books or my blog I am a husband to an amazing woman, and a father to two fantastic young adults. I am also a corporate finance professional that spends the rest of time helping executives and business leaders improve and grow their business. It is some of this experience which has helped bring this story and the next to life.

Please also check out my blog at
www.DavidEGordonAuthor.wordpress.com

Acknowledgments

Cover by DeLaine Roberts at www.DRGraphicExpressions.com

Formatting by Lou J Stock at www.ljdesignsia.com

Editing by Claire Allmendinger
Bare Naked Words Author Services
http://www.bnwauthorservices.co.uk/

Other Books By David E. Gordon

Cutter
Another Cutter
Cutter Returns

312 CUTTER